The House of All Sorrows

RICHARD GADZ

Deixis Press

First published in 2025 by Deixis Press
www.deixis.press

ISBN 978-1-917090-13-1 (HB)
ISBN 978-1-917090-14-8 (PB)

Typeset using Sabon LT Std by Palimpsest Book Production Ltd, Falkirk, Stirlingshire

Cover design by Deividas Jablonskis

The House of All Sorrows

RICHARD GADZ

"The Westwych House massacre of June 1897
is a subject I do not, cannot and will not discuss,
either in public or in private"

– *Memoirs Of A Successful Career*
by Dr. J. Utterson, 1938

"One droppe ef Moonwort! Lour! Hir deathful taste
Can manflesh webben unto wolf ad crabb ad snake"

– from St. Aelfrid Of Wessex's
Wikked Historie Significate, c.1172

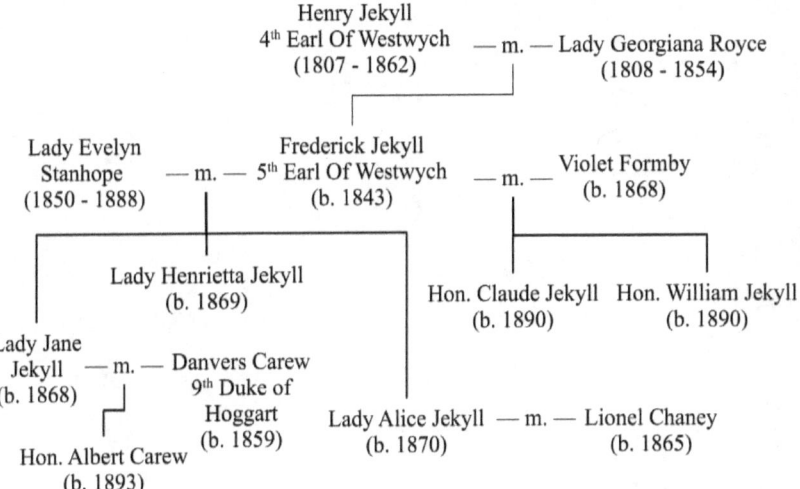

Henry Jekyll
4th Earl Of Westwych — m. — Lady Georgiana Royce
(1807 - 1862)   (1808 - 1854)

Lady Evelyn   Frederick Jekyll
Stanhope   — m. — 5th Earl Of Westwych   — m. —   Violet Formby
(1850 - 1888)   (b. 1843)   (b. 1868)

Lady Henrietta Jekyll
(b. 1869)   Hon. Claude Jekyll   Hon. William Jekyll
                                       (b. 1890)   (b. 1890)
Lady Jane
Jekyll   — m. — Danvers Carew
(b. 1868)   9th Duke of
                        Hoggart   Lady Alice Jekyll — m. — Lionel Chaney
Hon. Albert Carew (b. 1859)   (b. 1870)   (b. 1865)
(b. 1893)

The Jekyll family tree at the time of the disaster, June 1897

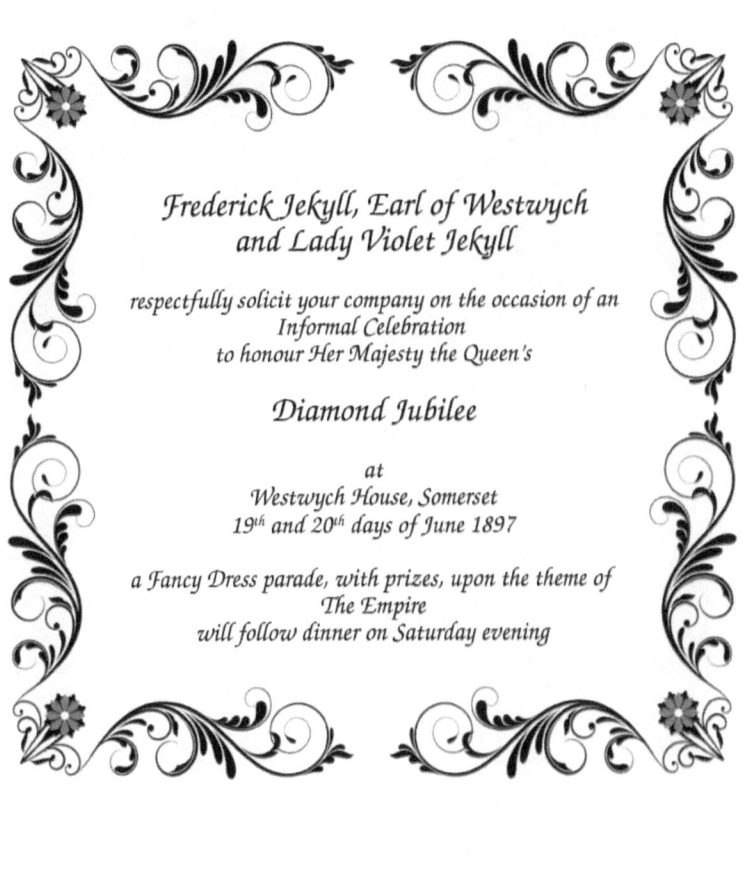

Frederick Jekyll, Earl of Westwych
and Lady Violet Jekyll

respectfully solicit your company on the occasion of an
Informal Celebration
to honour Her Majesty the Queen's

Diamond Jubilee

at
Westwych House, Somerset
19th and 20th days of June 1897

a Fancy Dress parade, with prizes, upon the theme of
The Empire
will follow dinner on Saturday evening

Whitechapel, London
early hours of 9th November, 1888

Mary lay back on the rumpled sheet which covered her bed, resolving to count her blessings while the man standing in front of the fireplace finished buttoning his waistcoat. The man was short and stout, with a bushy ginger beard and an air of fussy decorum. He glanced around the mildew-laced walls before hoisting up the large unopened can of ale he'd had with him when he and Mary had met, half an hour and a couple of streets ago.

He tapped his billycock hat to his head, his ruddy features shimmering in the fading, flickering glow from the narrow fireplace. He turned awkwardly on the spot for a moment, not knowing if he should say something, not wishing to appear rude, suddenly raw and self-conscious now the embers of his desire were as sputtering as those in the grate. Mary flopped her head sideways, looking blankly at him, still trying to think of a blessing to count.

Less than a mile away from her, and getting closer, a well-tailored figure in a tall hat stalked rapidly along the district's dark alleyways. Gripped tightly in his hands was a reinforced cane, obtained by his manservant for the purposes of beating back any mugsmen or other ruffians he might encounter on these night-time searches, any chancers who might think a toff an easy target.

He barely felt the air's intense chill, his breath clouding, for his mind focussed on finding the woman, the woman, the woman. He had seen her, glimpsed her, surveyed her hunting grounds. Several times recently, on nights like this, he had taken hold of some innocent female, thinking he'd found her, only to realise his quarry had eluded him again and that the search must go on.

On and on, through the stinking miasma which clung to this hideous place, these teeming, squealing, wailing streets where darkness of every kind watched from a thousand windows. His footsteps were made unsteady by the road filth underfoot and his lungs rasped heavily on the noxious vapour which soaked the night, but he hurried doggedly on. Flower And Dean Street, across the tramlines, Dover Street, past the Ten Bells pub, Hanbury Street, Devon Row, the Five Beggars, around Lame Street and the market square.

He would find her, he must find her.

In her single room on the corner of Miller's Court, Mary slid to her feet. Wrapping a coat around herself, she unbolted the door and the stout man left in a gush of outside air. He merged into the blackness of the covered passageway outside, his hastily re-tied boots clumping back towards Dover Street and the thin streams of humanity who meandered through the early hours.

Mary picked parts of a skirt and a battered hat from the pile of old clothes her most recent room mate had left behind, and dropped them onto the weakening flames hoping they were dry enough to catch. The light in the room was reduced to a vague glow.

She didn't want to strike a match to her only candle, not with so few remaining in the box. She retreated to the creaking bed, pulling the sheet around her, wrapping the blocks of ice which had taken the place of her feet.

Ought to go out again. Still time to catch a punter. Better chance of a posh one, this time of night.

The thought sent her mind tumbling back to better times. Not so long ago. Discreet parties in Pimlico, polite conversation and formal dancing, occasions when the name Mary Ann Kelly was a mask she wore lightly, coquettishly. Suppers at the Alhambra, or The Argyll Rooms, even Jimmy's in Regent Street. Before Paris, and being Marie Janette. Before making one too many enemies. Before this squalid, misery-smeared room. Before the nightly scraping together of—

She hadn't even been aware of closing her eyes, but now they snapped from sleep. The creak of her door. Had she heard the creak of her door?

The room was almost completely dark. Only the faintest blur of light came from the fireplace now. How long had she been asleep? Couldn't have been long. She normally slept through bumps and shouts from the woman upstairs, and through fights out in the yard, through all but the noisiest of regular disturbances, but now she was rubbing the fatigue from her eyelids because the familiarity of what she'd heard, its closeness, its suddenness, seemed to announce the arrival of someone in her room.

But there was only silence and darkness. She turned to the window which looked out over the tiny cobbled yard which was all Miller's Court amounted to. Beyond was pitch black, all moonlight swallowed whole by the height of the surrounding buildings and the low, fetid pall of cloud. She caught a faint shine, the ebbing glow of the fire, in some of the window's little square panes of glass. The rags stuffed into the lower left pane, broken during an argument with her Joe, were undisturbed. Reaching through that gap to grope for the bolt was how she locked up and let herself in these days, since she'd lost the only key, so rags still in place meant no unexpected visitor.

She nestled into the oily smell of her pillow. Her own imagination, that's what she'd heard. No more than that. She tugged the sheet tight around her and the seconds ambled by.

Until, suddenly, she sat up again. Another sound had broken the silence – it *had*, she'd heard it distinctly! – different this time, almost like a hiss of steam. She frowned, peering deep into the dark where nothing stirred.

Whatever it was, it came from *within* the room. Of that, she was certain.

She'd bolted the door. When ginger-beard went out. She'd bolted it. Hadn't she? The last of the gin fuzz in her system slunk away.

The sound came again, softer this time. Longer. By the door. Low down. Not a hiss, but a sharp inhalation. A sniffing of the air, of the room, of her presence, her body.

There was some animal in here. Somebody's dog got out. Some mangy wretch.

"Yaaa!" she cried loudly, waving an arm, hoping to scare the beast.

Nothing stirred. Mary strained to see the creature, to make out any kind of outline cast by the meagre light from the grate.

She caught a shifting of shadows. It moved. Slowly. Smoothly. Her heart raced.

It wasn't a dog.

"Hee hee," said a voice quietly. A woman's voice.

Completely unnerved, Mary scrambled back against the bedstead. Its joints groaned and squeaked. She gathered the sheet around her.

"Who's that?" she shuddered. "Who is it? Who are you?"

The shadows flexed, remaining low, close to the floor.

"I have come for you," whispered the voice.

Mary's breath caught in her throat. Her hand flashed out and scratched around beside the bedstead, fingers grasping. "I got a poker! I got it here!" she trembled, remembering it was over by the fireplace. "I got a poker! I'll brain you with it! Stay away from me!"

The shadows coagulated into shapes. At infinite leisure, a female face emerged into the failing yellow-orange gleam. Dark, wildly matted hair; skin streaked with dirt; a jawline strangely heavy. The creature's lips parted slowly into a gaping grin, revealing two prominent lines of long, bloodied fangs. Its eyes were fixed on Mary, unwavering, motionless, as red as rubies, its head held low and level in a predatory posture.

Behind the face, sinuous movement was wrapped in what

had once been smart and fashionable clothes, now torn and grimed into dishevelment. The beast advanced on all fours towards the bed in a slow, steady prowl, its arms and legs splayed. Mary could see its hands stepping across the damp floorboards, and in her fright it seemed as if they weren't hands at all, but clawed paws, like a tiger's or a lion's.

Helpless with terror, she watched the weird thing crouch at the foot of the bed, gathering itself, getting ready to spring.

For the briefest moment, there was stillness. Mary felt her will dissolve into fear, sensed the final moments of her life slip away into the past. This creature, was this Jack? Was this Leather-apron, the East End horror the bobbies couldn't catch? She had solved the mystery for them! She almost smiled to herself.

The beast leaped, fangs bared. Mary screamed.

The sound was heard three twists of an alley away. The well-dressed man whipped around on his heels, instantly alert. He ran towards Miller's Court just as the piercing scream was suddenly severed from the night.

The beast was half animal, half human. Across its skin and through its muscles, it struggled to find itself, in form and mind. A fluid of fur and muzzle, brain and instinct, it knew only hunger, a burning for flesh which had first shocked and then delighted the remnants of the woman it had been.

It tore at its prey, so intent on its lust that it didn't notice the well-dressed man arrive, paid no attention to the flinging open of the door and the bite of cold air which flooded the room. There was only the smell of blood and the reddening of the sheet and the glistening sprays upon the walls.

The man gripped his cane and, knowing he had no time to hesitate if he was to subdue his quarry, swung it heavily into the back of the creature's neck. The beast roared, knocked sideways. The man flung himself onto the monster's back, getting a tight hold of it around the throat and using his weight to pull them both off the bed and onto the floor.

With his free hand, the man snatched at his pocket, pulling out a brass hypodermic syringe he'd prepared on each and every night of his long search. The beast shook and scrambled beneath him, still stunned by the blow it had received, conscious of attack but momentarily unable to fight.

The needle plunged deep into the muscles of the creature's arm. The expression on the man's face was a tangle of sorrow and duty, like a veterinary surgeon ending the suffering of a wounded patient.

Slowly, the beast grew still and its breathing became shallow. The well-dressed man slackened his hold and turned the creature over, to cradle it in his arms. Rocking slightly, he staggered to his feet. The beast was caked with the blood of its dead prey, but beneath the blood its features appeared to have softened, to have become human. It hung limp and gasping in the man's embrace.

He pulled the creature to his chest, his head dipping to kiss its forehead. "Evelyn," he said softly. "Oh Evelyn, my dearest."

The beast's eyes fluttered. It spoke hesitantly, but with a smile. "You were right, my love. I was so alive."

Chapter 1

Jack Utterson's journal

Fri. 18th June 1897. Train depart 1:20pm
Paddington – Bristol, arrive 3:55pm.

I was glad to be leaving London for a while. Apart from
the fresh air and brighter skies which always accompany a
journey outside the city, I was looking forward to an agreeable break from my normal routine of work. Relations with
my colleagues in the department and, I regret to say, with
Mr Bittlesham in particular, had become a little strained
since the regrettable incident with the Saxon relics. After
that, it seemed as if no amount of apologies, however
sincere, or offers to repair the items damaged, could improve
the mood of my superior. What made the matter all the
more vexing was that it happened so soon after the unfortunate misunderstanding about the display case. Had this
not been so, it might not have become such an item of
common gossip among the museum staff!

However, I was soon much relieved to discover that Mr
Bittlesham's professionalism was of a standard which set

aside any personal animosities. When he summoned me to his office on the morning of the following Tuesday, I was expecting to receive a reprimand, but instead he informed me that I had been chosen, on his personal recommendation, to conduct a special mission to the West Country. Naturally, I was delighted to be given this responsibility, and silently thankful that my career was safe in such impartial hands, but I evinced ignorance of such an interesting opportunity having been available. Whereupon, I was told that the normal round of interviews had been bypassed since I was both eminently suitable for the position and free of the domestic responsibilities which would seriously dilute the attentions of other applicants. It would be left up to my personal discretion as to the length and purview of the task, and I would be able to draw my regular salary by arrangement with a nominated bank in Bristol.

Thus, the 1:20pm from Paddington! I treated myself to a new Mappin & Webb suitcase, settled up with my landlady in Battersea and was rather moved to find so many of my colleagues not only aware of my imminent departure but enthusiastic well-wishers.

The journey to Bristol was both agreeable and picturesque. I shared a compartment with only one other passenger, a fascinating chap, a retired engineer who, it turned out, had worked on the London sewerage system and the Thames embankment back in the 1860s. He relayed many remarkable stories about the complexities involved and the upheaval caused. All this, while the simple beauty of the countryside rolled past and the gentle rattle of the railway carriage was punctuated by hoots from the steam engine.

The engineer alighted at Bath and, once we'd said our

cheery goodbyes, the train chugged onward through Keynsham and the last few miles into the Bristol station. I was feeling content, even elated, to be starting a fresh chapter in both my life and my profession. I was looking forward, with great eagerness and anticipation, to the challenges which lay ahead of me.

How my mood was to change!

Fri. 18th June continued. Bristol 4pm – 5:52pm.

Billowing clouds of steam were huffed out across the platform by the cooling engine, and I emerged from them to find myself on a large station concourse where the usual array of gates and ticketing offices had been festively decorated with all manner of flags, banners and bunting. So elevated was my spirit and so rosy my outlook that I momentarily misinterpreted all the gaiety as being for my benefit, a jamboree of welcome, until I came to my senses and realised it was of course in honour of the imminent bank holiday and the Queen's jubilee celebrations!

Red faced and chuckling to myself, I made my way through the jostling throng of passengers and eventually navigated my way out of the building to find the point from which my onward connection to Hagstow was due to depart. No sooner had I got there than the rough-looking fellow in charge of the carriage informed me that repairs to the vehicle were underway – *by whom?* I wondered, since here stood the vehicle intact and unattended! – and thus departure would not take place until half past five o'clock. One or two other travellers were already huddled on benches close by, looking thoroughly dejected and resigned to a long wait.

A liveried officer of the Great Western, sitting on a low wall and seeing how disconcerted I was at this news, kindly directed me to a small stall selling street maps of the city. A gentleman like myself, he said with a crooked and toothy grin, might pass a pleasant hour in a walk around nearby Queen Square. The carriage driver laughed at these words and agreed enthusiastically, so I furnished myself with a map and, determined to remain buoyant despite the delay, set off on my unexpected excursion. The Temple Meads station itself was a landmark to which I was confident of finding my way back, the place looking so castle-like and reminding me so much of the environs of the Tower in London!

I made only a brief detour from the correct route, due to initially mistaking one turning for another. (Suspecting my error, I asked directions at a long line of sadly ragged women I took to be queuing for bread but who, to my great embarrassment, were in fact anxious wives and mothers waiting to view an unidentified corpse fished from the Avon by the police.)

I soon located what was definitely Queen Square, according to the sheet of paper in my hand, but which was not the scenic garden so particularly described by the railwayman. The area was little more than an extremely busy thoroughfare, surrounded by crumbling Georgian architecture which loomed over meagre shops and dwellings divided from each other by dark, morbid alleyways.

I took it that the railwayman must either have been thinking of a different Square entirely or else had evidently failed to pass this way in quite some time! Checking my pocket watch – 4:27pm – I stood in a fret of indecision over whether to simply turn back and wait or to make the best of things and follow the map a little further in the hope of finding somewhere more agreeable.

As I stood, the heavens opened. The day had been pleasantly warm and the sky, despite some clouds, had been bathed in a hazy Summer radiance but now a bleak carapace rolled overhead as if some huge, soaking wet tarpaulin was being hauled from one horizon to the other. Large raindrops began to plop and spatter and almost everyone within sight rushed to scurry indoors or vanished down some gloomy passageway or other.

Annoyed by my ill fortune, I sped for the closest cover. A signposted opening between two sadly dour mansions declared itself the entrance to a market, but beyond this entrance I found only a dizzying confusion of tiny back-streets, all crammed with fellow shelterers.

The elevation of the surrounding buildings was enough to stave off the worst of the heavy rain, but the milling press of humanity in all directions made the atmosphere horribly humid and malodorous. The sheer number of tall and bulky people around me made movement in a chosen direction all but impossible, and the many screaming infants and squawking old crones made thinking all but impossible too. I quickly became thoroughly lost and was pushed along in the flow until a slightly wider, slightly less crowded side street appeared beside me and I wriggled my way free.

A roll of thunder boomed overhead, loud enough and

close enough to feel in my boots, and with a shudder I looked about me for somewhere I might take refuge for a few minutes. The street was a drab and decrepit one, with wooden boards half-covering one set of leaded shop windows and nothing but a miserable heap of rags behind another. A stream of rainwater, browned by the muck it was washing along the channels in the road, was collecting into a puddle at my feet. A handcart, its cargo tucked tightly under cover, rattled along towards me and it was as I stepped aside that I noticed the sign over a dilapidated shop on the opposite side of the street: "Jemmison's Cabinet Of Curiosities."

Behind the window was propped a wooden board announcing "A thousand MARVELS from the FAR ENDS of the WORLD! Be ASTOUNDED for 6d!" in elaborate letters. Behind the board was a broad, threadbare curtain, through which peeked slender glimpses of lamplight.

What on Earth made me cross the street and go inside, I have no idea. It wasn't the sort of place I'd ever in my life frequented before. I dislike circuses and unfailingly find fairground sideshows of every kind to be shoddy and disappointing. I suspect it was merely my desperation to escape the crowds and rain for a moment or two. Whatever the reason for my decision, I very soon regretted it.

As I opened the door and entered, a bell tinkled above my head. I hadn't realised how wet I'd become until I removed my hat and tipped rain onto the floorboards.

"Oh, I do apologise," I said, purely by force of habit, as I became aware of someone approaching from the other side of a second curtain. This one was drawn right across the shop's low, narrow interior and was far more intact and opulent than the one which covered the window. It looked like it had been cut down from one of those huge red draperies you see in theatres.

The man who appeared, casting a swathe of the curtain aside with a flourish and stepping out of the shadows, was fat and rosy-faced. Curled moustachios underlined a bulbous nose which was topped with an impenetrably thick pair of spectacles beneath a domed and sparsely furnished cranium. His clothes were theatrical, even flamboyant, but all too obviously worn and repaired almost to the point of disintegration.

"A most good afternoon to you," he wheezed warmly, flashing teeth of assorted shades. His voice was as round as his belly but peculiarly glottal, as if engaged in a struggle to escape his tongue. "Mr A. E. Jemmison, proprietor. I thank you for visiting us. On such a vile afternoon. Most sincerely."

"I must confess," I said, with a sheepish smile, "I came in here largely to escape the downpour."

He beamed, emitting a sound that was half giggle, half rattle in the throat. "Then Fate herself has brought you to my door! Most fortunate!" He launched into a prepared speech which had the effortless monotony of one learned long ago and endlessly repeated ever since. "The Jemmison Cabinet of Curiosities is without parallel in the annals of Mankind, a collection of marvels and mysteries from every corner of the Earth—" His lungs heaved like a pair of old bellows and his grubby fingers jutted out ready to receive coins. "—An unforgettable journey into the realm of the strange and unusual. All for sixpence. Children half price. Prepare your senses for astonishment on such a— thank you, Sir."

21

His grand encomium was cut short the instant I dropped the money into his hand. Reaching up and unhooking an old oil lamp from a beam beneath the ceiling, he heaved around and beckoned me to follow him.

As I passed around the flap of curtain which he held aside to allow me through, a dreadful smell of caged livestock filled my nose and I instinctively raised the back of my hand to my face. However, what lay beyond the curtain were not farmyard enclosures but racks of shelving. At first, I couldn't see any of it clearly because the light from the lamp swung widely as Jemmison walked, sending wild shapes and shadows lurching like a boat in a storm.

After shuffling a dozen feet past the curtain, he hung the lamp up again at what was clearly the first designated stopping-point on the guided tour. The lamp's yellow glow finally settled down and I looked around myself at row upon row of boxes, glass jars, oddly shaped objects and unfamiliar curios. There were a large number of small mammals and birds, stuffed and posed, not one of which I could identify. There were ugly specimens of what I took to be sea life, encased motionless in glass. There were tableaux depicting various species in brutal and inappropriate combat with each other. Above all these, on a roughly plastered wall, hung a line of mounted heads as might be seen in a grand home or hunting lodge, except that these were the heads of nightmarish grotesques. One appeared to be the first few feet of an immense serpent.

"Nature is a powerful and peculiar mistress," muttered Jemmison, gently pointing out one or two of the weirdest pieces. "She never rests. Always moulding. Always changing. Watching the tiny fleas. Who live upon the surface of her planet. Killing those. Who dare to bite her. Playing jokes by birth and circumstance."

I shuddered despite reassuring myself that many, quite possibly all, of these things must have been faked in the same manner as one of those nasty seaside mermaid exhibits, cobbled together from bits of fish and monkey. Some of the glass jars contained similar items preserved in liquid: a little rodent with two heads (made from squirrels?); a plant-like thing with multiple eyes (sheep's I reckoned); an extracted heart which beat with a steady rhythm (animated by a hidden pump, clearly).

"These treasures," wheezed the proprietor, "have come down to me from my father. Mr G. E. Jemmison. He in turn inherited them from his father. For many years the Jemmisons travelled with the carnivals. Showing freaks, collecting marvels. Until too many marvels had been amassed. Too many to transport. Couldn't part with any. Settled here when I was a younger man like you."

Looking closer, I could see that the shelving and other furniture was all made of wood salvaged from the carnival wagons the man's family had owned. Here and there, up the side of some shelves or beneath a row of exhibits, words using the same emphatic lettering as the sign outside the shop were visible in chipped and faded paint.

"Indeed?" I said.

He mistook my politeness for interest, and all but danced his way along a rickety table holding a selection of larger items. His fingers fluttered nervously over a large, ornately decorated box, about the size of a tea chest, its lid sealed shut with metal bands and a layer of wax around the joins.

"This. See here. Obtained from a mystic in the Orient,"

breathed Jemmison, his voice quivering. "Trapped inside is a fiend. A demonic spirit. Would possess you in a second were it to escape. Would drink the blood right out of your warm body. A vampyr."

I saw nothing sinister about the box, unless the layer of dust it lay under was meant to convey a frisson of terror? Jemmison moved on to a birdcage which hung on a length of string from the ceiling. He kept beckoning me forward until he judged me close enough to the object, then tapped loudly at the bars.

A human hand jumped up at the spot he'd touched! With a startled cry I took a sudden step back, a hand to my chest. I bent to look under the suspended cage. Whoever was operating this horrible marionette was certainly dextrous and well-concealed.

The hand had been made to look half decayed, and it stank exceedingly. It scrambled about like a fat spider, its grey, blotchy fingers pattering against the floor of the cage, or scratching at the bars with a thumb almost worn down to the bone.

"Still alive," chuckled Jemmison. "My uncle, Mr D. K. Jemmison, acquired this in London. Some years back. Got it from the police, if you please. Last relic of a corpse that walked."

"I see," I said, now feeling slightly revolted and wishing to be elsewhere. Why did I ever set foot in this place? "Thank you for an interesting, er, show. However, it's now . . . two minutes to five by my pocket watch and I do need to retrace my steps and return to the station."

"Oh, but there is so much more to see, through here," urged Jemmison, his breath rasping. He unhooked the lamp and lumbered over to an open doorway. I hesitated for a moment but was quickly forced to go with him or be left in darkness.

On the other side of the doorway was a second chamber, about the same size as the first but for the most part containing larger and more alarming items. I flinched as the lamplight swung past a human skeleton with a greatly enlarged skull.

"Most remarkable treasures," grinned Jemmison, nodding slightly as if to elicit my enthusiasm. The lamplight flashed blankly in the lenses of his spectacles. "A winged fairie, pickled in vinegar, just there, see. The teeth of a mighty sea monster from the Indies. Kaiser Wilhelm of Germany's original left arm."

I had no desire to be rude to the man, especially since he was so evidently down on his luck, but I also had no stomach to indulge him further. "I agree, Mr Jemmison, this is a truly extraordinary collection, however I'm afraid I really must be on my way."

He plucked at my sleeve. "Come, see Cyril. If you must go. See him first. It will take no more than a moment of your time. Come. Pride and joy of the collection. Mustn't miss Cyril."

He seemed almost pitiful, deeply anxious to draw another sixpence from a visitor impressed by his pride and joy. As I pen these words I wish, fervently and sincerely, that I had not at that moment felt compassion and given in to his entreaties.

"Very well," I said, with what I hoped was more than a hint of impatience. My pocket watch itched in my hand. "Briefly."

With a wheezy twinkle of pleasure, he hurried past a teetering stack of crates, the glow from the lamp pitching left and right enough to make me feel giddy. I followed him into a third room, this one containing a heavily shuttered window and a bolted door beneath which crept grey daylight and the hiss of the rain outside.

This room was the source of the fusty zoo-like smell I'd encountered earlier. To one side were a couple of old chairs and a slim sideboard. To the other side were wooden stalls, separated by planks which had been nailed together to form partitions. Those into which I could see were empty. Straw was scattered across the floor and heaped up between the partitions. It crackled underfoot.

"He's our only complete live freak at the moment," said Jemmison. "You'd swear he was human."

"Human?" I said, my nerves suddenly twitching. Naturally, I was expecting to see a tame goat with faked fins or some other poorly assembled chimera.

"Rosita left us recently. Hair on every inch of her. Shaved and got married. And poor little Billy passed through the veil only this last month. The famous Multiple Boy, he was. Just the one left now. But he's the greatest Curiosity in all the world! This is what the kiddies keep coming back to see."

He shuffled aside, holding the lamp high above his head. For the first time, I got a clear view of what was the other side of the last partition.

"I give you, Cyril the Centaur!"

Tied to the nearest wall with a thick rope was what at first glance appeared to be a small pony, but one with flesh that was pinkish and rounded, like that of a pig, with none of the tautness of outline normal in a young horse. The animal's tail flicked lazily and its back legs appeared to be malformed, bending to the rear instead of forward.

It was when the lamplight fell upon its hooves that a nauseating wave of fear surged up through every nerve in my body. For its hooves weren't hooves at all, but quite unmistakably hands and feet! They flexed upon the straw bedding beneath them.

I felt myself recoil in shock. I struggled to comprehend what I was looking at.

The animal shook its long equine neck as it snorted at a passing fly. The upper part of its face was terrifyingly human, its eyes apparently those of a normal man, set quite close together, but its jawline was elongated and distorted such that its mouth hung low and its nose was flattened into an ugly snout. Its ears seemed human too, but its scalp grew in long tufts, pulled back into a rudimentary mane.

Was this some miserable wretch stripped to his skin and adorned with theatrical hokum? It was not. To my absolute horror and disgust I could see that it was not.

My mind reeled. This was a creature whole and living, the actuality of its form and presence evident in every movement, every muscular twitch. And yet it was a nightmare. I staggered, feeling sick and faint. Not a man, not a horse either, but some hideous mockery of biology.

It dipped its head to drink from a bucket of water on the floor.

I collapsed onto one of the chairs on the other side of the room, one hand pressed to my temples and the other to my stomach. Jemmison grinned down at me. "What a beast, eh? Never seen the like."

I leaped unsteadily to my feet. "What can– How in God's name has that hideous creature–?" I cried, unable to properly order my thoughts.

"One of a kind," he nodded. "Pride of the collection."

"You, Sir, are a disgrace!" I cried, words suddenly tumbling out of me in a stream of horrified agitation. "However this animal– whether deformed– or diseased, or bred in some foul way– is beyond any boundaries of decency– paraded in this manner!"

"And unforgettable, like I said," smiled Jemmison. "You paid your pennies."

The animal whinnied softly. Jemmison patted and stroked it. "There, he likes you." For the merest fraction of a second, I caught a look in Cyril's eyes. A look in which I sensed . . . I know not what. I turned away.

Utterly distraught, I dashed headlong for the street. Somehow, I crossed those first two rooms without collision, at speed and with only diminishing splinters of Jemmison's lamplight behind me.

"There's no monies returned!" he called.

Flinging the curtain aside I ran out of the shop and into the rain.

Chapter 2

At the same moment Jack Utterson was leaving Jemmison's Cabinet Of Curiosities, Lady Violet Jekyll was standing on the front steps of Westwych House, looking out across the green, densely wooded undulations of the hills which fell and flowed away, like a vast rumpled blanket, to form the landscape of the valley below.

Westwych stood roughly half way up a long, sinewy rise of tors and elevations which swept from east to west along the northern ridges of the Somerset Mendips. Behind it rose a spectacular vista of trees, high scrubland and rocky outcrops. Its position, embedded into the hills, made it visible for miles from one direction but hidden if approached from any other. There was no gatehouse or fencing to mark the official boundaries of its grounds, mostly because the surrounding geography was so changeable and unruly that any management of lands more than fifty or sixty yards beyond the house was impractical. Some outhouses for storage, two sets of stables and a large, well-stocked kitchen garden marked the limits of the Westwych estate.

As if to compensate for its lack of acreage, the house itself was a towering, cathedral-like structure, with walls of yellow limestone laid in irregular courses enhanced by lacings of red brick. No tendrils of ivy or other climbers softened their asceticism. Every entrance had its pointed archway, and all but a few of the windows were tall and narrow, many filled with stained glass. Multiple projections and recesses gave the whole building a complex, grandiose look. Steeply pitched and angled roofs, sharply cut by gables and redundant chimney stacks, formed an outline more castle than house, more defensive than domestic. It was a stern, ominous dwelling, hammered into the landscape with defiance, existing alone in an aura of misfortune and sorrow.

A gravelled driveway lead up to it from the nearest road, ending in a wide terrace which stretched half the length of the building. From the terrace, towards the right hand side of the house, rose the wide front steps from where Violet Jekyll was surveying the valley. Here, the rolling storm clouds that glowered over Bristol were still only an approaching smudge in the sky.

"Your Ladyship?"

"Hmm?" Lady Violet turned on her heels. She was a strikingly attractive young woman, with glinting doe eyes and a puff of dark, wavy hair. "Oh, Miss Tippel, we have duties to attend to, have we not? I was away with the faeries for a moment there."

The willowy old housekeeper bobbed her head in several directions and posed her lips in a selection of curly smiles, her ring of keys forever tinkling at her side. Secretly, Violet Jekyll always thought of Miss Tippel as a skittish giraffe.

She led the way back indoors, Miss Tippel's loping gait and bony features following in her wake.

The entrance hall of Westwych House was designed to inspire awe. A large and impressive vestibule, filled with floral stands and decorative details, suddenly opened up to the left into a grand, marbled atrium which instantly diminished that large and impressive vestibule to a mere cupboard by comparison. The ceiling of the atrium was very high and vaulted, with plaster mouldings of roses and lilies in bloom, all of it painted in intricate shapes and vivid colours. Three enormous windows overlooking the valley dominated the south-facing wall, their leaded designs depicting swirling patterns of vines and branches, so that each window cast shafts of brightly tinted daylight which inched from corner to corner with the progression of the day. Beneath the windows stood a line of antique monk's benches, remnants of the Jekyll dynasty's earlier residences.

Jutting out into the atrium, forming a hefty peninsular between two arches which led deeper into the house, was a tall arrangement of glass enclosures set into a very large, darkly solid rectangular wooden frame. Behind the glass were environments mimicking jungles and deserts, in which Frederick Jekyll, Earl Of Westwych, kept a selection of reptiles and arachnids. He considered his vivarium a vital part of his scientific research, but everyone else in the household – his wife included – considered it a dangerous nuisance.

"I've asked him to at least *cover* the thing while the visitors are here," said Lady Jekyll. She and Miss Tippel clacked across the marble floor of the atrium, their faces shiny in the mellow late afternoon sunlight, the busks of their tightened stays creaking. "He knows perfectly well what happened when the Cornishes arrived last New Year. But he won't even consider it. So that's that, I suppose. Silly sausage."

Miss Tippel slipped a notebook and pencil from the front pocket of her pinafore, and quietly recorded how silly a sausage the Earl was being. They took a wide detour around the whole slab-like structure, more by habit than actual caution, and proceeded under the arches and along a wide corridor, soon reaching a hallway and the foot of a fat, carpeted staircase which was interrupted by two large landings on its way up to the next floor. Throughout the stairwell, scenes of West Country life hung beside portraits of family members ancient and modern: Frederick, 5th Earl, brooding and bearded; Henry, 4th Earl, bright-faced and surrounded by some of his archaeological discoveries; Lady Violet, Countess of Westwych, sitting at her writing desk; Lady Evelyn Jekyll, Frederick's first wife, painted on the last birthday before her death.

Lady Violet spun to a halt in the hallway, one splayed hand reaching out at full stretch towards the top of the stairs. "Do we yet know if Henrietta is bringing a guest?"

Miss Tippel scurried through her notebook. "A secretary companion, m'lady, a Miss Augustine."

Lady Violet drooped slightly. "So the last bedroom *will* be taken."

"It will, m'lady."

"Then we must hope for no surprises." Her hand moved down on to the ground floor, to point at the first of several doors visible from where they stood. "Frederick's study, he's keeping locked as usual. Have we a record of when he last let one of the maids in there to dust?"

"Just this last Tuesday, m'lady."

Lady Violet was pleasantly surprised. On to the second door. "The morning room, I'm afraid we should lock too. We all know what Sir Godfrey gets up to." Third door. "We can put activities for tomorrow afternoon in the library. There'll be enough space, do you think?"

"Oh, yes, I'm sure, m'lady. The chaise from the morning room could be moved in, to avert any seating crisis?"

"A rush of the clevers, Miss Tippel!"

Miss Tippel twittered. "Thank y'm'lady."

"Are there fresh decks of cards?"

Scribble. "I'll check with Mr Poole."

Lady Violet leaned an inch or two towards the house-keeper and whispered. "Because I'm looking forward to watching the men get amusingly competitive over a hand of Nap."

Miss Tippel squeaked a little. "And might I enquire, m'lady, if you're planning to beat all comers at the mah jong table?"

Lady Violet beamed at her. "Oh, of course, Miss Tippel. Of course."

Miss Tippel was delighted, and bobbed her head in acknowledgement. Lady Violet's winnings usually meant a quietly administered bonus or two for most of the staff.

Visible through the open fourth door were a couple of maids, scattering damp salt on the rugs ahead of a vigorous brushing. "The drawing room can lie fallow," said Lady Violet, "unless Alice has the mystical vapours descend and wants to start reading palms and whatnot. Now . . ." Fifth door.

She crossed the polished parquet and entered the dining room. Miss Tippel clicked on the electric lighting, a miracle of modern science which never failed to thrill her, even now, and the chandeliers glittered dimly overhead.

This room was the largest in the entire house, a magnificent, rectangular chamber with ornate cornices encircling the high ceiling and polished mahogany wall panelling to head height, topped with crimson wallpaper patterned in a subtle damask. A bulky wooden table, on carved, elephantine legs, stood in the middle of the room and ran for most of its length. Neatly tucked in, at exact intervals along both sides, were chairs of matching solidity and solemnity, with high backs and plushly stuffed seats.

Lady Violet considered the décor with a flitting eye. "I fear this room is looking rather dated," she said in a softly subdued voice, as if the room itself might blush with shame at the news. Her gaze settled on the new, imported phonograph atop a small sideboard in the corner, a Berliner Gramophone, its bare arrangement of cogs and handles topped by a curling funnel.

"Jilks assures me he's been practising its operation, m'lady," said Miss Tippel. "The music that comes out of it is quite steady now." She paused, looking at the machine nervously. "Not so eerie."

"Cheaper than a quartet, at least," said Lady Violet, smiling ruefully. "I expect it'll be one of his Lordship's five minute hobbies, just like his mechanical carriage. Goofy goose."

"Should I ring for Cook, m'lady? She told me earlier she's settled on menus."

"No, let's pay *her* a visit," said Lady Violet. "We'll be like a general and his adjutant walking the field before a battle."

Miss Tippel soundlessly concurred. She thought nothing

of the lady of the house breaking protocol by entering the servants' domain because, unlike her husband, the lady of the house quite often left broken protocols lying about the place. The servants took it in their stride.

The kitchen, sculleries and larders of Wychwood House were contained in a one-storey annexe built onto the right hand side of the main building thirty years earlier. They had previously been in the basement, but the 4th Earl, Frederick's father, had wanted the basement to himself, to house his scientific researches, an indulgence carried on by his son. The annexe, much of it roofed in hinged glass panels, to let light in and excess heat out, was joined to the house by a dog-legged conduit which efficiently kept cooking smells from drifting.

The household's resident cook was Mrs Cook. The late Mr Cook had been endlessly entertained by her alignment of surname and career, and frequently in fits of laughter over her maiden name which, you'll never guess, complete coincidence, no relation, was *also* Cook, can you believe, but his wife never understood the joke. She possessed an inhospitable countenance, a hairy skin and truly impressive culinary skill, but no sense of humour. Secretly, Lady Violet always thought of her as a disgruntled bulldog.

The kitchen was a chaos of steam and industry, filled with the clanking of copper pots and bowls, the clatter of buckets, the click-clack of knives. Maids with rolled sleeves and sweating faces criss-crossed from one work area to another in a tightly choreographed march towards deadlines. When they noticed Lady Violet, they straightened their backs and drew weary forearms across their brows in front of her.

Mrs Cook approached, wringing a tea towel's neck in her hands. "Yes'um?"

"Miss Tippel tells me the Jubilee celebration menus are set?"

"Yes'um."

"Of course, Cook, I trust your judgement implicitly, but if you could reassure me about tomorrow's dinner? Not too many courses, when there's the fancy dress afterwards?"

Mrs Cook slapped the tea towel to her shoulder. "Pea soup, clear turtle soup, turbot and smelts with Dutch sauce, croquette of chicken but might be lark pie depending on the butcher, roasted pork, potatoes, French beans, compote of fruit, a raspberry water, vanilla cream."

"Excellent," said Lady Violet.

"And early, y'said m'um,"

"Yes, around half past six, to accommodate the fancy dress. In the letters I sent out with the invitations I stressed informality, so I wondered if the dinner should be *à la française*?

Cook eyed her levelly. "More modern *à la russe*."

"Quite right, that's what they'll expect, *à la russe* it is."

"They're not staying past luncheon Sunday, m'um."

"No, once the Duke of Hoggart's party are back from church, I'm sure most will be heading to London for the Empire festival and the Jubilee parade on Tuesday. Lady Alice and Mr Chaney may be here until Monday, but nobody else. That we know of."

Cook threw a nod in the direction of the yard outside the open back door, beyond which was the kitchen garden. "Biggest pig'll be slaughtered for tomorrow. What's not gone by Monday'll be cured, m'um."

"Excellent." Lady Violet looked around the kitchen at

the ongoing activity. "And what are we having for dinner this evening?"

"Duck," said Cook.

Lady Violet and Miss Tippel were half way back to the main house when Lady Violet suddenly stopped in her tracks and wagged a finger at herself. "I've just this moment remembered, would you ask Sweetman if she'd write the menu cards again?"

Scribble. "She'll be honoured, I'm sure, m'lady, especially with such distinguished guests coming. She was so excited last time."

"She did a beautiful job, her lettering is so very neat."

"I'll enquire of Monsieur Moreau if he might check her spelling. Accents tend to confuse her."

"Even so, her work is exemplary. Even Frederick remarked on it, and we all know how blind he is to such things. Where is his Lordship, by the way? Do we know? Has he gone into town yet?"

Miss Tippel discreetly informed her employer that the Earl was currently addressing a serious issue which her Ladyship . . . might recall? From early this morning . . .?

"Oh. Yes," said Lady Violet, feeling indelicacy flush her face and neck.

The serious issue was being addressed in the Earl's private study, a darkly furnished room with a view down into the valley almost as commanding as the one from the atrium. Despite the study's over-burdened shelves and the profusion of books and papers on the desk, both of which announced an urgent energy in its occupant, it was a room with an overwhelming atmosphere of melancholy.

Frederick Jekyll, 5th Earl of Westwych, sat with his hands steepled beneath his chin. His face was sombre, half hidden behind neat moustaches and beard. He had a heavily lined brow, under which burnt intelligent, penetrating eyes, and thick hair which had once been sable-dark, now streaked and smudged in white. He was of medium height and average build, but his presence took up considerably more space than his physique.

He glared at the two uniformed servants in front of his desk, a footman named Harris and a laundry maid, Bingham. Both stood with their hands worming behind their backs and their gaze resting anywhere but on the Earl.

"I'm afraid your excuses are wasted on me," said Jekyll, his voice deep and resonant. "You know perfectly well that I accept none when the rule concerning access to the basement is broken."

"We were curious about—" stumbled the footman.

Jekyll cut him off with a look. "I'll thank you to speak only when asked a question, Harris. Your conduct has rescinded the household privileges you've enjoyed."

For half a minute or more, there was utter silence.

"I find it hard to express my disappointment," said Jekyll. "Not only do you break the cardinal rule of this house, the *one* cardinal rule, but in doing so you make a mockery of the kind leniency shown to you by Lady Violet following your disgraceful behaviour last week! You should thank whatever deity you happen to favour that I believe your claim not to have acted on behalf of a third party. And with that being so, then why? Eh? For heaven's sake, why? What were you hoping to achieve? Steal my life's work and make a run for it?"

"No, m'lord," said Harris and Bingham in rapid unison.

Jekyll leaned forward a little on his desk, his voice simmering with controlled anger. "What was wrong with the family silver, I believe that's the usual choice for staff pilfering? Last week and this, you have both played to the very worst clichés of your stations."

The footman opened his mouth to speak but thought better of it. Jekyll sat back, his hands gripping the arms of his chair. "I propose to waste no more time on ingrates who would deliberately throw away decently paid, advantageous positions under this roof! It beggars belief!" He rubbed at his forehead wearily and sighed. "You'll both leave at once, needless to say without written characters. Mr Poole will take you as far as Hagstow in the brougham, since I doubt we can trust you not to ransack the plate room on your way out."

"Thank you m'lord," muttered Harris and Bingham.

A tall, angular figure stepped forward from behind the dismissed servants. Poole, Westwych House's steward in charge of the house and the grounds, was every bit as glowering as the Earl but unlike his master was peculiarly elusive, the sort of man who faded from thought the moment he was out of sight. The rest of the staff tolerated rather than liked him, making fun of his bald head and his glass eye, resenting his unwavering adherence to the Earl, and finding him uncomfortable company because of his reserved demeanour and his tendency to brood. He dressed in the same formal style as his employer, albeit several degrees cheaper in order to maintain a correct, respectful visual gap in status.

"Before you go, Poole," said Jekyll, "ask the kitchens to bring me whatever mice they have."

"Yes, my Lord," he said.

"All caught alive, I hope?" said Jekyll.

"Apart from one, I believe, Sir. It was discarded." His attention turned to the two servants. "Out."

As he left, ushering them away, he glanced back at Jekyll who gave him the briefest and shallowest of nods.

Chapter 3

Jack Utterson's journal

Fri. 18th June continued, village of Hagstow,
arrive approx. 7:40pm.

It was close to six o'clock before the carriage left Bristol. I
had no stomach to complain since it had been so thoroughly
turned by that scoundrel Jemmison! Every seat was taken,
some twice over with children sitting on their mother's
knees, and every passenger was soaked with rain. The air
in the carriage quickly became dank and thickened.

Although the downpour had eased a little, my mood most
certainly had not. To add to the misery, the road leading
out to the villages south of the city was so pitted that each
traveller in turn found themselves almost flung into the arms
of their neighbour. However, this circumstance, combined with
the drenching we'd all received and our delayed departure,
fortunately fostered a grumbling bonhomie amongst my
fellow sufferers which at least helped to pass the time.

After a short stop at a village beside the river Chew – I
was relieved when three passengers got out, then dismayed

when five climbed aboard – the carriage made a winding progress through craggy hills and narrow passes. By now we had overtaken the glacially advancing rain, and the ochred light of a summer's evening bathed the landscape in sensuous colours which shone all the brighter for being freshly washed. I tipped back my head, to rest it against the top of the seat, and at last managed to re-warm my thoughts a little.

I was the only passenger to alight at Hagstow, so took a while to find my bearings. My new suitcase, poor thing, having been tied to the rack on top of the carriage, was already beginning to look like the sorrowfully road-battered one it had replaced. The weariness of travel made it feel even heavier than when I'd left London.

At first sight, Hagstow was a picturesque little community. The road running through it divided up a generous scattering of one and two-storey cottages, most of them built to a similar design with overhanging tiled roofs and stubby chimneys. Within a short walk of my starting point there was a narrow river which cascaded around a low, ragged promontory before winding down a gentle incline towards an opening into a spectacular valley some distance to the south-west. Around the village, trees of great age were interspersed with lively copses and spreads of heather which shivered in the evening breeze. As I walked, I heard the cluck of chickens coming from many a rear garden.

Few villagers were in evidence, but a sturdy, bloom-faced man carrying a canvas bag of tools kindly directed me to Hagstow's only inn, The Tethered Goat, where I'd arranged for lodgings for the duration of my stay in the area.

Apart from its slightly larger size, and the weathered board on the front wall, there was nothing to distinguish the inn from the cottages which nestled up to it on three sides. On the fourth side was an open, overgrown area, upon which an unusually low and incongruously situated barn pointed to the inn's history as a coach house.

Hauling my suitcase into the inn, I found a cosy, low-ceilinged interior. An L-shaped bar took up one corner, opposite a large, unlit inglenook fireplace. Waving foliage was visible through the small windows, and most of the floor was taken up with an assortment of basic tables and chairs. A handful of villagers were gathered around a table near the bar, glasses and tankards in hand, talking amongst themselves.

I took a few hesitant steps forward, not wanting to disturb their deliberations. "Excuse me," I ventured, when a couple of inquisitive looks came my way, "might the landlord be available? Mr Prendick?"

Before one of them could answer, a sonorous voice came from the doorway behind the bar. "Aye, I'm right here." Prendick was a bear of a man, tall and muscular, with the most prodigious set of side-whiskers I've ever seen. "You the London chappie?"

"Yes, I'm Jack Utterson." I smiled. "I sent a letter of enquiry on the fourteenth?"

"This'll be the scientist," said one of the villagers, in the friendly, vowelled tones of the local accent. "You working for the Earl?"

"No, I have the honour of being on official business for the British Museum."

An expression of mildly impressed approval passed

43

silently amongst them. "When I was a lad on the docks," said another villager, a white-haired grandfather, "I lumped for Brunel, he was science. You building more ships and bridges, then?"

"Er, no, my field is a different one entirely, I'm afraid. The project upon which I'm engaged is to catalogue Neolithic and Chalcolithic anthropological data along the Lulsgate Plateau, with reference to the transition away from a nomadic Mesolithic culture."

The landlord and his customers nodded slowly. Prendick scratched mightily under his arm as he spoke. "Since you're our only visitor at the moment, Mr Utterson, you gets the bigger back room. You want some hot water sent up?"

"I'd be much obliged, thank you."

"Y'ungry?"

"I am, Mr Prendick, I haven't had a bite since this morning."

"Come down in a bit. Give it an hour, mind." He craned his bull-like neck to one side, to look over my shoulder. "Lizzie, show the gennerman up."

I turned to see that a very personable young lady was just now entering the room in my wake. She was trimly built, with kind eyes and a generous mouth. Her hair was long and of a flame-red hue, tumbling about her neck and shoulders in a way quite unlike the complex arrangements common to women back home.

She reached to pick up my suitcase but, in an effort to maintain propriety toward one of the fair sex, I snatched at the handle. I think I accidentally gave her the impression that I was guardedly keeping my belongings to myself. I tried to mumble an explanation but scarlet mortification gummed my words. She led me behind the bar and, via a narrow passageway, up equally narrow steps which creaked loudly underfoot.

"I hope you weren't getting a mouth pie off my da and his cronies?" she said.

"Oh, no, not at all," I said, trying to ensure the heft of my suitcase didn't knock gouges from the walls.

"They gossip like fishwives," said Lizzie. "Since your letter came and they saw the word 'scientist' they've concluded you're a distinguished colleague of the Earl's, up at the House."

"Oh. I'm so sorry, I didn't mean to give a false impression."

"Don't worry, I told them you couldn't be. If you were, you'd not be staying at the Tethered Goat in Hagstow, would you? A'least you've stemmed all their endless yammering about African gold rushes and Mr Marconi's doings in the Bristol Channel."

On the upper floor, a low door opened onto a modest but pleasantly appointed room, with night stand at one end, brass bedstead at the other and an antique, well-worn armchair positioned close to the bed. The ceiling sloped under the building's eaves, such that the top of the window was at chest level.

"Delightful," I said, "I'm sure it will suit me perfectly."

"You'll be staying a few weeks, your letter said?"

"For a month or two, at least, possibly longer. I'm not at all sure how long my work will take."

"What's your work?" said Lizzie.

"I'm here to catalogue Neolithic and Chalcolithic anthropological data along the Lulsgate Plateau, with reference to the transition away from a nomadic Mesolithic culture. I have an assistant curatory role at the British Museum."

"You're not that much older than me, are you? You must have had lots of schooling for a job like that?"

"Ah, no, in fact, er, to be perfectly honest, I have an Aunt Carrie whose third marriage is to a member of the museum board of governors. On the day I reached five and twenty she, and most of the rest of the family, issued a stern proclamation that I was to stop dithering and make something of myself come hell or high water."

Lizzie laughed heartily, the backs of her fingers brushing her lips. It was a sound which dispelled my blushes entirely. "Speaking of water, I'll get you that hot jug, Mr Utterson."

"Oh, please, um, Jack . . ."

She nodded and smiled as she closed the door behind her. Alone now, I set down my case and stood for a moment in quiet contemplation. I find that a few minutes of stillness can be quite restorative after hours of constant activity.

Enjoying the peace, I admired the decorated, gourd-shaped bottle which stood on the window sill. It was of an opaque green glass, similar to ones I'd also seen on the window sills downstairs, and I realised – based on 16th century examples I'd encountered in the course of my work – it must be a witch-bottle, as used in apotropaic magic to ward off evil. I was quite amused by this evidence of such a quaint old custom. I was indeed in the countryside!

Opening the suitcase on the bed's colourfully quilted coverlet, I began to unpack. I wasn't sure where to place my clothes, since there was no armoire in the room, so I folded them as best I could over the bars of the bed's tall footboard. I took particular care when unpacking the extensive range of folded maps which the museum had been kind enough to loan me. These maps, covering the extensive hills and valleys of the area, were to be my indispensable tools over the coming days and weeks. However, since there was no table in the room either, I placed them in as tidy a stack as possible on the floor beside the armchair.

I sank into the chair – several inches deeper than was intended by the manufacturer, I'm almost sure – and weariness quickly put me into a doze. My nap was one of those unusual instances, occasioned by sheer fatigue, when sleep blinks in and out without any bodily awareness. I had the peculiar experience of seeing the daylight at the window suddenly change angle, becoming lower in the sky and redder in complexion. At the same instant, a tall white jug of water appeared to wink into existence on the night stand. It was still warm, so I can't have been asleep for more than thirty minutes or so. By my pocket watch the time was five and twenty past six.

I freshened my hands and face to dispel the remnants of my exhaustion, and made my way back downstairs to the bar. A warm aroma of cooking drifted up to me and I grew hungrier with each step.

The inn's tables and chairs were now full of people. As I emerged from the passage, their hubbub of conversation dropped almost to silence and every eye was upon me. Feeling as if I was suddenly a specimen under glass labelled 'a Common or Garden London Chappie', I attempted a cheery nod at the room. I was much relieved when the chatter returned to its previous level. Mr Prendick appeared and directed me to a table where a number of locals were gathered, including most of those I'd encountered earlier.

Outside, a distant roll of thunder heralded the approach of what I took to be the Bristol storm, on its snail-like progress southward, although the fading daylight which bathed the interior of the inn was still that of a warm summer's night. Motes of dust rushed and pirouetted in its soft beams.

As I sat down, welcomed by raised glasses of cloudy ale, I noticed for the first time a photograph hung up on the whitewashed wall behind the bar, elaborately framed in black and with a black ribbon tied in a bow at its lower edge. The picture was a formal and evidently expensive cabinet card showing Mr Prendick standing to the left, a decade or two younger and a stone or two lighter, while to the right stood a little girl who must have been Lizzie. Between them was a woman, eyes closed in death, posed in a sitting position and dressed in a plain style. The facial similarities between this woman and the adult Lizzie were both obvious and heartbreaking.

"Rabbit stew," announced Mr Prendick proudly, setting a large steaming bowl and a full tankard in front of me. "It's yesterday's but t'is still good."

"Thank you, I'm sure it's splendid," I said, a little nervous of the oily patterns glistening on its surface. Looking at it, I decided to temporarily postpone my question about what alternatives to beer might be available.

"Oi, Jim!" cried the old man who'd worked for Brunel, playing to the room from his seat opposite me. He waved a finger at my bowl. "Where's mine, then?"

"I'm not wasting decent stew on you, Bern," said Prendick, "it's s'posed to go in your belly, not your beard." Half the room was set cackling.

Bern was already onto other matters, nudging a couple of his neighbours who were new to me. He was a frail old stick, but his eyes glistened and his lips were red and mobile. "London," he said to them, pointing across the table at me as if to confirm the novelty of my presence.

The others around the table took that as their cue to companionably probe my knowledge of the city, its landmarks, its people, its fashions and its mode of life. I answered their questions as fully as I was able, but – oh, in fact the stew was surprisingly delicious – but on the whole they seemed disappointed that the lives of the London citizenry, except in surroundings, differed little from their own. The two people Bern had been nudging, a burly husband and wife named Woolcot, were particularly interested in whether I'd been to the Royal Palace. I said, rather wittily I thought, that the only Palace I'd visited was the Palace theatre on the Strand, but they didn't appear to appreciate the remark.

For my part, I learned – oh dear, the ale, rather strong – I learned that Hagstow wasn't quite the rural enclave I'd expected; that while many of the locals worked on nearby farmland, a growing number were employed in modern industries, drawn by the greater regularity of income this afforded them; that the poor harvests of recent years had increased this tendency and that, consequently, the overall population of the village was sadly in decline. I began to understand why the arrival of someone like me, someone who might bring with him new perspectives and possibilities, would be the subject of curiosity.

"You're not here to work for the Earl, then?" said the man sitting to my right, a scruffy, droop-lipped fellow the others addressed as Tolly.

49

"No," I said. "Miss Prendick mentioned this Earl to me earlier, but I'd never heard of him before. Would he be the local landowner?"

There were nods. "Lives at Westwych House, a couple of mile up the hills," said Tolly. "Decent enough gennerman. At least, he's not stoked up the rents on his farms the last few years, not like most of his sort. That's 'cos he's got a factory in Bristol making his money. Bicycles. My lad left to work there, last winter."

"Aye, Jekyll's not so bad," muttered Mr Woolcot opposite me.

There was a hesitant tone in both their voices, the reason for which became clear when Mrs Woolcot added: "Lizzie's friend Ada, she's second housemaid at Westwych, she reckons Lady Violet is nice as you please but Jekyll's a gert moody one. Bit odd. Bit peculiar."

"He's reckoned to be one of these great amateur discoverers you hear about," said Tolly, "only he don't seemed to have discovered nothing yet."

"Proper scientific enquiry shouldn't be hurried," I assured him. "Or so I'm told."

Toddy shrugged. "Long as he keeps hisself to hisself. Don't bother us, we don't bother him."

A sudden rhythmic tapping at the window marked the arrival of the heavy rain. Daylight rapidly drained from the sky.

"I reckon he's inventing a new transport, innit?" said old Bern with a chuckle. "Bicycles today, flying wings to tie on your feet tomorrow! He's got a horseless carriage up there at the house, he has."

"Has he really?" I said. "I should very much like to see

one of those. Is that his line of enquiry? Machinery and so on?"

"Your guess is as good as mine," said Tolly. "Bern might even be right, for all anyone knows. Whatever he does, there's high-up gents come to see him about it now and then."

I finished the last of the stew. "Has the Earl been at his researches for a long time?"

"Ever since he inherited," said Bern. "And he inherited young, wasn't even twenty years of age. Lady Georgiana, his ma, was already long dead. And it were a sad day when his father Henry Jekyll passed. Over thirty year ago, now, 1862. Always stop an' talk, Henry would, never had any airs an' graces about him. He died when he fell in a deep gully up in the hills, broke his leg, couldn't move. It was eleven days before they found him."

"How awful," I said. Immediately, my nerves began to prickle, knowing my work would be taking *me* up into the hills. "Was he out for a walk?"

"No, he were a great amateur discoverer too, his passion was local history. Wrote a couple of books, he did. Frederick, tha's his son, tha's the Earl now, he was going to carry on what Henry started, but I don't reckon that lasted long. Quite soon he took to his secrets. Last time I saw Frederick were at Lady Evelyn's funeral, and that was nine or ten winters back."

"Lady Evelyn?"

"His first wife," said Bern. "Good woman. One of the Dorset Stanhopes, proper landed people, respectable. She had some illness or other and went raving mad. The Earl fell to pieces when she died, by all accounts. Biggest funeral you ever saw, black draped carriages, plumed horses, extra mourners, the lot." He looked around. "Where's Lizzie at?" He rose to his feet, cradling his empty glass to his chest, the creak of old bones showing on his face.

"Perhaps it's no surprise that the present Earl is taciturn," I suggested, "with such tragedy in his past?"

"We all have our sorrows," muttered Tolly. "The rich don't feel them no worse than the poor."

My nerves continued to prickle. "The previous Earl's unfortunate fate . . ." I said. "Are falls of that sort common? Accidents?"

Tolly's demeanour seemed to falter slightly, and I felt I'd asked an awkward question. "Accidents? No," he said. "But the old Earl'd be off to the middle of nowhere, on his own. Lots of groundholes and the like up there, y'see, so it can be treacherous. He went where nobody with sense has any business, rooting about where there's caveman remains, turning up bits of pottery and arrow heads and the like. Ancient, lonely places nobody goes. The hills are best avoided."

I felt a dreadfully cold sensation run through me. Outside, the rain was forming quick rivulets down the window panes. A stiff wind, as yet inaudible above the room's hum of talk, was shaking the bushes. Bern returned with his glass refilled and eased himself down, taking care not to spill a drop.

"Wha's best avoided?" he said.

"The hills," said Mr Woolcot beside him.

Bern looked at me, his open mouth showing amidst his white beard. "You been talking about the hills, Tolly? No wonder young London's looking a bit peaky all of a sudden."

I heard Tolly mutter darkly under his breath. He raised his tankard to his lips.

"Don't go scaring the lad away, Bern, he's only just got 'ere," said Mr Woolcot.

"If he's only just got 'ere," said Bern, wagging his head to imply impeccable logic, "then he won't know what's needed to know if he's staying, will he?"

"About the hills?" I said. I forced a smile which rapidly felt rigid.

"Pay him no attention," said Tolly, glowering somberly, "he's off on his evenin' wheezes."

Bern twisted on his seat to face Tolly. "We've not got reason to hide nothing, have we? No, right. So!"

A gust of chilly air suddenly lapped at my legs, and I noticed that the inn's customers were beginning to thin out for the night, leaving in groups of two or three, each turning up their collars as they opened the door to the lane outside and briefly let in the sight and sound of the driving rain. Short farewells from those remaining followed them out.

Bern sat back slightly, adjusting himself around his neck and arms. Mr and Mrs Woolcot did the same, the expectant arrangement of their faces declaring them agog to hear what Bern was going to say, no matter how many times they'd heard it before.

"You're science, right young London? Well, I don't know if there's science in black magic and monsters or not–"

Immediately, I couldn't help but glance at Mrs Woolcot, and then at Lizzie, who seemed to have divined what was being discussed and had drawn up a stool, to sit with her arms crossed on the table.

"–but we've enough of it around 'ere to fill any museum."

I whispered to Bern, as low as I could. "I say, is this a suitable subject to be aired with ladies present?" For a hesitant second or two, there was genuine bafflement around the table, followed by a snorting burst of laughter from every one of them, aimed at me, which I have to say I found rather offensive.

Mr Woolcot jabbed his wife in the ribs. "'Ere, Dora, you'd better bugger off, then."

She swatted him across the shoulder with the back of her hand. "I's a modern lady!"

"I don't know as it's a fit subject for *anyone*, lad," said Bern, "I'll keep my peace if you'd rather."

"No, please," I stammered, feeling a flush at my cheeks, "you're quite right, any historical information might have a bearing on my work."

He took a long drink from his pint and smacked his bright lips wetly. Tiny dots of moisture scattered themselves across the table. "This part of the Mendips is full of stories going back hunnerds of years, as far back as you like. Hagstow isself, the name means a meeting place of witches. There were claims of witchery 'ere for centuries, regular as ninepence. They had witch trials in this very village, and at Pinstone down the road, in Queen Elizabeth's time and then in the Civil War days. O'course, there weren't no such thing as witches then, and there ain't now, s'all nonsense, but people believed it 'cos of the weird things that got seen about."

"Weird things?" I said in a low voice.

"This whole parish's always been called an unquiet place." He raised a finger to point in various directions and draw paths in the air. "F'r instance, the road going east, out past Radstock, that's haunted by a highwayman as was hanged there in the days when this pub was a coaching house. All the time, people hear hooves running up beside 'em when there's nobody there. Or, f'r instance, you go into the woods, behind the cottages that way, you go in there, sit an' listen, you won't hear a bird, you won't see so much as a hedgehog, there's summin about it that gives you the shivers. People have seen lights in there, in the dead of night, and sensed they was being watched in the daytime. It's no wonder wild stories get started. I thought I seen summin meself, when I were a boy. Went in those woods to show me mates I weren't frit, and nearly wet meself."

"You're not above that now, on the ale," snorted Mr Woolcot.

Bern ignored them. "Because, I saw a shape. Kind of hunched. It didn't walk, it just glided along, slow and level. Soon as I got the use of me feet back, I scampered out of there like a startled rabbit. Afterwards, long time after, I felt like such a fool when I realised I'd scared meself over a cloud's shadow moving through the trees, but at the time I thought I'd seen one of the creatures that live in the hills, I thought one had come down looking for food."

As if the blood in my veins had not run cold enough that day, now it froze with horror. "Creatures?" I said.

"That's one of the reasons it took so long to find the old Earl back in '62. For three days, nobody'd go up there, Earl or not. His lawyer had to offer five guineas a head in the end. Every age in history has reckoned these hills are occupied by dark things. It was faeries and goblins way back in the Medieval. Then witches, like I say, for a long time, brewing up their horrors to terrify all and sundry. Then there's testimonials in the parish records from the seventeen hunnerds – you can look 'em up – about the restless spirits of dead miners roaming the land. That's when they were starting up a lot the mining west of here, ochre and coal and all sorts. In the days when I saw shapes in the woods, seventy, eighty year ago, the creatures we was all scared of were troglodytes. I reckon us kids got that idea from a story book, we thought there were hairless boggle-eyed flesh-eaters who come creeping out of the caves. These hills are riddled right through with holes and tunnels, and most of them have never been explored."

"Thank goodness such superstitions don't extend into our modern scientific age," I said, unsteadily.

"Don't they?" said Bern. "Today, some think there's been wolves up there for near a decade now, that maybe they haven't died out in England like we're told."

"It *may* be possible?" I frowned.

"May be," he shrugged, "but isn't. In Hagstow, we say it's not wolves at all, but a werewolf. Tha's people who's cursed. People who turn by the light of the moon into murderous brutes."

He paused, as if weighing up my reaction. An unsettling and nervous frisson suddenly seemed to circle the table, as if those present were thieves anticipating capture, or soldiers fearing the moment of discovery by merciless enemies. I wasn't sure how to reply. "As a cautionary tale for the children?"

"No, young London, it's a fact."

I was thoroughly perplexed. "Why would you say so?" I shuddered. "If you sensibly dismiss local fables of witches and goblins, why believe in a different notion every bit as absurd?"

"Because we've seen it," said Bern. "Least, Tolly has."

Tolly's voice was a whisper. "That's why I'm saying the hills are best avoided," he said. His tone implied a great reluctance to speak, as if this one brief utterance had escaped him for the sole purpose of cutting short my scepticism. His implacable countenance – mirrored in the rest of them around the table! – gave me no doubt as to his absolute sincerity.

"End of June, '88," nodded Bern. "We had a clear, cool night, no cloud, all the stars of Heaven in the sky and the full Moon shining so bold you could see for miles down the valley. One of them beautiful still nights, y'know? And close on midnight, half the village gets woken up by the most blood-curdling howls you ever heard. Like a wolf, but not a wolf, a sort of God-forsaken scream. Not in pain, mind, it was like the biggest, nastiest beast in all the world calling its territory."

"I was fifteen year old," muttered Lizzie. "I was only awake to hear the last of it, but that sound haunts my head to this day."

"On and off, it was," said Tolly, "just here and there, like. But each time, you felt it go right through you. Me and–" He leaned back and twisted around, looking for someone. "No, he's gone. Me and Pat Ollis, he had the blacksmith's at the time, we went up the hills a little way with shotguns. A dozen or more men waited just outside, here.

"We didn't take lamps in case it drew attention, but the Moon was so bright we didn't need them anyway. We weren't planning on going far, we was scared solid like everyone else. About a quarter of a mile we'd crept along, maybe more, and then we saw it. If you climb the first ridge that you come to on the road north, you can see three or four higher ridges further on. The top one was clear as day in the moonlight. Running along it, heading away from us and up the slope, was an animal. It was a good distance away, and it was in view for no more than half a minute, prob'ly not even that, but we had sharp sight of it.

"It ran fast as lightning. Sometimes like a man, sometimes bounding along like a wolf. But it wasn't neither, it was all the wrong shape. Great big back legs, with thinner ones at the front, and its head was round like a man's. It was as real as you or I, but I tell you it was no beast of God's creation. What we'd have done if it'd been coming our way, I hate to think. Soon as it vanished, we ran like all the flames of Hell were at our tail.

"At first, everyone thought we made it up, just to frighten 'em for laughs. Then they said the howling was putting ideas in our heads, getting us jumping at nothing. But I know what I saw, and so does Pat."

"It wasn't long, though, before most of us believed," said Bern. "Next day, there was a sheep found, not far away, torn to pieces like you wouldn't believe. From that night, and for the ten years since, if a sheep or a goat gets loose and goes astray in these hills, it don't come back. Not ever. Same for dogs, and you'd think a dog'd be clever enough and quick enough to keep hisself out of trouble, wouldn't yer?"

"M-Might not the same hold true for many wilderness areas?" I could feel my heart beating nervously in my chest. "Animals might get lost in the, er, Scottish mountains? Or Exmoor?"

"Aye," agreed Bern. "'Cept that some also get taken from

the farms around 'ere. Cows, even, and all that's left is a drag of blood on the field. Not often, only couple of time in a twelve-month, like. Tha's not thieves, thieves walk 'em out, quiet. Tha's summat 'ungry."

"People have gone missing too," muttered Tolly. "Three times since '88. They went over the hills. No trace, nothing, and they weren't crossing no wilds, like the old Earl back in '62, they were going by regular tracks."

"One of them were a cousin of Noone's at the baker's," said Mrs Wolcott, tipping back her glass to finish her ale.

"T-Then this . . . beast has been seen again?"

"It has and it hasn't," said Bern. "Things have been seen, and heard, but none of it like that first night. Chap from down in Wells – wha'was his name? The joiner. Aye, Bill, thassit – he was staying in this inn and he saw what he said was like a great big spider, all legs, the size of a barrel. Crossed his path in the dark, sudden like, scuttling. What set him yellin' was he swore it had a face, like a man's, only with a dozen eyes. That were a few years ago now, mind. There was summat like a huge cat seen along the same ridge where Tolly and Pat saw the werewolf, it were letting out these fearful shouts and growls. The Spring before last, Pat's eldest lad and his girl were out courting – this was in the daytime – up on the other side of the rise past Pat's place, where they couldn't be seen. They come racing down, eyes like saucers, saw some creature slithering through the long grass, covered in scales and spines. A man, they were certain, but his arms and legs curling like an adder's tail in season. There's been other sightings too."

"Is it your opinion," I said, clearing my throat, "that a

succession of these . . . were-creatures have periodically been at large in the area?"

Bern shrugged. "P'raps tha's indeed how it is, a moonlight curse that catches the unwary from time to time. Or p'raps it's some forgotten evil from long ago, makin' monsters when it stirs in its sleep. P'raps Mother Nature's had a look at all the digging and burning and changing we done to build the world, and She don't like it. Nobody knows."

I was feeling thoroughly unnerved. The rain continued to splash the window panes as I watched them.

Conversation around the table was already finding its way to other topics. Bern was entreating Mr Prendick to relent on the subject of the rabbit stew, to no avail, and Lizzie was making arrangements with Tolly over some repairs her father evidently wanted done to the roof. The matter-of-fact, almost casual way in which they'd related these stories about the hills, and the equally straightforward way in which they now turned their attentions elsewhere, left me in a state of mind somewhere between confusion and terror.

Deciding that my frayed nerves were becoming altogether too close to an ungentlemanly visibility, I excused myself on account of my long and tiring journey. I was warmed by Lizzie's "goodnight, Jack," delivered with a gentle smile and a sidelong flick of her eyes, and I made my way back up the creaking staircase.

It was barely a quarter past ten o'clock, but the day had exhausted me utterly. Nevertheless, I found I could not rest. Circulating in my mind, unbidden and unresolved, was the feeling that Tolly's and old Bern's recollections were entwined with the dreadful centaur-thing I had seen exhibited only hours before. Had it once been an inhabitant of the hills I was to survey? Was its existence *proof* of my dinner companions' extraordinary claims?

And the look I had seen in its eyes . . .

I had little sleep that night.

Chapter 4

As Utterson stirred restlessly in his bed, Frederick Jekyll's steward Poole was locking up the household brougham for the night. He leaned into the carriage and looked slowly around its interior, an oil lamp held up above his head, before clicking its door shut and leaving the stable block to cross the wide yard at the back of Westwych House. Bundled under one arm were two sets of clothes, belonging to Harris and Bingham, the servants dismissed by the Earl that afternoon, and their small cases of personal effects.

The day's waves of rain were finally abating, leaving heavy drips to fall from guttering and slither between cobbles under a black, lumbering sky. Poole's steady footsteps were barely audible beyond the sphere of lamplight in which he walked. An innate, unselfconscious stealth was his habit and his preference.

Before re-entering the house he paused to unlock the boiler room, close to the rear entrance into the kitchens. He threw the clothes and cases, ready for burning, into the coal store beside the robust, rumbling furnace that ran

Westwych's heating and electrical systems, overseen by the Earl's personal engineer, Monsieur Moreau. Moreau himself was in town tonight, seeking entertainment, but the hot heartbeat of his well-maintained machines pulsed on, powering the lights which gleamed gently behind many of Westwych's pointed, narrow windows.

And behind a line of the tallest windows, on the other side of the house, an electric candelabra shone overhead in the vaulted entrance hall atrium where the Earl kept his collection of animal specimens. Jewels of light reflected in the vivarium's large, glass panels and along the dark, polished woodwork of its bulky, slab-like frame.

It had three adjacent compartments in all, spanning the full width of the frame so that two sides of each compartment were glass, two wooden. The first was filled with foliage to mimic the jungles of South America. Inside, spiders lurked under leaves or clung to bark, males the size of dinner plates keeping themselves at a distance from the larger females. The next was brightly lit, partly filled with sand and blanched desert vegetation so that the Arabian scorpions would feel at home.

Frederick Jekyll stood beside the compartment housing snakes, each just under six feet in length, in an environment of black Australian soil. Their dull brown winter colouring had lightened into the patterned yellowish olive of the summer months. Their small, ridged heads were motionless, their black, bead-like eyes watching the Earl as he watched them. They seemed to sense that prey was near.

Jekyll held a wooden box containing the live mice trapped in and around the kitchens over the course of the previous week. He reached up to the top section of the compartment and slid back a small hatch.

The mice began to scramble frantically over and across each other as he opened the lid of the box. One by one, he picked them out by the tail and dropped them through the hatch. With the hatch resealed, he turned a circular dial. The mechanism which dropped the mice into the compartment was one he'd designed himself, just as he'd designed the traps which caught them and, kept in drawers under each compartment, all the equipment he used for handling the vivarium's inhabitants: clamps and gloves for the snakes, tongs to hold the scorpions, thin sheets to administer a light electric shock when it was time to harvest their venom.

The mice tumbled into view behind the glass, landing on a tilting arrangement of small platforms which delivered them uninjured down onto the soil. Instantly, they scattered, leaping high over the snakes' thick bodies in a panic to find shelter. The snakes' wavering tongues smelled the arrival of meat and slowly their heads turned to follow the scent.

Poole appeared at Jekyll's side. The manservant chose his words carefully since nobody, not even Lady Jekyll, dared use the word 'pets' in the Earl's presence. "Was sufficient food collected, Sir?"

"Yes, thank you Poole," said Jekyll. He closed the wooden trapping box. "Harris and, er . . .?"

"Bingham, Sir."

"Bingham. Safe and sound?"

"Yes, Sir, they should wake in an hour or two."

"I'll inject them with the new formulation shortly." Jekyll handed Poole the empty box. "There's a great deal to do before our visitors arrive. In the morning, go into Bristol and get a replacement for Bingham. Harris's work can be divided between the other men, we might as well save a little tax. Also, obtain a further two for downstairs, both males in good health."

Poole's stolid demeanour flickered momentarily. "Two, Sir?"

Jekyll's gaze met his. "Major Ruck and the accountant sewn to his breeches will be expecting to see progress. Since we can't show them a great deal of that, we can at least show them industry."

"Understood, Sir."

"For the same reason, I shall want Moreau to impress them." A harder edge entered his voice. "He *is* aware of tomorrow's timetable, isn't he?"

There were few people in the world Poole actively disliked, but Moreau the engineer was one of them. He tolerated the Frenchman's casual attitudes only under sufferance. "He's off on some jolly, Sir, but he'll be ready . . . You know how he is."

"Mmm," growled the Earl. He turned on his heels. "That will be all."

Poole, hands behind his back, nodded in the direction of the feeding snakes. "I have a similar duty to perform first, Sir."

Jekyll paused for a moment, as if steeling himself. "Yes, of course." His voice became soft, filled with something which might have been weariness. ". . . Thank you, Mr Poole. I'm most grateful."

"Sir," said Poole quietly.

The two men went their separate ways, Jekyll upstairs and along the landing to the nursery, Poole out to the pigsty at the far end of the kitchen garden.

Jekyll opened the nursery door with immense care, to avoid any creak in the hinges or floorboards. He leaned inside, through as narrow a gap as possible in case the light from the landing caused a disturbance. The room's warmth bathed his face, and as his eyes grew accustomed to the dark he could make out the shapes of two small beds, separated by a large rectangular rug. In each bed, a hump of sheets ended in a splash of unruly young hair against pillows.

By Jekyll's reckoning, he'd made one serious mistake in his life, a mistake so bad it had led to the funeral of his first wife, Evelyn, leaving his daughters motherless and a leaden guilt forever pressing on his soul. Yet, without that mistake, without that burden of guilt, he would never have married Violet, never discovered the simple truth that even the most agonising pain of heart may eventually be eased. The nursery's occupants, their twin boys Claude and William, were living proof of that. Every day, for seven years now, they had shown him that hope still existed in the world. Jekyll withdrew, the serenity of the sleeping twins having lifted his spirits while, out of sight in the far corner of the nursery, the boys' stately nanny continued to snore peacefully on her fold-out palliasse.

Directly above the nursery, up in the servants' quarters at the attic level, Lizzie Prendick's friend Ada had spent the last half hour rearranging the furniture in her shared room. Now she was taking a break, partly because she was bloody well tired, partly because she was fed up and irritated. Little enough bloody space in here as it is! Every bloody time there's a house party! Every bloody time! Why couldn't visitors' staff bunk down in the bloody stables?

Some snooty cow would be put in here for tomorrow night, she just knew it. Some *duchess's* servant girl, oh how lovely, a *duchess's* girl, how vastly superior you are, what with you being a *duchess's* girl. Well *she* could bloody well slot in under the eaves and bang *her* bloody head on the roof trusses of a morning.

Ada, being *second* housemaid at Westwych, thoroughly resented the inconveniences which no *first* housemaid would ever be expected to endure. She stood surveying the awkward traffic jam of beds, all that her lugging about had accomplished, puffing aggressively at a freshly-lit Ogden's and stuffing the little packet back into her skirt pocket. She crossed her doughy arms, face glowering, dark mop of hair in an uproar, cigarette plucked and planted back and forth between pale, pursed lips.

She was distracted by a faint glimmer at the attic's dormer window. Her eye level was only slightly above the level of the windowsill, so she hoiked herself up on tiptoe to look down the slope of the roof into the rear courtyard.

There was Poole, lamp held out ahead of him, leading a large pig on a short length of rope, out of the kitchen garden and towards the old outbuildings a hundred yards away. The newer stable block, used these days to store the household carriages and the Earl's new automobile, was as tidily maintained as the house itself, but the older stables beyond, half hidden among the trees, lay shabby and alone. And were utterly forbidden territory, like the basement.

Ada took a long drag of her tab. She sniggered to herself, imagining the pig was really Mrs Cook, stark naked on all fours. Oh, you fiend, Mr Poole!

Her fleeting smile faded, watching Poole disappear from

view behind the chimney stack at the edge of the roof, to reappear on the other side thirty seconds later, the faint glow of the lamp preceding him, the pig trotting heavily behind. A cortege in the twilight.

Ada took a final drag. Wasn't that the sty's biggest porker? The mottled one? Cook had wanted that pig for tomorrow's menu, hadn't she? Of course she had.

The second housemaid knew better than to question such things. She knew better than to make a fuss. Extinguishing her cigarette on the window frame, she deposited the tiny stub that remained into the little tin she kept for dog ends. Ah, nearly enough in there now to make a new gasper. She returned to her furniture lugging.

If odd things were seen by the servants at Westwych House from time to time, none of them discussed it. If the kitchen garden invisibly lost half its produce, comment was never passed. If any attempt to enter the basement or the old stables meant instant dismissal, nobody objected. Working conditions here were markedly better than in most grand houses, so why upset the apple cart? The Earl had his secrets and his eccentricities but, well, didn't everyone of his class? If, now and again, terrible sounds were heard in the dead of night, the howl of a wild beast or a scream of dying terror, why seek an explanation in the face of silence?

Chapter 5

Friday's rain dragged a sullen mantle of grey behind it, so that Saturday's dawn, despite being only two away from the Summer solstice, was almost as sullen and chilly as a sunrise in mid-Winter. Hagstow stirred and went about its business, dressed in an extra layer.

By Jack Utterson's pocket watch it was 7:32am when he set out from The Tethered Goat, with a full pack slung over his shoulder and a self-consciously forced sense of adventure in his heart. He made his way up and along the ridge of land behind the village, then down the other side and off across the steadily ascending, haphazardly undulating hills. At regular intervals, the folded map he clutched in one hand was unfolded, consulted, and folded up again, after which he would stand and stare at his compass for a minute or two, turning a little this way and that to orient himself.

Against the vast landscape of wildly irregular rocks and hissing grasses, he was a tiny, isolated figure. The hills soared and dipped in all directions, punctuated by sudden limestone escarpments, worn bulbous by time and wrapped in patchy lichens. The earth underfoot, cold where the wind had worked on yesterday's rainfall, squelching in mossy sags and sheltered hollows, grew firmer on the higher, drained slopes. The chilling breeze groaned softly, shaped into mournful song by narrow passes and steep slopes. A lonely place, desolate and feral.

By 9:14am, Utterson was convinced he'd lost his bearings. He pulled up the collar of his tweedy overcoat and kept glancing up at the moody, swollen sky as if expecting a handy signpost to dip beneath the clouds and point him in the right direction.

He dithered. It was something he was very good at, his most obvious and natural skill. He hated dithering, he hated his own lack of diligence and assuredness, but every time he solemnly resolved to do better he seemed to end up making a worse show of himself.

The museum had *entrusted* him. This survey was *important*. He had a serious *responsibility* to his superiors and, yes, indeed, to science itself. Yet he couldn't even find his first prehistoric site, on his first map, on his first day! It was there, *there*, clearly marked as evident on the ground. A long, rocky face to the north – tick, correct. Two low hills to the south-east – tick, correct. A flat, sheltered area between them, containing an early Bronze Age stone circle dated approximately 3000BC – nowhere in sight.

Utterson sighed, turned on the spot, looked at the map, looked at his compass, cross-checked with a different map. Rapidly losing his patience, he flopped down onto the grass, rooted through his pack for the bread and cheese wrapped up for him at the Tethered Goat, and bit savagely into them.

From where he was sitting, nothing but the sky was

visible beyond either the rocks ahead of him or the steeply rising slopes behind. He could imagine himself a thousand miles from anywhere, alone in some endless, windblown wilderness. His mind was suddenly drawn back to the unnerving tales he'd been told the previous evening, of witches and werewolves, and he cast a rapid eye around the close horizon, telling himself that stories about monsters were an interesting anthropological phenomenon and no more than that. Nothing more, despite the creeping feeling of something preternatural, something watching and lurking, which seemed to permeate these hills, a feeling he'd been trying hard to ignore for an hour or more. Suddenly, just as it had prevented him from sleeping last night, now the image of the half-human pony he'd seen in Jemmison's horrible menagerie conjured movement behind every stone, every patch of ground cover.

With an involuntary shudder, Utterson sprang to his feet. A strategic withdrawal, for the time being, he decided.

Gathering up his pack and slinging it onto his shoulder, he marched with purposeful strides in as straight a line as the rolling of the hills would allow, heading directly back to Hagstow. And if he found he wasn't heading directly back to Hagstow, well . . . then he'd surely spot the village from one hilltop or another.

He'd been too eager to start his work, he hadn't accounted for the confusing topography of the area. He hadn't taken into consideration the fact that so many sharp rises and falls looked very different *in situ* to the apparently simple arrangement of contour lines presented on paper. He needed to be more systematic in his approach, that was all. He should prepare more thoroughly so he'd properly understand, in advance, how map and landscape corresponded, and so he'd be–

There was a sudden crunching sound underfoot, the snapping of twigs beneath leaves, and one of his legs gave way beneath him. With a wailing cry, he tumbled forward, thrusting out his hands and clawing deep into the grass to prevent himself falling any further. His left leg dangled in empty space, kicking frantically, while his right leg, pulled up almost level with his chest, gripped the soil as tightly as his arms.

His heart galloping, he consciously steadied his nerves, repeatedly reassuring himself that the majority of his weight was in contact with firm ground and that he wasn't about to slip. Very slowly, he turned his head to look down.

His leg was hanging over a crevice in the earth. The sides of the crevice, roughly three feet apart, were solid rock, its edges blurred by centuries of rain but its depth impossible to gauge because it fell away into pitch darkness a yard or two past his boot. Little clatterings of disturbed pebbles rolled from under his other leg and bounced away into oblivion.

With infinite care, Utterson raised his left leg and pulled himself clear, slowly rolling onto his back. He shut his eyes for a moment, hugging his pack to his chest in an effort to stop trembling.

Good God, he'd come within a hair's breadth of suffering almost the same fate as . . . His blood running cold, the previous night's tales filled his head again. The terrible, lonely death of the old Earl – Frederick? No, it was his father, Henry, that's right. Fallen, trapped, lost.

Sitting up cautiously, then rising unsteadily to his feet,

Utterson surveyed his surroundings with dread. He looked back at the hole into which he'd nearly fallen. How could he have been so careless? It was such an obvious, livid crack, slotted into the long lines of visible strata which poked up from the grass for a hundred yards or more. He walked on, breathing deeply to quell his wailing nerves, eyes kept firmly on the ground ahead, all the time struggling to dismiss thoughts of Henry Jekyll's last hours, cold and alone.

But then he also remembered why the Earl had been here in the first place. An amateur anthropologist, the villagers around the table had implied, someone engaged in the sort of prehistoric studies which might very probably dovetail with Utterson's own. Since Utterson needed a more organised approach to fulfil his commission from the museum, then perhaps *Henry's* projects already contained the necessary groundwork? Perhaps this terrifying near-fall was serendipity in disguise, pointing the way towards efforts which might complete or even build upon Henry's legacy?

Utterson progressed – guardedly, steadily – back to Hagstow with a renewed optimism swirling in his head. If the old Earl's premature death had left the poor chap's life's work incomplete, then it made perfect sense for a fresh eye to revive it and expand upon it, to give it the life and meaning always intended. Didn't it? Of course it did!

He arrived back at The Tethered Goat at 10:41am. Throughout his walk back, it never once crossed his mind that stepping on those twigs and leaves, placed so neatly over a split in the ground, might be anything other than simple misfortune.

Lizzie Prendick was leaning over the bar, a newspaper spread open in front of her crossed arms, while her father pushed a broom around amongst the tables. She smiled at Utterson as he entered, his pack bumping the door frame and a chair or two.

"H'lo, Jack, thought you'd be gone all day."

"I anticipated as much myself, Miss Prendick," said Utterson brightly, "but I was, er, examining an interesting paleolithic find when I remembered the discussion we were having yesterday, about the previous Earl of, um . . ."

"Westwych."

"Westwych, yes. Henry. His awful accident."

"You watch yesself," growled Mr Prendick, opening the door to sweep a little pile of dust and detritus out. "Not going far off the paths up there, are you?"

"Oh, no, no," said Utterson. "I was remembering that someone mentioned the old Earl's scientific endeavours, and said he was a great amateur discoverer. In the field of anthropology, I believe?"

"Old remains," said Lizzie. "Stone Age stuff."

"Precisely right, Miss Prendick." Utterson's beaming grin and enthusiastic nod were wildly out of proportion. Lizzie's smile curled coyly. Her father sighed and shook his head a little.

"In fact," said Utterson, "he was engaged in much the same area of study as I am, on my survey for the Museum."

"Oh, tha's what all yer blather meant, is it?" muttered Mr Prendick to himself, carrying his broom off into the kitchen.

"The old Earl's caveman axes look like no more than bits of chipped stone to me," said Lizzie.

"You've seen them?" said Utterson. "His archive is extant, then?"

74

"The library up at the House is full of his things," said Lizzie. "Bits of pottery, some bones, all his books and notes. I've seen it when I've been up there working, they sometimes have extra people in to skivvy when there's something on. My friend Ada showed me."

"Do you suppose," said Utterson earnestly, "that the present Earl . . . Frederick—?"

"Frederick."

"Do you suppose he'd be amenable to my looking over his father's work? It seems almost providential that such a resource should be so nearby. It would be a way to keep Henry's work alive, so to speak. Since I have the authority and backing of the British Museum, the present Earl would be assured of my good intentions and professional standing. Do you think?"

Lizzie wrinkled her nose. "He might? No harm asking, I suppose."

Utterson checked his pocket watch. "I'll collect my card from upstairs and call at Westwych House in an hour or so."

Lizzie leaned forward a little. "Best not today. They're having a weekend party for the Royal celebrations, lots of family and guests."

"Oh."

"But, I do happen to know that the Earl will be at his factory in Bristol this noon. There's talk of the workers getting a jubilee bonus."

"Your friend Ada is a fountain of knowledge."

"No, I heard that from Tolly, his son works there. Give him a shout, he'll take you up into town in his trap for a shilling or two, he's going today anyway."

"That would be most helpful, thank you."

Lizzie turned, stretching back to face the opening into the kitchen. "Oi! Da! Give Tolly a shout, willyer?" From out of sight came a grunt of concurrence, followed by the sound of a window opening and a piercing two-note whistle.

"I'll let you know how I get on," said Utterson.

"Do," smiled Lizzie. "I'd like to make sense of all those pots and bones myself, be able to tell a caveman's axe from a bit of old rock."

"I'd be delighted," said Utterson, slightly breathless. "It really is a fascinating subject. When you hold an artifact made thousands of years ago, even something as simple as a rudimentary tool, it's as if you can sense the distant past, as if there's a connection across the centuries with whoever made or used this item. It gives you a—"

Lizzie was pointing over his shoulder with her eyes. Tolly stood in the open doorway, slouched in inconvenient distraction. "C'mon then," he said. "Is' out of me way, mind. I'll be wanting five shilling."

Chapter 6

An extract from Henry Jekyll's unfinished and unpublished memoir

Studies Of Early Man In The North-Eastern Mendip Hills

One is easily and agreeably sidetracked by the colourful folklore which abounds in this part of the world. I hope the reader will forgive a short digression here, for there is much of interest in charting the influence which one particular legend exercised on the Bronze Age communities located at references C, D and E (see *Map IV*).

The roots of many a superstition run deep into prehistory, and this is indeed the case with 'moonwort' (a 9th century word, see *Appendix II: semantics*), the mythical 'changing flower' also known as 'warpweed,' said to have been used by ancient cultures in both pagan and seasonal rituals. Its use is believed to be the original inspiration for stories of werewolves and similar shape-shifting entities.

This plant, goes the legend, is the rarest ever discovered.

It grows only underground in caves, and then only under very specific conditions of air, temperature and moisture. So scarce are these conditions, and so delicately balanced are the plant's requirements, that moonwort cannot be cultivated; it must be carefully preserved wheresoever it grows, and cropped with extreme caution so that one does not interfere with its natural development or damage its overall structure.

Its supernatural power to change human physiology is evoked by ingesting a tincture, or oil, extracted from the plant, whereupon one's entire body takes on the appearance of one's 'inner beast,' most often a wolf or a large cat. In some versions of the myth this change is temporary, in others permanent – depending, one suspects, upon the narrative demands of the storyteller!

To the modern scientific eye, it is clear that moonwort was akin to those plant based drugs known today to induce delusions, such as are used among certain desert nomads and tribes of South American forest dwellers. However, as the reader will appreciate, even the very earliest surviving accounts of moonwort's dramatic properties were written at too great a historical distance to be reliable, filtered as they were through spoken traditions, like a parlour game of Russian Gossip spread across hundreds of years. In fact, one might doubt if moonwort ever existed at all because, by the arrival of the written word, all specimens and known locations had evidently been lost in the mists of time.

Nevertheless, belief in the plant and its alleged effects, whether those effects were actual or imagined, is evident in the ground as far back as the late Neolithic period. Note the animalistic, half-human aspects of carved shamanic figures (see *Photographic Plates B, E, J, Q*) and the grave markings associated with high status burials (see *Photographic Plates C, G, K* and *Diagram XII*) most of which were found at sites B-2 and D-3 (see *Map III*).

One might be tempted to place alternative interpretations on these local discoveries, but for the fact that moonwort is known in the ancient traditions of at least three other cultures: those of Eastern Europe (specifically the areas bordering the Carpathian mountains), western Scandinavia and the north-west coastal region of Africa (specifically Morocco's karst landscape, falling partly within the current Spanish protectorate). Excavations in all these places have revealed artifacts not dissimilar to those found in our own region.

Seventy years ago, in 1790, claims emerged from Bukovina, now part of the Republic Of Romania, that a living specimen of moonwort had been found by an unnamed scientific emissary of the royal house of Habsburg. Interest was quickly aroused, but subsided with equal rapidity once it became clear that the specimen had withered away to nothing but loose strands within two days of its discovery, and before any rigorous examination could be carried out. Fortunately, an artist made three detailed drawings of it in its fresh state (reproduced in *Appendix III: supplementary material*). These illustrations certainly show an organism previously uncatalogued but, with no further data on the discovery being available, including the location of the find, nothing about it could be verified. A curious story which became no more than a footnote in an early number of Curtis's Botanical magazine.

Although it is entirely possible to dismiss the Bukovina

specimen as a fraud committed to gain notoriety, I myself am of the opinion that it wasn't. Fraudsters would surely have created something a little more lasting and robust, and would certainly have gone to greater pains to attach their names to it.

In his highly entertaining *Evidence Of Cultural Migration In Post-Mesolithic Settlements*, Professor Giles Hobbs argues that anthropological indicators such as the moonwort myth, belief in faerie folk or the adoption of occult rites were part of the Neolithic transition which swept the European continent, replacing hunter-gatherer cultures. I am inclined to agree but, trusting that one of our foremost men of science will forgive a dabbler like myself, I believe this falls short of the full picture in the case of moonwort.

The plant's cultural influence in the British Isles has never been widespread or long-lasting, with one noticeable geographic and historical exception: namely, the exact area of the West Country which encompasses my own studies. One cannot help but speculate on the peculiar endurance of the moonwort legend in our own region. It faded into obscurity everywhere but here, where it persisted for centuries, finding its way even into the *Wikked Historie Significate*, written in about 1172 by the generally reliable St. Aelfrid Of Wessex.

For what reason, one wonders? One is lead to the intriguingly amusing notion that there was, or possibly still is, a source of moonwort in these very hills, now lost somewhere deep within the many cave systems which honeycomb beneath our feet. A fuel of rumour, one might say, which kept the ancient stories a-burning all the way to the witch trials of the Tudor age.

The idea is not an entirely frivolous one. The folded formations of the Limestone anticlines which support and shape the hills are very much in keeping with the structural requirements alleged to foster moonwort's delicately balanced natural environment. Likewise, the flow of moisture through the rock. The presence of freshwater springs on lower slopes has always suggested the existence of subterranean systems some distance to the north-west of the Lamb Leer and Wigmore Swallet caves. My own survey efforts have revealed any number of hitherto uncharted slockers and dolines (see *Map V*), but it will be an explorer of far greater courage and hardiness than I who dares to venture inside them.

Chapter 7

A roomy, box-like brougham drew up outside the workhouse gate on Bristol's Fishponds Road and its springs rocked the carriage as Jekyll's steward Poole climbed heavily from the driving seat. Before turning his attention to the porter standing behind the gate, he opened one of the brougham's side doors, reached inside and swung down the padded plank at the front, to make extra seating space.

The porter, moustaches shimmering, touched a finger to his bowler hat. "G'day to you, Mr Poole." The buttons on his jacket struggled in various directions while the hems of his trousers made a vain attempt to reach his shoes.

He gave Poole a matey nod, which Poole ignored. "Good morning, Atkins, may I see the Master?"

As the railings clanged shut behind them, the porter whistled to a fellow bowler hat to take over at the gate for a minute or two. "Mr Timms is sick, Sir, we got a temp'ry Master for the time being, Mr Shunt."

"Then I'll see Mr Shunt instead."

They walked along the stony path which circled around

to the workhouse's tall, stark facade. The building was square and plain, laid out to the officially approved design with central blocks forming a geometric cross which divided the space inside the outer walls into four. The aim of the officially approved design, severe and municipal as it was, had always been to instil awe, to be a dark implication of courtrooms and shame, and this aim it achieved extremely well.

In front of the building was a long, flat area of land where men and women tended vegetable crops and dug soil. Their standardised, hard-wearing workhouse dress matched the hardness of their hands and faces. A uniformed superintendent in a peaked cloth cap kept a beady-eyed watch over them from a low wall, a cigarette jutting up from sloped lips.

Poole and the porter walked almost abreast, the tall steward's speed and uprightness silently exerting the higher status of his employment, the porter's pattering footsteps huffing along beside him. Poole's familiarity with this place had long since removed the frisson of fear which greeted every visitor, the involuntary shudder transmitted from the whitewashed walls and the scuffed, dark woodwork, welcoming them to a new hell, of scarred lives and limbs, of broken minds, of ruin, of Authority.

The two men climbed the squeaking staircase to the upper floor. They stalked along a high gallery overlooking the echoing dining hall, where long tables waited to be crammed with residents upon whom God Himself would glare down in judgement, in the form of stern sayings painted in booming capital letters on the walls. A queasy smell of boiled vegetables and ill health percolated throughout the gallery. Without slowing, Poole swerved a fresh stain on the chipped stone wall beside him, a violent splatter of half-liquid beside which was propped a mildewed mop. From elsewhere, reverberating down long corridors and out of scrappily furnished rooms, came intermittent shouts and yells, some angry, some begging, most of them incoherent through one madness or another.

A few more steps, doors and keys brought Poole and the porter into a comfortable sitting room, situated at more or less the centre of the building and dominated by a weighty, smartly-organised rolltop bureau. The porter's busy moustaches blew quick introductions, Mr Shunt, Mr Poole, Mr Poole, Mr Shunt, then he plodded back to his gate.

Shunt was a puffed, waxy gentleman with a high voice, like a helium balloon in a boldly patterned suit. He convivially ushered Poole to an armchair.

"Delighted to make your acquaintance, Sir, your reputation precedes you. I trust the Earl is in sound fettle?"

"He is," said Poole. "May I ask how long you expect to be Master here?"

Shunt glanced up over his spectacles, as he lifted the lid on a decanter case. "My appointment is, on paper, a temporary one but— Sherry?"

"No, thank you."

"—but between you and I, Mr Pile, I believe Timms may not return at all. His wife has priests stationed at his bedside in relays." He filled a sherry glass to the brim and raised it between thumb and forefinger. "I have just this moment returned from the eleven a.m. inspection of the men's sleeping wards. I generally find myself in need of a restorative. By the way, I understand from the Society columns that Her Ladyship is hosting something of a gala at Westwych this evening?"

"A private one," said Poole. "For reference, will you be pursuing Mr Timms' proposed policies?"

Shunt downed his sherry and gave a little twitch of ah-that's-better. "Oh, no no no," he said, his chin dropping to his neck for a second or two, "rest assured, Mr Peel, that when glasses are raised tonight in toast, it can be in the certain knowledge that my time in office will be as firmly rooted in continuity and valued tradition as that of the dear Queen herself." He slumped himself onto a chaise. "Not that I wouldn't gladly scrap a few petty-minded encumbrances. Eleven o'clock inspections, for one."

"No revised work schedule, I take it?" said Poole.

"Teaching cobbling and tailoring and such like? No no, that sort of thing runs contrary to the entire purpose of the workhouse system. What is to be gained in simply *giving* residents what they lack? It would be madness. This institution's stated function is as a *deterrent* to indolence. Always has been. If Timms' policies held sway, there would be swarms of loafers at our gate, demanding free apprenticeships, if you please. How would that deter? No no no, here we will continue to chop, dig and grind. The only effective way to cure the moral failure that fills our beds is to make it as unattractive and inconvenient as possible." He delicately placed his sherry glass on the bureau. "Besides, the Treasurer of the Union has already ruled that Timms's work schedule would adversely affect the return payable to the Board of Guardians, so it would never have seen daylight in any case."

"I hope," said Poole, "that my employer's arrangement

therefore comes under your heading of valued tradition, not petty-minded encumbrance?"

"Most assuredly," beamed Shunt. "I have the Board's support in saying that the Earl's benevolence is thoroughly appreciated. Indeed, I would relish the opportunity to express our gratitude to his Lordship myself."

"You know the full terms of the agreement?"

"Indeed," said Shunt, with a nod deep enough to be a bow. "Do you require a male or a female on this occasion?"

"Three. One woman, two men. All must be in full health, preferably experienced in domestic service, preferably able to read and write."

"Three?" enquired Shunt. "Additional staff for tonight's festivities? What an occasion it will be to behold, for all those so favoured!"

"Two will be passed on to a friend of the Earl's . . . on an estate in Yorkshire."

Shunt heaved himself to his feet with a grunt and paused at the door. "Might any be of about nine or ten years in age? We have half a dozen who were left here as infants and the Union are pressing me to secure a decision on them."

"I'm afraid not," said Poole. "We took one as hall boy about a year ago, but he couldn't adapt to life at the House. His grasp of language was poor and among other deficiencies he'd never encountered a spoon."

Shunt sighed. "Ah," he muttered, "never mind."

He galumphed away and returned about twenty minutes later, herding five residents ahead of him. The three men appeared to be in their late twenties, two of them brothers to judge by their rugged facial features, the two women slightly older. All of them moved with an inmate's timidly, as if their bodies feared unnecessary effort, and all had the efficiently clipped workhouse haircut normally sported only by children.

Shunt lined them up with a few barks and some wags of his fingers. Each looked mystified and uneasy about their summons to the Master's office, and equally suspicious of the dour, bald stranger who eyed them up and down from the armchair.

"Have any of you been in service before?" said Poole.

Three of them were about to answer when Shunt declared, "All. And all know their letters and numbers."

Standing, Poole indicated the two brothers and the shorter of the women. "These three."

Shunt waved the others away. "Be off about your business, thank you." Once they'd gone, he addressed the remainder with his hands clasped behind his back. "I have no doubt you have heard of the generosity shown to this institution by his Lordship the Earl of Westwych?"

They had. "Mr Tool here is the Earl's personal representative. You will be found employment at his discretion. Any insult to his Lordship's munificence through idleness will bar re-entry into this workhouse and any other within the purview of the Board."

He paused to let his words sink in. "Any personal property?" They hadn't. He turned to Poole, his voice softening. "May I enquire if transport–?"

"I have his Lordship's brougham outside," said Poole. His brisk manner took charge of the three recruits as if leading them on invisible ropes.

"I learn from Mr Timms's records," enquired Shunt with

quiet servility, "that exit paperwork is to be kept to a simple tabulation of successful discharge?"

Poole's good eye stared into Shunt's face. "His Lordship has always been of the opinion any public account of his charitable work would be vulgar and distasteful."

"He is a gentleman of rare distinction," said Mr Shunt. "I hope I have the pleasure of meeting him, on some occasion, at not too distant a point in time."

"Good day, Mr Shunt."

The steward and his recruits made their way back along the high gallery. Below, steaming metal cauldrons of pale stew were being hauled onto an end table. At the other extremity of the hall, a flock of old men, like decayed vultures, perched patiently beside a dying friend. Poole's recruits were silent and docile, shocked by this unexpected twist of fate, barely believing their luck.

Poole marched downstairs, indifferently passing knots of skeletal derelicts and pleading inmates offering up their grimy hands, their rags, their babies. They seemed to seep from the cold walls as if drawn by a psychic aroma of money, a telepathic rumour of kindness. The recruits copied their new benefactor, suddenly superior to their erstwhile kin now that their lives were no longer drowning in the sea of human wreckage, now that they had been chosen.

At the gate, the porter waved Poole a cheerful, unacknowledged farewell. Without a word, Poole opened the brougham's side door, waited while the recruits ducked one by one and stepped inside, and fastened the door shut behind them with a click of the handle.

Inside, one of the brothers sat on the upholstered flip-down plank while the others nestled into the rear seats.

Their knees criss-crossed. The padded enclosure of the carriage was quiet enough for them to hear themselves breathing.

The woman delicately ran her fingers along and smooth, dark lining beside her. "This is posh, innit?" she whispered. They smirked and giggled at each other, a dream-like elation beginning to glow between them.

"You ever been in one of these?" muttered the brother beside her.

The woman pulled a comical face, eyes stretching as she slowly shook her head. "I'm Emily," she said. "Em. Looks like we'll be workmates. What's your names?"

"Joseph Carter," said the brother on the fold-down, fingers poised at his chest. "That's James. Were you in there long?"

The brougham lurched into motion, the horse snorting as its hooves built up a steady rhythm.

"No, thank Christ," whispered Emily, watching the gate and the porter slide out of view. "You?"

"Five months," said Joseph.

Poole flicked the reins. With the brougham picking up speed, his hand reached down to check the small brass tap installed beside his foot rest.

He would wait, until the city was behind them and there was countryside as far as the eyes could see. Then he would turn the tap and release an oneirogen gas, a sedative derived from diethyl ether, into the compartment behind him.

Chapter 8

It was exactly noon when Poole steered the brougham southward, and at the same moment the end-of-shift whistle was sounding at the H & F Jekyll Cycle Company factory on the other side of the city. The forest of vertical drive belts that powered the workbenches slowed their high, febrile whine into an ever-deepening tone which gradually slid to a shudder and a sharp stop. The clanging noises of the metal presses and the assembly bays were replaced with footsteps and subdued talk.

One hundred and nine workers – machine operators, leading operators, section foremen, steel cutters, saddle stitchers and packers – traipsed through the jigsaw of shadows thrown by the webwork of machinery beneath the glass roofs. Dust and fibres swirled in shafts of midday sunlight.

The factory's normal Saturday routine had, for the first and only time since the present Earl had taken ownership, been shifted forward by one hour. On balance, the workers' chatter was ambivalent to the change: the novelty of going home early, and the unprecedented pleasure of not being docked sixty minutes' pay for the privilege, were offset by their impatience at having to line up in a time-consuming ribbon near the factory's smart main entrance instead of making their usual hasty exit via the goods yard.

Many of them had never seen inside the front, street-facing section of the factory before. They nosed with interest at the tall wooden panelling and the bicycles, current and discontinued, mounted onto the walls in a display no visitor could fail to see and appreciate.

Towards the head of the curling line of workers, while they shuffled through a self-generated fug of their morning's labours, the factory's overseer regaled them with long-winded expressions of his personal happiness on this joyous national occasion, his personal pride in the company's loyal celebrations of it, and his personal gratitude to the Earl for taking such a personal interest in these loyal celebrations. His face was fixed in the personal smile which beamed whenever his Lordship was in the building.

Frederick Jekyll stood near the double doors which opened out onto the street. Beside him was the company's chief clerk, manning a refectory table covered in commem-orative Diamond Jubilee china cups bearing a coat of arms and a portrait of her majesty beneath a protective arc formed by the words "Longest and Most Glorious Reign." As each worker filed past the Earl, the clerk handed Jekyll a cup, who handed it to the worker, who muttered a few words of thanks before looking into the mug to discover a specially cleaned shilling. One hundred and nine china cups having been dispensed, the one hundred and nine workers dispersed until Monday and the company's loyal celebrations of this joyous national occasion were concluded.

Jekyll and the chief clerk discussed the week's ledger for a few moments, until the overseer, hovering like a bee at a flower, caught the Earl's attention. "There is a gentleman here who wishes to see you, m'lord."

"On what business?" said Jekyll. "A company matter? He'd be better advised to speak to you."

"No, Sir, he asks specifically for a private interview. His card states he represents the British Museum in London."

Jekyll's heavy eyebrows lifted. "Does he now? What on earth might he want here, I wonder? Very well, as long as the fellow makes a quick account of himself, I'll see him."

The overseer opened the door into the sparsely furnished anteroom where visiting tradesmen were stored while waiting for appointments. As soon as the Earl entered, a slimly-built man, dressed for the outdoors and with an eager, almost puppy-ish manner, jumped to his feet and straightened his collar.

"Mr Jack Utterson, m'lord," said the overseer, passing Utterson's card back to him. Utterson extended a hand and Jekyll shook it with the casually nettled air with which the gentry greets strangers.

"May I be of help to you, Mr Utterson?"

Utterson cleared his throat and took a breath. "My apologies for the unorthodox nature of our introduction, Sir, I aim to explain my purpose as briefly as possible, I don't wish to detain you any longer than strictly necessary, I'm aware of your many commitments, but I'm hoping we may discover a mutual benefit relative to our respective lines of enquiry, that is as scientists."

Jekyll's expression darkened, the grim set of his mouth all but invisible behind his beard. "My field of enquiry?"

"You see, Sir, I have an assistant curatory role at the British Museum, and it is with the museum's express authority and backing that I am undertaking a survey, to catalogue Neolithic and Chalcolithic anthropological data along the Lulsgate Plateau, with reference to the transition away from a nomadic Mesolithic—"

"Your stated aim of brevity is falling short, young man," said Jekyll. "What aspect of *my* scientific enquiries are *your* concern, precisely?"

"Oh, Sir, of yours, none. I'm afraid I'm not conveying my intentions with sufficient clarity—"

"You are not." Jekyll's stern gaze examined Utterson in more detail. He noticed the obvious efforts Utterson had made to brush the dried mud from his clothes. "How is this 'survey' conducted? I no longer carry out field work."

"No, Sir, indeed, but your father did."

"My father."

"Yes, Sir, I'm reliably informed that his scientific findings have been preserved, and by a most fortunate coincidence my own studies, it seems, appear to overlap his to a substantial degree."

"Do they really?" said Jekyll with icy calm. He teetered on the edge of rage.

"They do, Sir," smiled Utterson. "I understand that, sadly, the late Earl passed on before he could publish the results of his labours and thus my proposal to you, Sir, is that both his work and mine be combined, entirely under the official auspices of the British Museum, naturally, such that, firstly, the museum's survey can be completed and, secondly, and more significantly, with your kind permission, that your eminent father's scholarship may finally see publication in its own right, so that he at last receives the full credit and recognition he undoubtedly deserves, in the eyes both of Science and of the public at large."

Utterson skidded to a verbal halt, his face awash with hopeful enthusiasm. Now that he was no longer putting all his concentration into the words he was saying, he quickly sensed Jekyll's reaction to them and his hopeful enthusiasm washed away.

"With my kind permission?" said the Earl flatly.

"Y-Yes, Sir."

"Mr Utterson, you do not need my kind permission, for the simple reason that my father's papers were all destroyed years ago. The few trinkets he unearthed proved to be worthless and of little scientific value. Your reliable informant is wrong."

"U-Um, but i-if—"

Jekyll's mood began to spill out into his voice. "Mr Utterson, are you deaf as well as impertinent? My father's frivolous hobby can be of no possible interest to you, to the British Museum, or to anyone else."

"Sir, I can assure you—"

"The only thing you need assure me of is your immediate and complete abandoning of any further interference in my family's private affairs, is that understood?"

"Sir, I would never—"

"Is that understood, Mr Utterson?"

"Entirely, Sir. I'm very sorry to have intruded upon your time." The overseer bustled Utterson away, growling under his breath.

Jekyll stood alone in the anteroom for a minute or more, silently staring at the lime green walls. His mind galloped angrily through the long airless corridors of the past, plucking at memories, assessing risks, digging into old wounds.

This man Utterson. No more than some minor functionary, surely? A threat? A spy? Or was he an innocent, ignorant of the truth, exactly as he appeared to be? Was he a dupe, sent to confront or confuse? No matter who or what he may or may not be, he unnerved Jekyll. Fortunately, the Earl had contingency plans in place, a mousetrap for spies and saboteurs, set up in the early days of the protective bargain he'd made with the War Office. Perhaps that trap was about to snap shut again?

He blinked and sniffed sharply, tugging his frock coat into shape as if giving himself a slap on the face, a reprimand for momentary panic.

He left the factory at an unhurried pace, accepting the discreet blandishments of the overseer and the chief clerk with good humour. His new motor carriage, a Leon l'Hollier Anglo-French, was waiting beside the pavement outside, his footman Jilks standing guard over it. He drove the automobile back to Westwych House himself, in a glowering silence, his mind running helplessly over and over the events of twenty years ago . . .

Chapter 9

Extracts from the private papers of Frederick Jekyll

dated February 1877

REFLECTIONS UPON IDENTIFYING THE PROBABLE LOCALE

I simply could not help but weep. In marking the final points of the search area on the map, thus completing a roughly trapezoid shape encompassing slightly more than one and one half square miles, I was unexpectedly overcome with emotion.

The cause, I believe, was the thought that for so many years, my dear father Henry had aimed to arrive at this same point. He followed the folds and strata of the hills, charted the myriad flows of water through the landscape, and cross-referenced evidence of every kind, from every era, back beyond the dawn of civilisation in these isles. How much further his work might have taken him, it is impossible to say.

I am aware that his death – so horrible, and so

tragically met in the pursuit of his studies – has relent-lessly driven my subsequent efforts to build upon his findings, to long past the point of mere obsession. I have given so much of my time and my attention to his memory that I am changed in both temperament and personality. For the worse, I fear. My Evelyn, my love, has been the most patient and understanding of companions. Without her warmth and devotion, I would be lost.

And so, with the search area defined after years of frustration and intensity, I wept. With relief, certainly, and from a sense of triumph, but also in the knowledge that I would, from here onwards, be surpassing my father's work. I would be exploring territory, both physical and metaphorical, that he never reached. Territory, it must be said, which he may not even have wished to reach. I wept because I was passing a mile-stone, but had a far greater distance to travel than I had hitherto come.

Through extrapolation from my father's detailed and exhaustive records, and through additional researches in many an arcane library, I was certain that the search area contained the ancient source of moonwort conjectured since pre-history to exist in the hills close to Westwych House. My father was never entirely convinced that the warpweed of legend was rooted in fact. He thought the truth would be revealed as far more prosaic, an unremarkable mix of exaggerations, wish-fulfilment and pagan ideology.

I did not. To me, there were too many coincidences, too many independently generated stories, too steady a crumb-trail of clues. Do we not live in a time of valiant discovery? Of constantly expanding knowledge of the world? I burned with but one ambition: to find moonwort and bring its fabulous possibilities into the modern age.

Naturally, I was at great pains to ensure that my findings remained secret. I took my beloved Evelyn into my confidence, but only to the extent of telling her I was in pursuit of rare chemical deposits. She is of much the same inquisitive disposition as myself but baulked at the considerable risks involved in my plans, and I promised her that I would not take so much as one footstep underground without proper preparation. Privately, my thoughts cried out that any risk was worth the prize.

dated March 1877

PLANNING THE DESCENT

Within the identified ground level search area I made a rigorous square yard by square yard examination of the terrain. I found three pot-holes where a cursory investigation with a few stones indicated depth. One had an opening aperture too small to admit anything larger than a dog, and I discounted it. The other two, although almost a mile apart, were both located in the shelter of overhanging rock, where nettles and under-growth had hidden the entrances all but completely. It took me some time to clear them enough for inspection.

The first of these entrances was roughly circular and

could be accessed without difficulty on my hands and knees; the second was an irregular vertical slit, some five feet tall, through which I could shuffle sideways-on. In both instances, I ventured inside by only a few feet and used a candle and a plumb line to gauge the formations ahead. The circular cave ended in a series of smaller holes and crevices which, although leading deeper into the earth, were all too narrow to allow further progress. The taller cave, however, twisted off to the left and then down through a large, oval-shaped opening from which came a distant echo of trickling water. I returned to the sunlight with my heart leaping from my chest!

Over several days, I checked and re-checked my initial findings, a feverish anticipation growing within me. I became certain that I had found a hitherto uncharted cave system lying in the precise patch of country upon which numerous disparate references to moonwort were centred.

I was extremely puzzled as to how such a cave system could have remained forgotten and unexplored for centuries, but enquiries into the equipment currently favoured for subterranean ventures gave me an immediate answer to that question: there was essentially none, bar plenty of rope and enough clothing to keep out the cold and the damp. Simple pragmatism solved the mystery of why only the largest and most accessible caves had ever been properly mapped.

The true scale of the dangers I would face was finally becoming clear to me. A fall, a trapped limb, even disorientation, all might mean death. And if I should die down there, my body – unlike my poor father's – would never be recovered.

Bearing in mind my promise to Evelyn, I considered recruiting others to accompany me, but very quickly dismissed the idea. With a quarry of such staggering value at the end of the hunt, nobody could possibly be trustworthy. Nobody whatsoever. The task must remain mine, and mine alone.

Naturally, in Evelyn's presence, I played down the risks in a manner positively flippant. She was, at least outwardly, reassured by my demonstration of the coils of stout rope I proposed to carry on my shoulders, the strong metal hooks to which I'd tie them, the thick leggings and waterproof layers in which I would snugly and safely be clad.

However, although she never spoke of it, I was aware that her most persistent anxiety was my less-than-candid accounting as to the object of my search. I should have known that no woman of her intelligence and sensitivity, no bond as loving as that which existed between us, could have failed to see through my half-truths.

My lack of candour had nothing whatever to do with my trust in her. Evelyn is the one person in this world whose discretion and fidelity are beyond any question. I would gladly place my life in her hands at a moment's notice and without the slightest hesitation. Nor did I doubt her capacity to share my vision, since she has always spoken with insight and curiosity when-ever other topics of a scientific basis have been subject to discussion between ourselves or friends.

I withheld the full story from her, told her nothing of moonwort, because there was still the possibility of failure. The probability, my father would have said. For if I found nothing, if all my efforts were a futile waste of time and energy, if moonwort was no more than a myth after all, I would not be able to bear the shame of Evelyn knowing the true extent of my failure. Years spent in a fruitless hunt for some unspecified treasure would be mortifying, but a mere passing discomfort compared to the utter humiliation of failing to bring moonwort to the world. Moonwort, in God's name! It would be a failure as complete as a lifetime's folly in pursuit of dragons or the fountain of youth!

I could endure any manner of disdain from others, but not from Evelyn. To have my darling wife think less of me, to be diminished in her eyes, and deservedly so, would be the worst failure of all.

dated April 1877

A RECORD OF FINDINGS
BENEATH THE EARTH

As soon as I had solved the problem of illumination, I was ready. I had anticipated needing as bright a light source as possible, since I could not afford to miss even the smallest indication of my goal, and at first I planned to take with me a photographer's Duboscq limelight, suitably adapted. However, the item's awkward bulk proved impossible to re-engineer, so instead I equipped myself with a basic Davy lamp, similar to those which have been used for decades in the local coal mines. I modified the fuel reservoir to allow for extended operation, and designed a seal to encircle the wick, to enable the lamp to be tilted by ninety degrees or more for short periods, should it become necessary in the confines of the caves. To compensate for the much reduced brightness of the lamp, in comparison to the limelight, I furnished myself with a quantity of magnesium strips, which I could light whenever I needed to see every detail of my surroundings.

I set out from Westwych House at dawn and reached the cave entrance within the hour. My supplies and protective clothing were a greater weight than I would have wished, but I had done all I could to keep the load to a minimum.

I entered the cave mouth, lit my lamp, and proceeded to the oval-shaped gap I had discovered earlier where I hammered a hook into the lip of the hole. Each strike seemed unnaturally loud, putting my teeth on edge and setting off reverberations in the pit below which travelled down, and down, into seemingly unending depths.

My nerves suddenly bristling, I tied the end of a rope to the hook and threw the rest of the coil into the darkness. I heard it hit solid ground after only a few yards. With great care, I descended.

The oval now some distance above me, only the faintest of natural light still reached my eyes. A gurgle of running water came from somewhere further below and I decided to light a magnesium strip. My fingers fumbled nervously with the matches but the strip eventually fizzed into life and I flicked it ahead of me.

Immense rock faces were much closer to me than I'd imagined. They were streaked and blotched in shades of yellowish-brown, large areas glistening with slime and jagged hulks of stone protruding everywhere. The wide ledge on which I stood curled over at a steep angle, leading down along an uneven but almost step-like gradient.

The strip burnt out after a quarter of one minute. The sudden return to the Davy lamp's dimness caused my nerves to quiver once more. I cut the rope behind me, leaving enough hanging to enable the climb back up, and picked a dry spot on which to prominently mark my direction of movement in white chalk.

The easiest way to negotiate the gradient was backwards, on all fours. The sounds of water I'd heard were coming from a stream which coursed across an overhead promontory and drizzled directly onto the spot over which I had to pass. Ice-cold splashes spat against my neck and the back of my head, trickling beneath my collar and chilling the woollen shirt next to my skin.

I continued crawling through ever-narrower passages, until the only way forward was via a low, horizontal crack beneath an immense block of limestone. I had to push all my equipment ahead of me and remove the outer layer of my clothing before I could squeeze my way through.

With every faltering step I took, fear tightened its grip upon me. I struggled against incessant, nightmare thoughts of entombment, thoughts of being trapped in eternal night, unable to see or breathe.

Despite the exertion, my fingers were numb with cold. The strangely odourless air felt thick and clammy in my lungs. Many times I found myself gasping, on the brink of a panic from which I could retreat only by forcing myself to halt for a moment and take long, steadying breaths.

As a distraction from terror, I busied myself with practicalities, marking my route at frequent intervals and constantly monitoring the level of the flame in my lamp: while it burnt just so, then all was well; if it burnt lower, then too little oxygen was present, what miners called blackdamp; if it burnt higher, the opposite danger was indicated, namely firedamp, an excess of ignitable gases.

I couldn't prevent myself feeling a horrifying, engulfing sense of isolation. I was overwhelmed with a perception of loneliness so profound I felt I was the only living being in existence.

Emerging into a space where the echoes of my movements suggested larger surroundings, I lit another strip of magnesium and almost cried out in surprise at what I saw. I was in a chamber of enormous size, fully fifty yards or more across, the centre of which was dominated by a pool of water, black as pitch and completely still. From the chamber's steeply angled roof hung a forest of needle-like stalactites, the lowest of which ended five or six feet above my head.

The magnesium's brief glare ended and I cautiously approached the central pool. Crouching down, I reached out and ran two fingers along its glassy surface. Ripples bloomed, crossed and vanished. I was awestruck, marvelling at the notion that mine may have been the first human disturbance of these waters in many thousands of years.

To my complete dismay, a tour of the chamber's extremities revealed no less than seven possible exits, excluding those impassable and excluding my own point of entry. A fresh roil of alarm began to stir inside me, curbed only by my decision to light more magnesium, in the desperate but logical hope that the men of pre-history must surely have reasoned in exactly the same way as I at this moment.

I beamed with relief when I saw that my supposition was correct. Just before the intense brightness sputtered out, I caught sight of a pale shape high up on the rock face to my left. My eyes readjusted, I scrambled over the rocky floor of the cavern and raised my lamp as high as I could.

It was a pictograph, a daubed image not unlike the cave paintings found in France and Spain. There were simple, curving delineations of a body, tail, and legs, topped by an oversized depiction of a head with pointing ears and an open mouth showing teeth. Surely, a wolf.

Proof! Unequivocal, undeniable proof.

The lamp began to shake in my hand, setting the meagre shadows a-dance as wonder and uneasiness battled for my heart. The pictograph lay directly above one of the exits, a smooth-sided gap which at its base was slippery with a slow, meandering trickle of moisture.

Breathing hard, I hooked the lamp at my waist and

felt along the edges of the cold, clammy rock with both hands. Finding a grip, I held on as firmly as my trembling fingers would allow, my boots hesitantly navigating the wet ground. I looked ahead, my eyesight straining in the lamplight. Sure enough, my footing slipped more than once, each time sending my stomach into a sharp lurch and a harsh crunching echoing off the walls.

The tall but thin tunnel into which I moved was so confining that it was impossible to turn around. I breathed dampness, the sound of each exhalation circulating tightly around my head. Taking a firm hold on its wire handle, for fear of dropping it, I unclipped the lamp and raised it up once more.

To both sides, a vibrant tableau of primitive paintings swirled! The colours of these figures were muted and their outlines somewhat chipped, but here were scenes of ancient life as visceral and vivid as if separated from us by mere seconds instead of by millennia. Beasts being hunted, and caught in covered traps. Figures adorned with ornaments, possibly shamen or ritual idols. There were others shown in two forms, as man and creature, leading the hunt, repelling invaders, leaping to the stars in the sky.

Above me, the rock faces rose cleanly into pitch darkness. Ahead, they appeared to gradually converge. It was difficult to estimate how much further into this crevice I'd be able to go.

A jutting ridge, at waist height, forced me to choose between again divesting myself of equipment and layers in order to squeeze around it, or to squat down and crawl beneath. I chose the latter, and cursed the decision when the ropes on my back immediately wedged me against the ridge like a vice.

I could move neither up nor down, forward nor back. I propped the lamp on a rock on the ground, to give myself room to push free, but with my arms ahead of me I simply could not find enough leverage.

I need not – I will not – describe my state of mind in that instant. A long wail of horror escaped my lips, so reedy and forlorn I didn't recognise the voice as my own.

Brute force alone saved my life. I shook and twisted and bucked with every atom of strength remaining to me. My yells of exertion were deafening.

I felt a crack against my spine. I froze in dread, fearing agonising injury, but then the ridge above me gave way, crumbling over the shredded fibres of rope that my abrasive movements had dragged against it.

For some minutes I lay face down, motionless, feeling the hardness of the stone against my cheek, my mind slowly regaining control of itself, my speeding heart and burning lungs gradually calming. It was when I finally uplifted my head, when I reached for the lamp and placed it behind me so that I had space to shift around, that I saw it. The glow.

How ironic that, had I been able to bring with me the brighter illumination I'd desired, I would probably never have perceived that pale luminescence ahead of me at all. In my addled mental condition, I at first mistook it for a trace of daylight.

The soft glow was roughly five feet away. It was a

blueish colour, harder than that of a candle but only fractionally as bright. It came from one side of the crevice, from a natural alcove in the rock three feet above the ground, angled away from my present position and otherwise entirely hidden from view.

Prostrate, pulling myself forward inch by inch, I drew level with the alcove. It was perhaps two feet deep, with a concave upper surface shaped by eons of water droplets into an inverted bowl, and a lower surface worn into a recessed cone or funnel. Sitting neatly inside this lower shape, mirroring its contours in a perfect fit, was a bronze cup. A man-made bronze cup, with a small V-shape for pouring on one side and a raised edge for holding on the other. It was filled to the brim with a pearlescent liquid.

Directly above the cup, growing downwards from the centre of the inverted bowl, was a lush crop of filigree plant tendrils, each one delicately curled, each ending in a tiny, slenderly petalled flower. It was these flowers which were the source of the luminescence. They hung loosely in the pitch black like little blue eyes.

Moonwort. Alive, surviving.

I longed to touch it, but dared not. I examined it by lamplight, noting that the plant appeared to have no central stem but grew its delicate, entwined tendrils from a series of nodules linked by a gossamer network of connections similar to blades of grass. The flowers were of identical size, and all shone in the same eerie way. Their petals had a fork-like structure, bending inwards as if invisibly holding something between them. I understood why when I saw that on five of the flowers a minute sphere of moisture was forming, poised on the petals' tips. These five spheres varied from less than a pin's head to a globule about half the diameter of a pea. None of them seemed anywhere close to the point when gravity would gradually bend the flower and drip the sphere into the cup below.

How long must it take for one small drop to form? Many weeks, if not months or even years, estimating by the proportion of flowers in mid-sphere formation to those not. How long had it taken the cup to be filled? How long had those who'd made this cup, untold centuries ago, waited for enough fluid to gather to enable their ceremonies? How often could they use . . . what was it, exactly? The plant's essence? Its power in distilled form? The liquid had to contain all the properties of the plant itself, else why make a cup at all? The moonwort itself, so notoriously fragile, could stay untouched here yet still provide its strange bounty.

And I, Frederick Jekyll, had rediscovered it.

I, in all the human race, had found it here.

Snapping out of my exultant reverie, I retrieved two sealed vessels I had brought with me. The first, lined with glass, was eminently suitable for transporting the liquid, and of sufficient volume. I steadied the trembling of my hand by resting my forearm against the cold rock, lifted the ancient cup from its resting place and slowly emptied the moonwort essence into the vessel. I capped it securely and reinforced the seal with the gauze that formed part of my small medical kit.

Not wishing to disturb the plant itself any more

than absolutely necessary, I picked off only a single flower, leaving the rest alone, and placed it in the second container. (I intended to keep it in a permanent preservative solution, but in the brief period between the plucking of it from its tendril and the reopening of the container upon my return to ground level, a period of only two or three hours, I was to discover it had withered and shrivelled into little more than brown, coiled filaments.)

The moonwort safe, I retraced my steps along the narrow crevice, across the large chamber, beneath the overhang, every moment consumed with rushing thoughts and eager expectations. Thanks to the thoroughness of my chalk marks, my return through the cave system was slightly quicker, if no less physically arduous. It was early afternoon before I gasped fresh air again. Never have I been more pleased to be dazzled by the light of day.

But I barely noticed. I existed in a whirlpool of plans.

Chapter 10

Emily felt funny. Funny.

Sleep. Had to sleep. Left the workhouse. In a carriage. Posh. Nice . . .

She felt consciousness return to her, felt the fog in her brain slowly lift, thoughts of cold and noise, of picking oakum at the . . . fog in her brain slowly lift . . .

There was a . . . dream? Faces, two men, same face, brothers, in the carriage. Looking out, head resting on glass, streets passing, trees passing, head resting, something, something, something . . .

She blinked and sniffed, then struggled to sit up when she realised she was sprawled awkwardly across the brougham's seats. Sleep still nagged at her and she had a throbbing headache. She rubbed at her eyes, pulling air into her chest sharply to wake herself up.

"How'd I nod off?" she mumbled. "Wha's time?"

"Out you get. We're here." Poole stood, as taciturn as ever, outside the brougham's open side door.

Events came tumbling back to Emily. "I'm sorry, Sir, I

don't know why I went off like that. Where's the other two? The brothers?"

"They alighted earlier," said Poole flatly, as if she'd be a fool to think otherwise. "At the railway station."

"Thought we were all goin' to work for the Earl?" Her headache made her wince. She remembered . . . something weighty, dragging past her legs . . .? Just a minute ago.

"They're to be employed by a friend of his Lordship. In Yorkshire. Out now, we don't have all day."

Apologising again, Emily climbed woozily out of the brougham, trying to identify the peculiar smell that was lingering in the carriage. A bitter sort of smell.

The brougham was parked at the front of Westwych House, close to the raised steps from where Lady Violet had looked out over the valley the previous day. Emily gazed up at the building, overawed by the vertical sweep of the windows, the sharply defined stonework, the pointed, austere, castle-like shapes which seemed to gaze back down at her in return.

She noticed that the brougham's fresh tracks, the narrow wheel indentations and hoof prints across the gravelled forecourt, showed it had driven way off around the far corner of the house before coming back to this spot. But her thoughts were pulled away from that subject by the unnerving stillness of Poole's glass eye, and by the novelty of seeing one of those auto-whassits, one of those motorised carriages, standing close to the front door. Poole was under instruction to place it back in the garage once all the guests had arrived for the festivities in a few hours' time.

He led Emily into the house at a brisk pace and snapped

his fingers at the second housemaid, who was cleaning the greenery in the vestibule.

"Alcock," he said. "This is . . .?"

"Oh. Emily Wells. Em."

"This is Wells. She replaces Bingham. Show her the ropes, she's to start at once."

"Yes, Mr Poole," said Lizzie Prendick's friend Ada, wearing the chiselled smile she reserved for those she didn't like. He nodded and stalked away across the enormous atrium, his footsteps drumming a steadily diminishing beat.

"He seems a bit fierce," whispered Emily.

"Thinks too much of himself, that's all. I'm Ada."

"H'lo. Em."

"Poole pulled you out of the Old Basty, did he?"

"Yes," said Emily, smiling weakly, her fingers touching at her hair.

"I knew 'cos you've no belongings," said Ada. "No shame if you've come from the grubber, most of those below stairs here came the same way. Tho' I'm from Hagstow. You been in service before?"

"Yes," said Emily, her eyes wandering at random, "but nothing grand like this."

"C'mon." Ada tugged off her work gloves, gathered her cleaning cloths and polish and jammed the lot into her apron pocket. She walked into the atrium, Emily at her heels, and opened a concealed door onto the unlit female servants' stairs. She glanced over at the Earl's vivarium, thought she'd better warn Emily about it, then changed her mind. "You don't want to look at that until you have to," she muttered, wrinkling her nose.

She beckoned the newcomer up the shadowy wooden steps,

pulling the heavy door shut behind them with a low bump. "Before I show you anything," said Ada, "I'll let you have the temp'ry bed in my room. We've got a house party later and I'm not having some snobby *duchess's* girl getting it first."

The click-clack of Miss Tippel's shoes, quick but wary on the well-worn stairs, announced the housekeeper's descent before she came into view around a bend in the stairwell. "Ada," she said, head bobbing with relief as if she'd been trying to track down a second housemaid for days, "help with the household's luncheon, would you, please? They're nearly finished, but today's changes of routine have left Doris on her own." The pinch of her lined face and the curl of her lips expressed a great deal more about today's changes of routine.

Ada jabbed a thumb over her shoulder. "Can I show Watts to her room first, m'um? Mr Poole says she's to replace Bingham."

Miss Tippel's upper body cocked to one side to get a look at Emily and her mouth formed a perfect U. "Oh! Hello dear." She introduced herself. "Come and find me later on, we must have a chat. Ada, did Mr Poole not mention replacing young Harris?"

"Not to me, m'um."

Miss Tippel tutted. The knitting of her brow summarised her vexation at all things Poole-related. "Cook's in a fury, the pig she wanted for tonight is away on its trotters." In answer to Ada's question, she fluttered a hand up the stairs: *yes, up you go, go on, but be quick about it, please.* She clopped down; Ada and Emily trudged up.

"What happened to Bingham?" said Emily.

"Got the sack," said Ada.

114

"What did she do? Are they strict here?"

Ada, suddenly self-conscious, wasn't sure what to say. Day-to-day living with the oddities of the house made her feel uncomfortable explaining them. To speak, out loud, about the blind eyes she and every other servant turned, would seem like complicity, perhaps even approval. She decided to take a scenic route to the truth.

"Well, for a start she couldn't keep her hands off young Harris."

Emily sniggered into the back of her hand.

"For a house this size," said Ada, "Tippel says we're a small staff. There's only about a dozen of us, but some have been here years, like her and Poole. Others come and go so quick you hardly get to know their names."

"They don't settle to it?" said Emily. "A lot don't these days, I'm told."

"Have a look at this," said Ada, slowing down as they slogged up the last steps to the servants' quarters at the attic level, where a narrow, green-painted walkway ran thirty yards in both directions. She pointed to a small metal plate fixed to the wall, then turned the switch poking out from it. Three incandescent bulbs glowed into life, hanging by short cords from points along the ceiling.

"Electric!" said Emily. "I've never seen it indoors before."

"All over the house," said Ada. "No candles, no stink of gas."

Emily approached the nearest bulb for a closer look, gazing in delight at its globular shape. "Isn't it dangerous? My da worked in Bristol for a couple of years, in that generator place at Temple Back. He reckoned he'd never want it at home."

"You can get a sort of hard nip off it sometimes," said Ada, "like a wasp sting, but the doctor from Bath who does Cook's leg reckons that's good for you."

"Do the wires go all the way into town, then?"

"No, it all runs from the boiler room off the back yard. Like the heating."

"Heating?"

Ada was enjoying herself now, presenting one wonder after another like a music hall magician. "We don't have to scrape out the fireplaces, and we don't have to get up in the freezing cold to light the buggers either."

"Eh?" Emily half-laughed.

"You look, as you go round the house. There's metal grille things fixed on walls and ends of beds and such. They're red hot, there's no need to light anything."

"What makes them hot?"

"Water."

"Eh?"

"Hot water, runs through pipes. Like that one, there." She nodded at a fat iron tube, bolted along the length of the wainscotting, which bent at ninety degrees and disappeared into the floor close to the stairwell. "Us girls on this corridor, we dry our smalls on it."

Emily giggled. Ada stepped across the corridor and grandly swung open a door. "And! Where there's hot water . . ."

Emily poked her head into what at one time had probably been a large storage cupboard, but was now a compact bathroom, slightly too small for the lavatory, hip bath and wash basin it contained. She looked back and forth between the porcelain fittings and Ada's grinning face. "This is for servants' use?" she said quietly, as if expecting it to vanish if anyone should overhear. "That's a flushing privvy, isn't it?"

Ada chuckled to herself, enjoying Emily's amazement. "One here for the women, one on the other side by the men's bedrooms. And the kitchens have hot water from taps, and there's two bathrooms on the upper floor for family and guests. By the way, you can't get to the men's rooms from here, if you're wondering."

"Bloody hell, this place is like you're already in the new century. No wonder you've got a smaller staff, there's sod all needs doing."

"His nibs designed the whole lot, plumbing, heating, electric, had it built from scratch."

"The Earl must be a very clever man."

"A very clever miserable git, sure."

"Did he build that auto-wassit parked at the front?"

"No, he bought that in Birmingham. But he's had it apart."

Ada led Emily to her bedroom, where her furniture-lugging efforts of the night before had finally wedged an extra fold-out bed under the eaves. "That's yours," said Ada. "Leave your jacket on it or something, mark your territory. Here." She pulled the cloths and polish from her apron and dropped them on the bed. "Right. Occupied, it's yours, when Lady Snot's dogsbody turns up, there's no room at this inn."

"Are many coming today?"

"Quite a few," said Ada, "but if you're doing Bingham's duties, don't worry, you'll hardly even see them. Although, I'd put a scarf round your hair, you know how nobs get the vapours if they see anyone normal. Tippel'll kit you out. C'mon, we'd better go and help Doris. With a bit of luck, we'll be just in time for awww, sorry Doris, household's finished lunch? Aww, we rushed down soon as Tippel said, sorry, tsch, oh well."

"What's the household like?" said Emily. "You say the Earl's a misery?"

Ada sensed they'd come to the end of the scenic route. The two of them plunged back into the gloom of the servants' stairs, Ada dragging the tip of a fingernail along each wall."

"He's preoccupied with his work, and everything what's not his work seems to annoy him. Except for Lady Violet and the twins. The boys are alright, they're quite sweet, even if they do have a lot of their father in them. They're seven years of age, they've got a nanny but Lady Violet's getting a tutor for them soon."

"What's Lady Violet like?" said Emily.

"Nice. Soft as shite, really. We reckon she's a lurker."

Emily looked blank.

"She talks posh," said Ada, "and she looks posh, but she wasn't born into money, You can tell she's not one of their breed. They think they're dogs in a world full of cats."

Emily looked blank again.

"The dogs tell the cats they'd be dogs if they weren't so stupid and lazy, so then the cats fight each other instead of the dogs, thus the world goes round and round in circles. I read that in a suffrage pamphlet."

"Are you one of them socialist intellectuals?"

Ada frowned. "Do you mind? I support Queen and country, thank you very much. But also the suffrage. So does Lady Violet, she knows that Sophia Fry."

"If she's not a toff, how did she marry the Earl?" Emily hastily checked her balance as Ada suddenly stopped half way down to the first floor landing.

The second housemaid spoke in a conspiratorial tone, twisting around and leaning her head upwards at Emily as if to make sure her words had as short a journey as possible between mouth and ear. "This was a long time before I started here, but according to Cook the Earl was in a terrible state when his first wife died. Lady Evelyn. But! Not one year later, he suddenly announces he's got married again, she's nobody anyone's ever heard of and she's twenty-five years younger than him."

Emily's eyebrows rose. Ada's chins made a momentary dip of confirmation.

"Cook reckons she's some tart he got pregnant and who blackmailed him into keeping her. But I don't think that's right, that doesn't sound like her at all. I think she worked at his factory and he took a shine to her. His grown-up daughters – his brood with Lady Evelyn – they hate her."

"Do they live here too?"

"No, but they'll be here for the party. Unfortunately. Jane, Henrietta and Alice. A cow, a snob and a loony. Jekyll dotes on them almost as much as he dotes on the twins, but he goes mad if any of them criticises Violet in front of him. Him and Violet do love each other, plain as day. Or, at least, something holds them together like glue."

"His Lordship can't be all bad then?"

"He's fine until you cross him." Her voice dropped to a whisper and all trace of levity left her face. "His workplace is the cellar, right? When we get downstairs I'll point out the passage near the plate room that leads down to it. But that's only to show you where you can *never, ever* go. Right? Never. You even set foot in that passage and you'll be out on your ear, no excuses, no character, nothing, you're gone within hours. The same goes for the old stable block out the back, past the yard. The newer block is fine, the old one is off limits. That's why Tippel said she wants a talk with you later. It's not just to go over your duties and your pay, it's to make sure you know the unbreakable rule. The Earl handles those sackings himself."

She drew herself even closer to Emily, who bent her knees a little to bring her face level with Ada's. She could smell detergent on Ada's uniform and Nuttalls' Rum & Butter drops on her breath.

"Bingham," mouthed Ada, "she was caught having a fumble with young Harris, like I said. But they only got a bawling-out and extra duties for that, which shows you how soft we have it here otherwise. What got them the push was that they tried to pick the lock on the cellar. I think, when the Earl sends anyone packing, they get warned off too, threatened, 'cos you never hear from them again even if they say they'll write. Mind you, that's just people, is'nit."

"What the devil goes on down there, then?" whispered Emily.

"Nobody can say for sure, but below stairs we reckon Jekyll's working on a cure."

"For what?"

"Whatever disease killed Lady Evelyn. Dunno what it was, but it sent her mad."

"Did it?"

"The Earl took her to a load of special doctors in London,

but it did no good. She died there. Going on bits and pieces Cook's picked up over the years, he's still tormented over her illness for some reason, so he's working on a cure to make amends. Involves all sorts of poisons. We're sure he tests it on dumb animals, down in the cellar. Because there's screams sometimes, in the night. Howls, awful sounds. Screams like you can't work out what it is. But that's his work and you say nothing, right? We've got it good here. We don't even have a rules board in the servant's hall."

"Is the cellar where Cook's pig went? To be tested on? I thought Miss Tippel meant it had been stolen, or got out?"

Ada's eyes widened as she shook her head very slowly. "Poole had it. I saw him myself, heading for the stables, from up in my room. He takes pigs, chickens, rabbits, endless vegetables. We've had goats sometimes and they go too. But you say nothing. Whatever old Jekyll does, Poole's in on it all, same as Moreau."

"Who's that?"

"Moreau? He's his nibs' tame Frenchie, his engineer. He runs the boiler room, the systems, Jekyll's gadgets. Smarmy so-and-so, he is. The pair of them can't do no wrong as far as Jekyll's concerned, they could get away with murder, I reckon. They definitely get paid extra, always seem to have plenty of cash. Moreau's forever off prowling in town."

Ada smirked like a little girl catching her governess on the flushing privvy. "Cook reckons Jekyll, Poole and Moreau might be jolly good chums on the quiet, like Lord Arthur Somerset and that Irish feller they just let out of prison. It'd explain why they're always locked away together."

Laughing, they clattered quickly down the stairs.

121

Chapter 11

Lionel Chaney's black, silver-topped cane tapped out the seconds as he strode down Gulley Row towards The Sailor's Arms. The street was a busy commercial one, close to the city's docks and lined with emporia of every kind: a butcher's with half-carcasses hung in a line outside; Elland Boot Repairs, Gents from 2/6, Ladies from 1/6; a corner chemist's shop, windows filled with tall white boxes of Hall's Wine, The Tonic Restorative Supreme; Stott's the baker's selling Fry's chocolates and Parkinson's biscuits in tins; the local Lipton's; a grocer's; a department store. Carts and carriages jostled for position, pedestrians sidestepped puddles of congealing mud.

Chaney felt uneasy in plebeian surroundings. Here, the sharpness of his clothes attracted looks, which he resented, and the rigour of his bearing attracted deference, which he encouraged. He was a solid, sinewy man, with a firmly curated head of sandy hair and a prominent chest. The turn of his lower lip and the slight asymmetry of his grey eyes gave him a quizzical air, as if constantly impressed by his own existence.

He described himself as an industrialist. He owned a business in London's East End, Pell & Blight Ltd, a bankrupt company his father had bought for next to nothing in 1879 and repurposed into a manufacturer of soap.

The Sailor's Arms turned out to be a shabby Georgian house at the less attractive end of the street. Chaney caught the reek of the docks and looked up at the forest of ships' masts rising high above the surrounding rooftops. Swoops of seagulls screeched and whirled overhead.

Inside, the pub was loud with male revelry that walked a knife's edge between good-natured and aggressive. The few women who rolled in the sea of bodies were either curled slyly around some hard, tattooed ball of flesh or else leading the sing-song from the top of a table.

Chaney steered around the rowdy drinkers by tapping them with his cane and mouthing humourless excuse-mes. He scanned the room through the thick haze of tobacco smoke and human emissions until he at last caught sight of the man he'd come to see.

The man he'd come to see caught sight of him at the same moment, raising a grin and a finger in greeting. Henri Moreau's regular looks and proportions conflicted with the distinct impression he gave of ugliness and deformity. In the way he spoke, with his tongue lapping at his teeth, and in the way his eyes seemed to be in half a dozen places at once, his whole manner was rat-like and guileful. His high hairline revealed a tall, protruding forehead and the fingers which slowly rotated his mug of ale were long and bony. A pewter plate, scattered with crumbs from the bread he'd used to mop up his gravy, was pushed forward on the table in front of him, knife and fork slung across it.

Lionel Chaney alighted like a bird on the grime-coated chair beside Moreau. "Why did you want to meet in this God-forsaken place?" he said, his shoulder nudged by the rear end of a rotund, guffawing reveller.

Moreau smiled. "I am known here, I have friends here," he said in a glutinous voice. "If anything should happen to me, if enquiries need to be made, then you, looking like that, you will be remembered."

"What a trusting fellow you are, Monsieur."

"A sensible precaution, when you have so much more at risk in this matter than I."

"Oh yes? And how do you get that?"

Moreau swallowed the last of his ale. "You are going to ask me to betray my employer, *oui*? If I comply, you will be betraying your own father-in-law, the Earl, and your wife, the Lady Alice, and very probably your country. I lose my job, you lose many things. I see by your face that I am correct."

Chaney bristled inwardly. Rehearsals of this conversation in his head had featured rather less frankness and rather more wide-eyed compliance.

"Yes," he said tersely. "I want Westwych's research. You anticipated as much?"

"You are hardly the first. In the past year alone I have been approached by representatives of two supposedly friendly nations. Perhaps you're here on behalf of a third?"

"That's none of your damn business, Moreau."

The engineer chuckled to himself. "I suppose not. How much will you pay? Bear in mind that I have never yet acquiesced to any such proposal. I have my price, the same as anybody, but that price must overcome my loyalty to the Earl. And I am a loyal servant. I received an offer of two hundred pounds during an interview last November, at which I learned that gentlemen like yourself do not like to be laughed at in the face."

Chaney blanched. He'd hoped to spend no more than fifty. Even his wife Lady Alice knew nothing about his plan to avert ruin, about the imminent bankruptcy of his business, about the legal and financial threats which haunted him. Pell & Blight Ltd had become an inescapable curse, a millstone around his neck like Coleridge's albatross. "Naturally, you've doubled the real figure as a negotiating tactic. However, I am . . . prepared to match it."

"*Non.*"

The two men stared at each other for a moment. Another round of drinks at the bar set the room cheering.

"What," said Moreau, "makes you think I would accept that sum from you, when I would not accept it from others? Others with clearer motives and deeper pockets. Why would you, *m'sieur*, a member of the family, do this? How can I be sure the Earl himself has not sent you here to test me?"

"That's absurd!"

"Then such betrayal must be worth a great deal more to you than two hundred pounds!" He jabbed an angry finger at the industrialist's chest.

Chaney felt a surge of indignation. Damn this ruddy man's impudence! This jumped-up French factotum! What right had he to question the motives of his betters?

"If there is one lesson life had taught me," he said at last with an imperious sigh, "it is that any human bond – of blood, love or loyal allegiance – dissolves in money. Kindness and devotion crumple beneath cold self-interest. Two hundred and fifty."

"I will have to vanish, quickly and completely and forever. The Earl is vengeful and has connections. I want five hundred, and not one shilling less. A large sum, I agree, so I will accept half today, and half when I am . . ." He swept a languid hand, ". . . elsewhere."

"Today?" said Chaney. He considered the bargain struck at £250, since he had no intention whatsoever of parting with another penny once Jekyll's work was in his hands. "You can smuggle the material out today?"

Moreau snorted loudly. "Now, *m'sieur*, it is you who are being absurd. The cellar at Westwych House is filled with scientific equipment, including distillation and purification apparatus I designed and built myself. The repository of the Earl's experiments runs to hundreds of boxes and thousands of pages, many of them pasted to the walls of his laboratory! You seriously believe you are buying a wagon loaded with booty? You're buying access to the Earl's work, you're buying entrance to that cellar. It would be impossible to 'smuggle the material out,' particularly today when the house will be filled with overnight guests!"

"Then why expect the money now?"

"Because you are one of those guests! What better opportunity will you have to slip away and enter the cellars unnoticed? Only the Earl, his steward Poole and I have keys, I will hand you mine on payment of the first half of our agreed fee."

"You are expecting to be given this outrageous sum merely in exchange for a key?"

Moreau shook his head, chuckling. "Ah, that starchy blend of ignorance and apathy which the English do so well."

Chaney pressed his lips together for a moment. Impertinent little swine! "Since my purchase is so nebulous," he said with exaggerated composure, "I want some sort of guidance on what I'm looking for. From all I've gathered through the family grapevine I doubt there's anyone, not even you, who knows the full details of what Westwych is doing except he himself, but you must have some idea of the direction in which his research is aimed?"

"I must admit," said Moreau, broodingly, "I am also curious as to his purposes. I see much but, as you realise, not everything. What do you suspect he's up to?"

Chaney had no intention of engaging in idle gossip with this mechanic, this servant, but his own curiosity prodded at him to test out his suppositions and observations. He glanced around the pub, but the ongoing carousal and its tuneless vocal accompaniment meant there was no chance of being overheard. "It's a poorly guarded secret that Westwych has been in cahoots with the War Office for a few years now. In fact, as I understand it, a pair of government emissaries are among tonight's guests."

"That's right," nodded Moreau, "I'll be preparing for their arrival as soon as I return."

"A military objective would accord with the build up of arms which is at present taking place on the continent of Europe. It would also lend credence to your claims regarding approaches by foreign governments. Many would say that the Earl's use of poisons, from that rather repulsive vivarium he keeps in the house, suggests he's developing some kind of toxin for use by the army, perhaps in the form of a lethal gas, or as a liquid with which to contaminate enemy water supplies. Such things are known to be in demand, deliverable via shells fired over distance, deployed to reduce troop numbers or to suppress insurgence."

"Entirely plausible," said Moreau.

"However, I'm personally certain that the reverse is true. Those same poisons can be of great value in the production of analgesics. I have heard privately, from more than one source, that a battlefield medication is greatly sought after, to offset the effects of more efficient weaponry. Extremely tricky work, apparently, and Westwych is a clever man. He's making a powerful alternative to morphine, a stimulant rather than a narcotic, to pep up the troops and keep them going through thick and thin."

"Also plausible, and indeed more in keeping with his Lordship's character?" said Moreau. "In order to find out, once the key has placed you past the door, your strategy should be to descend the steps and look immediately to your left. There is a small open area at the foot of these steps. The Earl keeps recent results in a bureau, an ongoing written summary which is the basis of the periodic reports he forwards to the War Office. Possession of this should furnish you with enough technical data to answer your questions in full."

"Very well. What's further back in the cellar?"

Moreau paused, choosing his words. "You'll have no need to find out. You'd require a cool head and a strong stomach. His Lordship's experiments involve living creatures, by necessity."

"I'm not the type to be squeamish," scoffed Chaney.

"I will have the key with me from around four o'clock, when I'll be carrying out maintenance work in the boiler room. You know where that is?"

"Yes, there's access from the rear yard? Westwych showed it off to me a couple of years ago. On my wedding day, as I recall."

"Then, until four." Moreau gave a brief grin and a curt nod, and slunk away out onto the street.

Chaney followed after only a few seconds, but by the time he emerged from The Sailor's Arms there was no sign of the Frenchman on Gulley Row. He strode back to his hansom, waiting three streets away, where Lady Alice, slapping down her *Tit-Bits* and her *Chatterbox*, asked him where on earth he'd been for the last half an hour and why his clothes suddenly smelt like a tramp's haversack.

Chapter 12

Extracts from the private papers of Frederick Jekyll

dated December 1878

With the liquid moonwort recovered from the cave safely in my possession, I conducted a rigorous revision of everything known relating to how it was used in ancient rites. In this, my father's groundwork was of immense help.

Unfortunately, these comprehensive enquiries produced exactly the same conclusion as my earlier and more casual readings had already implied: that there existed no firm recipe for the moonwort-derived substances brewed by the ancients, those substances which, when ingested, released the moonwort's transformative power. Some legends spoke of a green liquid drunk only on the night of a full moon; some described a paste, blood red, smeared onto the body; some listed common herbs; some listed ingredients exotic enough to make Macbeth's witches scratch their heads!

In the end, I had to admit to myself that my desire

to unearth a specific, usable answer was nothing but blind optimism on my part. All ancient sources on the subject are, as my father so trenchantly pointed out, at best unreliable and at worse pure fiction.

I purged my expectations of such unrealistic flights of fancy. Results, I admonished myself, would come only from the hard work of experimentation through the scientific method, not float conveniently off the pages of some bygone myth. My principle, my lighthouse, was the certainty that moonwort *did* have the properties ascribed to it, that *somehow*, in combination with catalysing chemical agents of *some* kind, a secret lost for centuries could and *would* be regained.

I itched to begin my experiments. The scratching of that itch almost killed me.

One night, after much futile poring over academic texts concerning biocatalysis and the actions of organic enzymes, I resolved to establish what might be termed a basic or prime level for my work by imbibing some of the raw moonwort essence myself and observing the effects. It was fortunate that I took the tiniest of doses. I dipped the point of a sterilised pin into the moonwort and placed it flat upon my tongue.

I was feverish and bedridden for a fortnight, in a permanent state of wakeful exhaustion. Pain coursed through my nervous system like knives let loose to cut open my body at will. By the time I recovered, I was cadaverously thin and barely able to walk.

As might be expected, my darling Evelyn feared for my life and made frequent entreaties to our doctor in Bath. By good fortune, I was sufficiently alert – and

131

our doctor sufficiently incompetent – to convince them both that I was suffering from a virulent bout of influenza. I did not, even then, take Evelyn into my confidence regarding my discovery in the cave system, telling her instead that I had returned from my expedition with no more than a selection of interesting plasmodial slime molds, as lately classified by Herr Heinrich de Bary, possibly new species and worth mycological study under controlled conditions.

BEGINNING SYSTEMATIC WORK

I decided to withhold news of the moonwort's existence until such time as I could reveal positive, useful results. I was more firmly convinced than ever that such results would be obtained, for if the merest touch of raw moonwort had the proven power to hurl me to the brink of death, then the taming of that power must inevitably follow.

Mankind has mastered the energy of the electrical storm, domesticated the wild beast, spied high into the heavens, wrought the very minerals of the earth into the stuff of civilisation. Why, then, should the human form itself go unconquered? Nature has always dared us to turn her deadliest poisons, both flora and fauna, into medicines. I would do the same, with moonwort.

To that end, I set about a complete refurbishment of my late father's domain, the basement beneath the house, with a view to using it as a laboratory. All his Iron Age and Bronze Age treasures, along with all his notes and diaries, were transferred upstairs, to occupy a large display case in the library and closet space elsewhere on the ground floor.

Once emptied, I could appreciate the full extent of these cellars. Like many houses of this type, this had been the original location for the kitchens and bakery, and so is divided into a series of chambers. From the outermost chamber runs a long passage extension below ground, which emerges among the trees past the old stable block; it is a remnant of the days when the approaching road curved around behind the house, before it was shortened and made more direct, and was used for cold storage and to make goods deliveries easier.

I write these words in a basement which is currently rather chilly, rather musty and rather empty. The moonwort is safely under lock and key in a Brown strongbox visible from where I sit, and at my side is a pile of my reference books waiting to be organised onto a new shelf.

I recently began making extensive plans for various improvements to the domestic arrangements of the house, and I have engaged Henri Moreau, a Parisian engineer, a man of great skill and ingenuity, and of impeccable reputation, to assist with the practicalities. I'm sure he will prove equally invaluable for assembling the complex apparatus I will soon need for such tasks as chemical analysis and the refinement of blood serums.

I have bent Nature herself to my will!

The ceaseless labours of day upon day, month upon month, failure upon failure, so minutely catalogued in the rows of thumbed and ragged notebooks shelved above me, have not been in vain! I claim the first of many victories over the feeble restrictions of human biology!

When I first set up my laboratory, these brick walls were plain and unadorned. Above a workbench, I pasted up my starting line, my initial chemical analysis of moonwort, then beside it, some time later, the next step in my progress, and the next, eventually branching in every direction as I trod the slippery path to knowledge, until the walls have come alive with formulae, calculations and data. They dance to the music of my success!

One week ago, after a long day spent in anticipation while a crimson-purple liquid slowly coalesced beneath the smaller of the distillation tanks, I held up a half filled test tube to examine it against the electric light. Its contents shone: sharp, translucent, pure, like a ruby. In the liquid's colour, in its slight viscosity, I could sense the complex formula of its construction, the intricate balance of modified chemicals with moonwort at its core and the harvests of my vivarium adjusting its properties into perfection, like dressers in attendance on their monarch.

Not since that night, ten years ago, when impatience placed a tiny, near-fatal drop of moonwort on my tongue, had I dared consume the outcomes of my experiments. I had relied on chemical tests alone to inform me how they would react with a human subject.

No longer. This liquid passed every test I could devise. By any measure, this formulation was viable. The only rational proposition was to drink it. My fingers trembled. I took a firmer hold of the test tube to ensure I wouldn't spill or drop it.

I looked up at the clock on the laboratory wall. The household above me would be asleep. I smiled to myself at the sight of all the papers posted up underneath that clock, like a rising flood of calculus and reasoning poised to engulf it. Alas, poor timepiece, if only you could reverse your single function, change your nature and halt the ticking hours so that the flood might never reach you.

I laughed at the irony. The loudness of the sound in the hush of the laboratory instantly got me glancing around myself, as if I'd roused hostile observers.

Crossing to the steps leading up into the rest of the house, I checked that the door was securely locked. My heart raced as I paced for a moment or two, back and forth through the chambers of the cellar. The palms of my hands were sweating and I felt a strange tide of reticence and apprehension ripple through me.

On one of the laboratory workbenches there was a shaving mirror, of the type angled on a short stand, left there for occasions when work overtook my appearance. I placed it on top of the distillation tank, level with my face, and regarded my features. My smooth chin, my hawkish eyes.

135

Glory, or oblivion?

I shrugged off my jacket and swathed it around the back of a chair. I raised the test tube in my unsteady hand, clearing my throat as I did so for no apparent reason. Standing straight and firm, I put the glass tube to my lips. Heart thumping in my chest, I tipped back my head and swallowed the liquid in one quick draught.

It had an oddly sweet taste, like sugared aniseed. I delicately placed the empty test tube into a rack on the nearest workbench.

I felt a warming sensation. This quickly became acute, perspiration breaking out on my neck and forehead. It seemed to me that the air of the cellar was becoming unbearably hot. Suddenly, my breathing was laboured, as if my lungs were half-filled with water, and every muscle in my body flexed. A dull throbbing started to pulse in my blood, a fervour which grew to encompass every organ, bone, nerve and tissue.

I felt myself bathed in a seething, squeezing numbness. My eyesight became blurred and rolling, yet my mind remained perfectly clear. I marvelled that I felt no pain, while my thoughts reeled, aghast but unafraid.

I must have staggered, because I was suddenly off-balance, my hands gripping the edge of the workbench in order to keep myself upright. My skin seemed to swell and sprout. My legs ruptured the seams of my trousers as they fattened and pullulated, their joints reversing themselves into those like a dog or a horse. I stared through swimming vision at the claws into which my hands were warping. I felt my face contort and my mouth fill. Deep growls vibrated in my throat.

After what may have been several minutes, the crawling numbness which gripped my entire frame started to recede at last. My limbs felt heavy, yet teeming with energy. My sight settled, presenting my surroundings in fewer colours, a muted palette of greys and purples, but with a truly astonishing clarity and detail! Sharper, too, were my hearing and my sense of smell. I could detect the scent of my earlier self, my human self, as an almost palpable map of movement around the laboratory! My chest was larger, my breathing more sonorous, my height greater. Raising my hands up level with my new eyes, I saw they were furred and taloned, the fingers stubby, the palms thickly padded.

I took a step forward, on clawed feet. The overall increase in my mass made me sway uneasily. I approached the distillation tank and the shaving mirror perched on top of it.

My reflection elicited a breathy growl, for I could no longer gasp. My mouth and nose were distended outward, and behind thin lips pressed tall fangs. My ears were high and muscular. Coarse, matted hair covered me, but enough of my humanity remained, in the general cast of my features and the shape of my head, to yet identify me.

I was wolf, and I was Frederick Jekyll. I was a creature of cunning and instinct, of power and strength, of frenzy and hunger.

Stepping back from the mirror, a burning desire to escape the confines of the laboratory suddenly flamed within me. I stumbled into an array of chemical apparatus which toppled and smashed on the basement's flagstone floor. I rushed for the laboratory door and reached it in barely half a dozen strides, but my clawed hands no longer had the dexterity to operate the key. A harsh, feral growl escaped me while I scratched at the handle, leaving deep gouges in the surrounding wood.

Remembering the basement's other exit, the one past the old stables, I hurtled through the chambers of the laboratory and along the underground passage. This one was fastened with a simple metal bolt, easily dislodged. I flung the door open to the cool night air. Instantly, my senses were alive to the world outside. A thousand scents and intuitions plumed thrillingly in my brain!

I bounded up the short set of stone steps leading to ground level, emerging through a tangle of leaves and branches where the little stairwell had become over-grown from disuse. I paused, breathing deeply, feeling the soil beneath my bare feet.

My point of exit was a yard or two inside the edge of the woodland which rose with the hills behind the house. I glanced back at the building's vast, angular shape, black against the glitter of a starry sky. My home, yet it felt alien to me now.

I turned and ran up the wooded hill. I moved at great speed, sometimes on two legs, sometimes leaping along on all fours. I could smell the bark of every tree, the moisture on every blade of grass, the presence and position of every mouse, every bird, every insect. I could perceive the eternal mystery of the night itself!

Faster and faster, my throat roaring the air's song,

my heart beating the drum of the heavens. Out from the other side of the woods, down the steep valleys, over the high ridges of rock and scrub. The touch of the undulating ground, the breeze ruffling at my sides.

Above me, the Moon! Full and speckled and glowing and beautiful! Its lustre, bewitching!

I threw back my head and howled. I howled in sheer joy. I howled for this sensuous night and this physical form. Here was a freedom and a power unguessed, unimaginable. I felt my soul afire and my mind cleansed.

And I knew where it was, the sheep, long before it came into view. I caught the vibrations of its cautious hoofsteps on the slopes below me. I smelled its fear and its flesh. I deduced its mindless wandering away from pen and kin. It was for me, this animal. Mine. My prey. Born for my use, to fill my belly. Its only destiny, to be consumed as my inferior in the chain of life.

It tore at grass in the inky shade of the moonlight, all a-shiver. It found no comfort there. It tensed, sensed danger, looked up, was as still as the air.

My lightning speed, from downwind! Its muscles twitched, to flee, but I struck like a bullet in the darkness, knocked it flying, claws hooked into its flanks, teeth buried in its neck.

The blood, and the meat. Its round eye, dying, close to mine. No sound but the rip of sinew. No pattering heartbeat in the pump and gush.

Invigorated as never before, I tore across the soaring hills, the wondrous infinity of the open sky above me. How long I ran, I cannot say.

Eventually, I found myself back at the rear of the house. The night was black, the Moon fragmented behind the trees, and no light shone at any window. Instead of returning to the laboratory, I silently crossed the courtyard and stood looking up at the building, the bloodied claws of my hands resting against the stonework, feeling its immensity, its grandeur. Seized with the elation of the moment, my only thought was to find Evelyn, to reveal the truth to her at last, to share with her my glorious achievement.

I sped around to the front of the house, to the point directly beneath her bedroom window. It was slightly ajar, as is her habit in the Summer months. To scale the wall was the work of seconds, bounding swiftly from one architectural feature to the next, sharp talons holding me firm. With a single claw I opened the window to its full extent. Moonlight bathed the room inside, washing my sleeping love in its pale glow, the colour of marble statuary. She lay with bed linens askew, one foot emerging from her nightgown, her face tilted gently up toward the carved headboard. I slunk over the window sill, my gaze never leaving her while I reached down to steady myself. It seemed churlish to disturb this portrait of tranquillity, but I couldn't contain my feverish excitement.

Evelyn suddenly stirred, as if some psychic influence had alerted her to my proximity. Blinking, one hand placed to her tumble of auburn hair, she saw the open window, and then the regnant, more-than-human shape crouching beside it.

Sitting up with a start, she took a sharp breath which

remained poised at her slender neck until released into a shuddering gasp of fright. The shock of recognition swam in her rounded eyes as she stared fixedly at me. I moved away from the window slightly, so that the light of the Moon would fall more clearly across my head and neck.

Her fingers fluttered at her shaking lips. She trembled at the cliff edge of hysteria. Yet she was held back from panic by her swift intelligence and her strength of mind: in knowing me, now, she pieced together the bones of everything I had withheld. Her hand inched out over the folds of her bedsheets. Her voice was barely a whisper. "Frederick . . .?"

I longed to doubly assure her of my identity and that I, Frederick Jekyll, was no brute beast but a man improved, made *better* by releasing my innermost power. My long tongue and sharp teeth could not form the words, but she understood my meaning by the supplicant character of my movements.

Slowly, I rose and crawled onto the bed, my weight sagging deep into the mattress. Evelyn shivered, her face glistening in the rolling shaft of moonlight from the window, her misted eyes catching the dark stains of blood upon my claws and chest. Hesitantly, as if it would scald, she touched the thick hair at my temples and her jaw quivered in fear. But how well I know her heart! I knew that a fearless curiosity glowed inside her, almost as intense as my own! I knew she would exalt in my wonderful discoveries.

I embraced her. She stroked my neck, and we slept.

I awoke to bright daylight, and to my form entirely

human once more. However, the fearsome energy of the transformation remained, and on springing steps I descended to the breakfast table, where I devoured all but a few scraps of the entire buffet from devilled kidneys to kedgeree and all points in between, much to Evelyn's amusement.

We sat together and in hushed tones I related a full account of my experiments. I explained the reasons for my erstwhile unwillingness to take her into my confidence, and she stated that, in hindsight, she was glad of my decision because she might otherwise have been living in a state of tense impatience even worse than my own. How my Evelyn never fails to delight and astonish me! The brain of a mathematician, the nerve of a tiger, the beauty of a Summer's rose.

She asked, with nervous lips and jittering fingers, when she might try my moonwort formulation for herself. Not for several days yet, I reluctantly informed her, for the correct quantity of liquid had first to be calculated and distilled. The intimacy of our chatter, all hugger-mugger, seemed to perplex and alarm the servants, so with curling mouths we agreed to contain our excitement for the sake of appearances.

The burst of energy I experienced lasted some two or three days. During that time, I felt repeated urges for sustenance like that I'd found in the hills, but this was a craving readily assuaged by having Cook prepare some rings of black pudding, to be eaten cold.

Concurrently, Evelyn learned that local gossip was a-twitter. Villagers in Hagstow were speaking in fearful whispers of a werewolf seen racing over the hills by the light of the full moon, and a stray sheep found the next day, torn to pieces. Well, well, thank heavens for mad superstitions and a credulous peasantry! What devilry have they made of my nocturnal scamperings, I wonder?

For days I have itched as much as Evelyn for the moonwort mixture to be replenished, days spent describing to her how *alive* I felt! how unburdened! unbuttoned! unhindered! By tonight, the exact dose for her weight and musculature will have been refined.

dated November 1888

Each night, the dream is more horribly disturbing than the night before. More perverse, more accusing. I clasp my Evelyn in my arms, on the blood-soaked floor of that filthy hovel in Whitechapel. She looks up at me, her features melting back into humanity at last, her voice weakening, her eyes closing. "You were right," she breathes. "I was so alive."

I call her name, holding her tightly, rocking back and forth in agony and despair. And the sound of my wailing becomes her screams in the laboratory, with the moonwort tipped past her lips mere seconds ago.

In the dream, I try to return, to warn myself, I try to shout, yell, to break time's iron bonds, but her screams smother every cry and thought. She claws at her neck; her limbs fold; she thrashes wildly as her body twists and heaves. The laboratory is wrecked. She leaps and roars. I struggle to hold off her slavering, snapping teeth. Her voice fills my head, words she never uttered: my suffering is your fault, Frederick Jekyll, you caused my pain, you corrupted my flesh, you sent me mad! You sent me mad! You sent me mad!

I worm into consciousness weeping for my beloved Evelyn. Shame and guilt shroud my life, a waking nightmare from which there is not, cannot, must not be a single moment's relief.

It was nine hours before her body regained its regular shape. Her face, however, kept a strange, weirdly vulpine aspect to it, not so much in the arrangement of her features but in the hard-eyed, greedy expression which shocked all those who saw it. Worse, far worse, was the overthrow of her mind. Her character was altered beyond recognition. She would twitch and snarl, muttering darkly to herself at one moment and spitting curses the next. Food might either be eaten with bestial gusto or else thrown across the room. She would tear at furnishings and cocoon herself in blankets for days and nights together. The heartbreak of her condition was pushed beyond endurance by her inability to acknowledge our daughters, her own children. All three had always enjoyed her devoted attentions, but she no longer appeared to know them.

The girls, naturally, were extremely distressed by their mother's illness. Jane's recent marriage to Danvers Carew kept her away from the house, fortunately; she is a level-headed and sagacious girl, very much like her mother, and she accepted my assurances that this brain fever, no matter how serious and alarming, would receive the best treatment available to medical science.

Henrietta and Alice, being more sensitive in disposition, found Evelyn's sudden decline harder to bear. I was able to persuade Henrietta to return to her university studies in Oxfordshire, but Alice had no similar distractions, bar the society of the odious young Mr Chaney, and I fear her constant enquiries made me somewhat impatient with her.

My mood, in any case, steadily darkened as the days passed. I was so preoccupied with Evelyn that I startled myself, standing near the hanging mirror in the library one evening, by realising I had grown a beard. I have kept it, a mark of my burden.

I was forced to confine Evelyn to her room. The servants were openly fearful of her and she posed an obvious danger to anyone unaware of her situation. I spent most nights watching over her, a habit which proved fortuitous. On more than one occasion, suddenly and apparently unprovoked, she began to thrash and scream and within minutes reverted to the feral, predatory creature she had become in the laboratory! It was with great difficulty that I managed to prevent the rest of the household from witnessing her transmutations and to explain away the violent sounds which echoed through the house.

With tears in my eyes, I affixed strong leather restraints to her bed. Whenever I was not at Evelyn's side, I worked to reassemble the equipment in the cellars which had been smashed in the struggle following her initial transformation, but the sum total of what could be salvaged amounted to barely a dozen phials, a few copper pipes, and one of the glass refining tubes, which proved to be undamaged. Thankfully, my original supply of raw moonwort, from the cave, had been and remained secure in the safe.

However, I was able to recover a small amount of the specific moonwort formulation I had administered to her. I was at a complete loss to explain the disastrous effect it had wrought on her, when no such horror had resulted from *my* drinking the *exact same formulation*. As a test, I took three drops of it, certain of a result identical to my earlier experience, although of course milder in proportion to the much lower dose. Instead, my right arm and right leg took on the characteristics of cephalopoid tentacles! For the hours the effect lasted, I watched in utter disgust as they curled and wriggled, my head seized up with anger and dismay.

It was immediately evident that Evelyn needed help far more quickly than I would be able to provide it. Without revealing the true source of her malady – I conjectured an infection of enteric fever – I engaged every reputable medic in the district. They were able to soothe her febrile temper, but little more.

Exhaustion, and my failure to restore Evelyn's sanity, forced more drastic action. I arranged consultations with London's leading doctors and alienists, while Poole secured rooms at a hotel off The Strand. He and I alone accompanied Evelyn to the capital, keeping her partially sedated for the duration of the journey.

I told Poole the truth. He is discreet and highly efficient, in his own quiet way. I have impressed on him the need for secrecy, and guaranteed his loyalty by privately increasing his wages threefold. I suspect

I may need to do the same for Moreau, he has already correctly divined the purposes to which I've put some of the more specialised chemical equipment he's engineered for me.

Enquiries in London were fruitless. One after another, the greatest minds in the medical profession applied their remedies and medicines then declared themselves completely unable to cure my wife!

We were at the point of returning to Somerset when Evelyn escaped. On a sweltering night at the beginning of August, while in the grip of one of her increasingly frequent transmutations, she managed to evade us, slipping out via a window I had not been able to secure.

Day and night we scoured the city. Poole searched to the west, I to the east. The area south of the river Thames was covered by Miss Violet Formby, a nurse I engaged in London to administer to Evelyn's needs during her quieter moods. She was told only that my wife's mind was severely unbalanced. She proved herself to be a capable and observant participant in the search.

Our efforts were soon concentrated on the area around Whitechapel and Spitalfields, as the London newspapers became filled with ghoulish reports of unusually savage murders taking place there. It made an ideal hunting ground, a densely populated rat's-nest of the city's poorest, full of narrow passages, dark corners and lost souls. Any predator, human or otherwise, might feed their bloodlust with impunity.

I strictly forbade Miss Violet from setting foot in such filthy, crime-ridden streets, apprising her that no delicate or gracious person should be exposed to the sort of vile, corrupting scenes she'd most certainly encounter. Poole patrolled by day, questioning locals and showing them a photograph of Evelyn taken less than two years ago. I did the same by night. Both of us went armed with a steel-reinforced cane, which Poole wisely suggested might be useful as a discreet but formidable weapon where robberies and assaults are common.

Three times I almost recaptured Evelyn in the dingy alleyways which spidered between Whitechapel High Street and the market square off Brushfield Street. Twice she was human, once not, but each time she got away from me because we were out in the open and she could easily flee into the shadows.

On multiple occasions, befogged with fatigue and sick at heart of the stinking, grimy environs through which I stalked, I mistook some ragged harridan or other for Evelyn and accosted her, only to be swiftly rebuffed with screams or fists. As a result, at the end of October, a semi-accurate description of me appeared in the press as that of a suspect in the police's investigations into the Whitechapel killings!

My luck changed . . . my dearest Evelyn's luck changed . . . shortly after midnight on 9th November. The furtiveness of a stout, ginger-bearded man, carrying a large can, had set me lurking in the maze of backstreets beyond Devon Row and the Five Beggars public house, when a piercing scream echoed through the reeking yellow fog and was suddenly cut short.

I raced down a covered alley to a corner room in

what I now know to be Mitre Square. Inside, Evelyn didn't notice my arrival, too intent on tearing apart her final victim, later identified as a poor wretch named Mary Kelly.

I have no wish to dwell on the memory of that moment. It festers in my nightmares, as I have already stated. For weeks, I had carried around with me a syringe containing a lethal overdose of sedative. After a brief, violent struggle with Evelyn, I plunged the needle deep into her flesh. Poole and I emptied a large travelling case, placed dear Evelyn inside it, and were on the road out of London within a few hours. I disgraced myself with a flood of snivelling grief when I told Miss Violet that my wife was dead.

Why did my triumph turn to ashes? Why did Nature let me hold infinity in my hands, then dash it from my grasp?

Where did I go wrong? Where was the error in my work?

But I *will* defeat Nature's cruel caprices! I will set to work anew and I will crack open the secrets denied to me! At all costs. *AT ALL COSTS!*

Chapter 13

At the Tethered Goat in Hagstow, Jack Utterson was feeling quite annoyed. If not indignant. If not vexed. "I must say, the Earl was positively brusque with me," he said in a wounded tone.

Lizzie Prendick, with a glow of affectionate amusement, leaned over the bar on folded arms, looking across to where Jack was seated with his cup of tea, in an oasis of afternoon sun beside an open window. He'd been politely cordial when old Bern had plodded into the pub, collected his pint and dropped himself next to Jack in the otherwise empty room.

"I told yer he's a grumpy beggar," said Bern, lips smacking in the middle of his white whiskers as he took a swig of his beer.

Jack frowned into his tea. "What I don't quite understand is why he would lie about his late father's work in that manner. I thought he held the fellow in high esteem?"

"He told you all the papers and artifacts were destroyed?" said Lizzie.

"That is the very word he used. He was quite hostile. If, as you've told me Miss Pr— Lizzie. If, as you've told me, his father's anthropological findings are on open display up at Westwych House, why repel an innocent enquiry with such force? A simple 'not today, thank you' would have been sufficient. His reaction was rather suspicious, I think, as well as rude."

"Grumpy beggar," said Bern, cocking his head to one side to underline the wisdom of great age.

"Perhaps that stuff's no use to him any more?" said Lizzie. "Or its too full of sad memories? He *could* have got rid of it all, to be fair, it's a while since I saw it."

"But why?" said Jack. "It would be an affront to science! His father's papers could include material of immense value, he must see that, surely?"

"I think he sees his secret whatever-he-does and not much else," shrugged Lizzie.

"I'm still reckoning he's making a winged machine," chuckled Bern. "Fly to the Moon. Or it might be Seven League boots, for gettin' about."

"In our, er, discussion last evening," said Jack, "did someone mention there's official interest in the Earl's activities?"

"Yes," said Lizzie, "he has visitors from the War Office come to the house, now and again, so my friend Ada says."

"Well, in that case," said Jack, sitting up a little straighter, "I'm sure nothing, er, nefarious is going on. Although . . ." His voice tailed off and his expression ran through a short conversation with itself. His brow knitted and his hand dabbled as if he was catching thoughts in mid-flight. "On my way back from the Earl's bicycle factory, I was turning recent events over in my mind. You see, yesterday, before I even arrived in Hagstow, I was shown something, in the city, which disturbed me terribly—"

"Tha's some dirty folk in town, young London, yer needs be careful," said Bern.

"Shut yer trap, Bern," muttered Lizzie.

"It was an animal," said Jack. "Horrible, unnatural."

"How do you mean?" said Lizzie. "Like the things in the hills? You saw one too?"

Jack winced. "I don't know. In my agitated state, at the time, it's entirely possible I misidentified what was merely an exotic and unfamiliar species. I say this because, now I come to consider everything I've since learned, I'm wondering if the Earl's secret work is, in fact, of an agricultural nature? We're all well acquainted, I'm sure, with the debates in the newspapers about the current declines in farming, changes in production methods, problems over cheaply imported foodstuffs and so forth? It may be that the Earl is playing his part in combatting these problems by developing new breeds of farm livestock? Cross-breeding varieties from overseas, for example, to produce hardier strains or herds which are easier to maintain? This could explain his guardedness and the official interest in his research."

"Interest from the War Office?" said Lizzie, a sceptical squeeze to her face.

"It may be Ada was wrong in that one detail?" said Jack. "It might also explain the strange creature I saw, or many of the sightings in the hills? An animal may occasionally escape?"

Bern emitted a long snort of derision. "Escaped from Hell Farm, eh? Tha's a new one!"

"Every farmer breeds for better stock," said Lizzie, over the top of Bern's mirth and head-shaking. "It doesn't call for secrecy. And nobody's going to put a farmyard in a cellar." She smiled ruefully as Jack's shoulders slowly slumped.

"Yes, quite," he said, his cheeks flushing as he checked his pocket watch, "on second thoughts . . . I suppose it's only if the Earl's late father also concerned himself with animal husbandry that such deliberate obfuscation might be explained? It's hard to say."

Lizzie stood with outstretched arms, palms flat on the bar. "There's one way to know if those papers are still there. Go and look."

"I don't think the Earl is likely to welcome my card a second time any more than the first."

"That's not my meaning," said Lizzie. "Go and look when he's not looking."

Utterson was taken aback, and set down his teacup. "You're not suggesting I enter the man's house without his consent? He'd have just cause to have me jailed."

"There's a dozen or more entering his house right now," laughed Lizzie. "Delivery boys, guests' servants, a few from Hagstow as extra help for Lady Violet's jubilee party, all kinds, every last one a stranger to him."

"But they're expected," said Jack.

"I'm not saying to steal anything," said Lizzie, "just check if the papers are there. No harm in it. Then you'd know if he lied or not. You can't see the pottery and arrow heads, they're in the library and that'll be full of posh guests. But

I know exactly where the papers are kept, tucked away on shelves along the passageway to the cellar."

"What if he sees me? He met me only this morning, he knows my name."

"It's a big house. We can put my da's coat and hat on you as a disguise. It'll be like an adventure story in the *Halfpenny Marvel*."

"It's underhanded."

"I'll come with you. But if we're going, it needs be now. The posh guests will be turning up and there'll be every-which-road below stairs. We'll be in and out in a few minutes. Or less, even."

"I in't goin'," said Bern, raising his glass.

"You in't invited," said Lizzie.

Utterson checked his pocket watch again. He drooped and swayed with indecision, which Lizzie interpreted as enthusiastic assent. Grinning, she went to fetch her da's coat and hat.

"O'course," she said, paused in the doorway, "if you *do* want to steal it all later on, Ada will bag it for a few shillings."

"How riotously funny," said Jack, with a sarcasm mild enough to remain on the edge of courtesy. He umphed to himself. What a day he'd had, gallivanting to and fro. Make something of yourself, lad, his relatives had implored, en masse, at the end of their tethers, time and again. Forge a career, uphold the name of Utterson, find a path, do as you are told.

Would being Burglar To The Aristocracy do, he wondered? At least he'd have the pleasure of Lizzie's company for a while. And the most probable outcome, should he run true to form and not succeed? A sharp expulsion from the premises, certainly. A fate he could steel himself to endure twice in one day, he felt, if he had to, in the name of Science.

He was wrong, in every respect.

Chapter 14

Mrs Cook, the cook, dragged a spindly wooden chair outside into the sunshine, bumping it over the step by the kitchen door and swinging it to a stop a few yards onto the rear courtyard. She sat down with a low grunt and a squealing of chair legs. She lit her long clay pipe and puffed slowly, one arm tucked under the other, thick fingers delicately holding the pipe's stem, feet crossed beneath her seat.

Five minutes' peace.

Behind her, there was orderly chaos in the big, glass-covered kitchen annexe. Every vent and window was open, showing glimpses of movement, flashed reflections off pans, a heap of finely chopped carrots, a mushroom of steam, all of it boiled in a stew of voices, whacks, clanks, thumps, scrapes, hisses and running taps.

Seen from the kitchen, Cook looked every inch the poised bulldog out there, like an illustration by Cruikshank or Tenniel. She sniffed and batted at her nose. She puffed her pipe and sighed.

Four and a half minutes' peace.

A polished landau appeared around the far corner of the house, driven by a liveried footman and adorned with coats of arms. A couple of boys from Hagstow, earning a bob or two on helping-out duties, directed it to a space at the end of the yard, next to the carriage which had already brought Lionel Chaney and Lady Alice from the Bristol docks. The boys fussed around the landau and its horses, chipper and rosy-cheeked because they might cop a tip or two from some toff's manservant. They were slightly less chipper and rosy-cheeked when the valet left them unrewarded, heaving his way across the yard to the servants' entrance under the weight of two huge overnight bags.

Inside the house, at the dining room window, Asa and Lizzie Prendick watched the valet stagger out of sight. "He'll be the Duke and Lady Jane Bitch's," muttered Ada. "Cook's won the sweepstake."

"What were you betting on?" whispered Lizzie, following a curl of Cook's pipe smoke outside in the yard before turning to her friend.

"The order the three witches would turn up in," whispered Ada. "She reckoned Alice Fruitcake, Jane Bitch, Henrietta Upherself."

"What if Henrietta doesn't come after all?"

Ada frowned. "Tha's a point. Have to check the rules."

Their voices were all that broke the heavy silence of the dining room. The long, hefty table was now set out for dinner with white cloth, red runner, floral centrepieces, gleaming silverware and individual hand-written menu cards. They tiptoed to listen at the doors to the hallway. Muffled sounds of conversation came from somewhere nearby.

"Your mate Jack goin' to be alright, is he?" whispered Ada.

"He only needs a minute," whispered Lizzie. "I showed him the passageway and said I'd meet him at the back, by the kitchen."

They stepped out into the hallway, prepared to adopt an air of busy efficiency if Lady Violet or Miss Tippel the housekeeper were there, but the voices they'd heard were rebounding along the wide corridor past the grand portrait-filled staircase, and were coming from the cavernous atrium.

There, Lady Violet was greeting Danvers Carew, 9th Duke of Hoggart, and her step-daughter Lady Jane, just arrived in the landau now parked in the yard. Carew was a dapper, finespun man, pert and precise and with a habit of posing his upper body at an angle as he spoke. His pince-nez was kept on a cord so that it could fall off without damage whenever he pulled his hilarious comical-astonishment face. He felt this helped put others at ease the first time they met him. His wife Lady Jane, when describing him to a third party, pulled a different kind of face. She took after her father in many ways.

"Where *is* Father?" she said. "Not working today, surely?"

"I'm afraid so, we've even got some War Office guests coming, but he's around," said Lady Violet brightly, the edges of her smile jittering with nerves, as they always did when addressing any of her step-daughters. She secretly thought of all three of them as residents of her husband's vivarium, Lady Jane a fashionably-dressed scorpion, Lady Henrietta a bespectacled snake and Lady Alice a spider running around in circles.

"Are we first at the watering hole?" said Carew.

"Oh, Alice and Lionel are in the library," said Lady Violet, indicating like a tour guide. "We're putting everyone in the library for the time being."

"Until all the cattle are in the pen," said Carew.

"Yes," laughed Lady Violet. "The Hapgoods have arrived too, I think you've met them?"

"Hapgood?" said Carew, leaning slightly towards his wife.

"Sir Godfrey, and Delia," said Lady Jane. "I told you what he gets up to."

"Oh yes!" said Carew. "He's a hoot."

Striding footsteps announced Frederick Jekyll, appearing through the arches at the other end of the atrium. From just behind Lady Violet came whispers of excitement – the twins, Claude and William, had been standing dutifully silent, their nanny's hands resting on their shoulders, but now they looked at their mother pleadingly. "Mama?" they said in unison.

Violet's loving smile was all the cue they needed. They raced over to their father and launched themselves up at him, each grabbing hold of one of Jekyll's outstretched arms. He swung them round and round and they squealed with delight.

"Father, the human carousel!" groaned Jekyll through gritted teeth.

His strength gave out and his arms dropped, but the boys held onto his wrists, laughing together as they walked back to Lady Violet. "Heavens above, boys," said Jekyll, "you're getting too tall and heavy for that." The twins let go of him, giggling, and Violet's hand immediately clasped his, their fingers entwining. "I'll need to become a Hercules by the time they're eight!"

Violet gazed into his dark eyes, smiling. "Silly sardine." He kissed her hand and gave it a squeeze of reassurance.

A little hand tugged at Carew's trousers. The Honourable Albert Montgomery Carew, a sour and sickly child aged three years and eleven months, frowned up at his parents with wordless demands.

"Go along upstairs to the nursery with Nanny," said Lady Jane. "Play with your uncles."

"Yes, Mother," said the Honourable Albert Montgomery Carew. He let the twins' nanny lead him away, Claude and William running and jumping on ahead. He looked up at the Earl's imposing vivarium as he passed it, an expression of nothing in particular on his small face. Violet, feeling a vague curiosity, watched the child leave while Jekyll kissed his eldest daughter's cheek and shook the hand of his titled son-in-law.

At the same moment, out in the back yard, Cook also felt a vague curiosity, because the next arrival around the far corner of the house was a man on foot rather than another carriage. Alice Fruitcake's fella, innit? Her thoughts wandered into what she might do with her sweepstake winnings while Lionel Chaney strolled, in an inauthentically casual manner, as far as the entrance to the boiler room.

He didn't appear to notice Cook at all. He knocked, and the door was answered by Henri Moreau in a thick green work apron. The low roar of the boiler and the high, steady hum of the electrical generator spilt out across the yard. They went inside. Chaney emerged a matter of seconds later, and walked back the way he'd come, this time at a marching pace.

Cook sniffed, tapping out her pipe against a chair leg, idly jotting in her mental notebook under the heading Alice Fruitcake's Fella. She sniffed again, aware that the kitchen's heat had now faded from her meaty cheeks, returning them to blotchy pink instead of beetroot red, signalling that her five minutes were up. She got to her feet and dragged the chair back into the kitchen. No more peace 'till bedtime.

High up on the kitchen wall, the electric bell labelled 'LIB' jangled twice. Cook barked across to one of the scullery maids. "Tea. The Wedgwood china. Sharpish."

At the other end of the bell wire, in the library, Lady Violet's attention returned to her rapidly expanding house party. The library itself was square and high-ceilinged, its floor covered with a selection of brightly patterned rugs from the Far East. Mahogany bookshelves were filled with neatly arranged, evenly sized volumes, with Lady Violet's shelf of personally-owned novels in a less curated space near the windows. While recent Jekyll family portraits hung on the house's main stairwell, here in the library were paintings of earlier generations, plump Georgian beauties and stern, bewigged men on horseback. To one side stood a tall, glass-fronted cabinet showcasing row upon row of the late Henry Jekyll's Iron Age and Bronze Age artifacts, in much the same way as the room's tasteful scattering of sofas and armchairs showcased the ladies and gentlemen of Westwych House's informal celebration.

Danvers Carew stood behind a low Chesterfield on which lounged his wife Lady Jane and her sister Lady Alice. Opposite them lounged the Hapgoods, a pair of slender thoroughbreds with fixed expressions of recently insulted virtue and one oddly prominent physical feature apiece, ears for him, feet for her.

"Yes," Lady Delia Hapgood was saying, "he's done well, he's to be elevated to the Privy Council in the Jubilee honours on Tuesday."

"Is he the one who galloped to the altar the other week with another of those American heiresses?" said Carew, busying himself with his cigarette case and holder.

"No, that would be the Duke of Mirstone, your Grace," said Sir Godfrey Hapgood. He rocked with a sudden burst of laughter. "There can't be many American heiresses left in America by now, surely? Still, the man's got twenty-nine thousand acres to keep up."

"Anyone for a few hands of Nap?" said Carew. "Or Beggar-my-neighbour? Are there enough of us yet?"

While he was speaking, one of the Hapgoods reached over, tipped back a book on Violet's shelf to show the title and exchanged withering looks with the other Hapgood. Violet didn't see this, because she'd noticed Lionel Chaney's absence.

"Alice? Where's Lionel?"

Alice brushed back her flighty blonde hair with one hand and waved the other in mid-air circles. "Gone for a walk in the grounds, so he said."

Carew jabbed his cigarette holder in the direction of a nearby side table. "Don't think I haven't spotted the Mah Jong set at the ready, Mother-in-law," he grinned. "I am going to win back my money!"

"You're welcome to try," smiled Lady Violet. She looked around herself. "And I seem to have lost track of Frederick, too. Again."

Frederick was still in the atrium. Within minutes of each other, all eight of the remaining guests had alighted at the front steps and been conducted inside: Viscount Horace and Lady Gertrude Froome, pronounced 'frum'; the two War Office visitors Major General Harry Ruck and Mr Jasper Stoppard, along with their wives Maude and Enid; Jekyll's daughter Henrietta, a New Woman of tightly clenched severity; Henrietta's secretary companion, Miss Maria Augustine, "a radical novelist and exemplar of the feminist ideal" – *London Daily Examiner.*

It was Enid Stoppard, keen to make a good impression, who ooh-ed and ahh-ed intense interest in the vivarium and asked the Earl for a closer look. Jekyll was genuinely pleased to oblige, unconsciously smarting from the continued absence of comment on his Leon l'Hollier Anglo-French parked so conspicuously outside. He began with an overview of the vivarium's bespoke design and construction. All except the Stoppards drifted away to the library, led by Lady Henrietta, who stage-whispered a remark which included the word 'pets,' just to irritate her father.

"Each type of creature inhabits its own little environment?" said Mrs Stoppard. She peered in, nose almost to the glass, eyes twinkling. "You see this, Jasper?" Her husband was a dowdy, weaselly man with a sharply trimmed moustache and a genius for almost-completely-concealed embarrassment.

"The aim is to mimic their regular surroundings," said Jekyll. "If you place a hand on the glass beside these scorpions, you'll feel that it's very warm."

She did so, and it was. "How marvellous."

"The hatches you can see above are for feeding purposes.

163

At various points around the house and grounds are specially designed traps, collecting flies and other insects for the arachnids, mice and the occasional vole or sparrow for the snakes."

"Do they eat the vegetation too?"

"No, all the plants you see here are also cultivated for their poisons. This one is Water Hemlock, a member of the carrot family, native to North America. Those are castor bean plants from Africa, and the tropical Rosary Pea behind those rocks – you see, there? – is rich in toxic proteins."

Mrs Stoppard dabbed at the neckline of her brand new dress, which had cost three weeks' worth of her husband's wages. "May I ask, your Lordship, what is a protein?"

"A chain of amino acids," said Jekyll, "as described by Fourcroy, Berzelius and others."

"I see!" said Mrs Stoppard, none the wiser. She eyed the snakes in the compartment beside her with fascination. "Hello there." One of them curled up the glass, eyeing her back. Behind her, Mr Stoppard's embarrassment was almost completely concealed.

"It seems rather unfair on their part to be so plainly coloured," she said, "the unwary native must have to watch his step!"

"These Inland Taipans are rather shy, in fact, and extremely rare. None have been seen in the wild for over twenty years. Their method of killing prey is interesting, they raise their heads and strike multiple times with great accuracy and efficiency."

"Gosh. Are they especially poisonous?"

"One bite generally contains enough venom to kill a hundred adult men."

"Fancy that!" said Mrs Stoppard. The information made Mr Stoppard feel slightly sick. "Are these spiders as deadly?" she said, her puckered, oval face gliding sideways to loom into another compartment.

"Not so much," said Jekyll. "They're *Phoneutria fera*, more commonly the Brazilian wandering spider, these were collected in Suriname—"

"Oh, they wander quite a way, then?"

"They're found throughout north eastern South America. I'd like to keep some blue-ringed octopi and Japanese stone-fish, too, but marine habitats would require more time than I could give them. When I need those particular venoms I have to purchase them. All these specimens I milk myself."

"Good heavens, how do you do that?"

"With care," smiled Jekyll.

Mrs Stoppard was tittering at length, and elbowing Mr Stoppard to follow suit, when Poole suddenly appeared at Jekyll's side. His mute scowl told Jekyll much.

"Do please excuse me," said Jekyll to the Stoppards. "If you'd like to join the others . . .?" When they'd gone, after copious thanks for such a thrilling lesson, no really, most instructive, Poole informed his master in a low voice that a guest had been caught attempting to enter the basement.

Jekyll's face was stone. "Where is he now?"

"I wasn't quite sure what to do with the gentleman, m'lord," said Poole. "I've locked him in the plate room for the time being."

"You acted correctly, Poole," said Jekyll. He thought for a moment, huffing through his nose like a bull. "I presume the servants are eating now, with the guests' dinner being served earlier than usual?"

165

"Yes, Sir, they'll have sat down a few minutes ago."

"Then I'll deal with this straight away, while there are fewer eyes about."

As they hurried away, neither of them – nor anyone else in Westwych House that evening – could have foreseen the disaster this event would set in motion, and which almost none of them would survive.

Chapter 15

The narrow, windowless plate room, close to Poole's private quarters on the ground floor, was relatively empty at the moment. Most of the silverware it normally contained was on the long table in the dining room, and several valuable items of jewellery normally kept cased were on Lady Violet.

The man held captive paced beneath the thin, yellow glow of a bare lightbulb. He breathed deeply, self-consciously, to quell the fear rising in his gut and the intermittent shuddering of his bottom lip. He flinched as a key clattered in the lock.

The light threw deep shadows down the faces of Jekyll and Poole. The Earl momentarily registered surprise before his expression lapsed into anger. "You? How dare you ignore my admonishment! Not a guest, in fact, Poole, but a familiar face none the less."

Jack Utterson's voice was thick with nerves. "I-I thoroughly appreciate how reprehensible my p-presence here seems, Sir, but as I tried to explain to your butler here, I was in no way intending to steal anything, or to invade the privacy of your household, but merely to look at, er, that is, to see with my own eyes what was—"

"Be quiet!" snapped Jekyll with sudden force. "I had enough of your inane chatter at the factory this morning! Uppingham, is it?"

"Utterson, Sir, and I sincerely appeal to—"

"I said be quiet! It's perfectly obvious to me now that my suspicions were correct and that you're working on behalf of a third party, your actions are tantamount to proof."

"No, Sir, your Lordship, I only wished to—"

"Whatever you wished, Mr Utterson, you wished in vain." He turned to Poole. "We'll put him downstairs."

Poole nodded and took hold of Jack sharply, one hand gripping his collar, the other tightly twisting Jack's arm behind his back. Jack was too frightened and astonished to make a sound.

The plate room was locked up again and Jekyll led them the short distance to the passageway where household staff were forbidden to set foot, pausing here and there to check that none of the servants were astray from their dinner in the kitchen.

To one side of the passageway, shelves were stacked with files and notebooks compiled by Jekyll's father, the documents Jack had been tentatively examining when he was caught. Jack eyed them helplessly as he was frogmarched past, his thoughts filled with relief that Lizzie hadn't been with him. He sensed, correctly, that he was about to discover why the Earl had tried so firmly to deter him.

Jekyll pulled a long key from an inside pocket. A heavily reinforced door at the end of the passageway was immediately re-locked behind them. Beyond were steps curling down to the basement level underground. Their footsteps were loud in the confined space, the stone surfaces around them becoming darker and more age-spotted the deeper they went.

At the foot of the steps was a small area containing a battered-looking bureau heaped with books and loose sheets of scribble-filled paper. To one side was access to the boiler room, securely bolted. Straight ahead, a second locked door, even sturdier than the first, which opened onto pitch darkness.

Jack struggled to free himself. Strange growls and bumps emerged from the dark, and a peculiar smell hung in the cool air, a sickly blend of chemicals and offal. Jekyll clicked a switch beside him and banks of electric lights, arranged in clusters along the edges of the low ceilings, bloomed into life. Here was the first of the cellar's two main chambers.

The sounds increased in intensity. They were coming from the next chamber, past a wide archway of bare brick. Jack wriggled violently but the tall steward held him firm. As the cellar door was locked behind them, he noticed a series of aged gouges around the handle, as if something large and clawed had once tried to escape the laboratory.

The chamber was filled with scientific equipment. Jack could identify some of it as being used in processes of evaporation and electrolysis, but a series of metal tanks and intricate glass tubings were joined across a dozen worktables in a way which was a complete mystery to him. The walls were lined with handwritten sheets, floor to ceiling, several layers thick in places, in an endless, branching chain of equations, diagrams, notes.

Jekyll ran a hand over the copper tanks and liquid-filled flasks. "Moreau has checked everything for our after-dinner visitors?"

"Yes, m'lord," said Poole, propelling Jack towards the second chamber. "He's in the boiler room at present, some routine maintenance on the furnace and the hot water steam pump."

Jekyll nodded. "Put Mr Utterson in the isolation cage."

Jack suddenly felt his insides twist into knots when he saw what was in the second chamber. Eight large cages, made of fat, rust-peppered iron rods like those he'd seen in zoos and circuses, were bolted to the flagstoned floor, four on each side.

Six were occupied: two by Harris and Bingham, the footman and maid Jekyll had sacked the previous day; two by Joseph and James Carter, the brothers Poole had recruited at the workhouse; one by an earlier workhouse recruit; one by a servant dismissed three months ago for persistent drunkenness.

None of them were human any more: Harris was a six-legged bag of flesh, with two mouths full of curving fangs; Bingham's body was covered in eyes; one brother was mostly reptilian, with a long tail and a crocodile-like head; the other was scaly and insectoid, spines bristling along its back; the earlier recruit had become a semi-wolf, its legs greatly elongated; the dismissed servant was a huge, furred beast somewhere between ape and lion.

Jack's terror at the sight, sounds and odours of these creatures was beyond his capacity to express. One thought cut through his mind – that this place, without any shadow of doubt, was the source of all the stories about monsters sighted near Hagstow in the past few years, and the source of the hideous 'centaur' he'd seen at the museum of curiosities in Bristol.

The creatures stared at him as he was pushed past the cages. He didn't know what horrified him the most, the haphazard signs of residual humanity in their bodies or the ferocious hostility of their gaze. In a state of shock, he allowed himself to be manoeuvred past another brick archway and into an empty cage that stood apart from the others, largely out of sight behind a protruding buttress. His senses partially returned to him with the loud clanking as Poole locked the cage and stepped back, hanging a small ring of keys on a wall hook well out of any captive's reach.

Jekyll stood in front of the iron bars with no more ceremony than if he'd been addressing one of the kitchen staff. "Well, Mr Utterson, we find ourselves in highly unusual circumstances. There are pressing demands on my time this evening, so it will be later tonight when I take some blood and tissue samples from you, and inject you with a formulation to study its effects on your body's chemistry. Until then, I suggest you get some rest. In an hour or so, immediately following the celebration dinner upstairs, I will be down here in discussion with others. You'll remain where you are, out of sight. If you speak, or otherwise indicate your presence, you'll die shortly afterwards. You're alive now only because I want the truth about who you are and in whose employ you are, and because I require more test subjects than usual at present. Do you understand all this, or are you going to simply gape at me like a fish on a slab?"

Jack took a weak hold of the cage bars and tried to say something. "W-What kind of—? T-This is a—"

"I can see I'll get little sense out of you," sighed Jekyll.

He turned and strode past the other cages. The half-lizard snarled and flung itself against the bars, clawing at Jekyll, but its upper limbs were too stubby to reach him and he didn't react to the creature in any way.

Poole was beside what used to be Bingham. The sacked maid was standing upright and very still, wearing only a grubby chemise which was bloodstained in two streaked patches around her middle where she'd plucked out a couple of the blinking eyes covering her entire body. She held one hand raised, as if in greeting, and had been doing so for several hours, her arms and fingers seeing somewhere far away.

"This one's not got long, m'lord," said Poole.

Jekyll regarded her stoically. Behind his mask of indifference, familiar leering goblins knifed at his heart – bitterness, frustration, regret, sorrow. Another failure. Another chaos of reactants where there should have been order!

A thread-like rash of tiny blisters, the avatar of oncoming biochemical breakdown, was evident all over what-was-Bingham. "If you'll pardon the liberty, Sir," said Poole, keeping his voice low for Jekyll's benefit, "you can't let this one go, not until there's fewer people about, and you don't want a dead one when the War Office gentlemen come down."

Mask firmly in place, Jekyll looked away from the cages and into Poole's worried expression. "You know the rule. They die free."

"Sir, are you—?"

"They die free. Whatever else goes to the boiler room is irrelevant, I will not have them put in the furnace like

172

household garbage. We can only hope this one survives a couple of days yet."

"Very good, m'lord." Poole had never agreed with Jekyll's policy of setting failed experiments loose in the hills, once they were judged to be close to death, but he knew his master well enough to accept that argument was pointless. Jekyll's stated aim was to let them end their lives unchained, to taste fresh air and feel the ground beneath their feet one last time, but in Poole's opinion his employer's motive was intractability, a desire to shake his fist at Nature, to show a hardened defiance.

Jekyll and Poole left the laboratory, switching off the lights and securing the doors as they went. What-was-Bingham's approaching death prompted both of them to think back a fortnight or more, to the last reject sent to die in the bleak, lonely hills, a lumbering crab-beast – Jekyll mulled over the data gained from analysis of its blood, Poole pictured it as it must be now, eaten by crows and foxes, decaying into the soil. Jack Utterson was out of sight and out of mind.

Chapter 16

The party guests had dressed for dinner in their allocated bedrooms and were now sprinkled artistically across both the library and the drawing room.

Lady Alice, as she often did on special occasions, soon felt spirits from the Beyond moving within her and so the curtains in the drawing room were almost-closed to create an atmosphere suitable for a séance. Half a dozen guests, either seriously interested or charmingly amused, sat in silence while she composed herself, sitting at a card table with her palms flat against the baise. As she closed her eyes, she noticed with annoyance that her husband Lionel had apparently gone for *another* walk in the grounds? All day he'd been disappearing like this. What the devil was he up to?

She breathed deeply for several minutes. Her delicate features melted into a tranquillity which echoed the Classical busts of Nyx and Artemis on the mantelpiece. Her severe sister Lady Henrietta peered over her spectacles with an indulgent smile.

"I see the realm of the dead," gasped Alice. "The spirits, they gather around me. They guide me into the great unknown . . ." Slowly, her face tilted upwards. "Do you not hear it? The music of the spheres? These are echoes of another time, clearer than I have ever seen before. The spirits lead me, they show me, they beg of me. I see what may be, and what must be." Her fingers trembled over the table's surface and her head dipped, turned, gradually rolled.

Sitting beside Henrietta, Miss Augustine the novelist slid last week's *New Age* across her lap. She held it close to her face, in order to read in the low light.

Alice, her eyes tightly shut, suddenly fluttered like a startled bird. "Burning! Burning! In a future inescapable! Land scarred and pitted, filled with rain and with blood! Oh, the dead! They rise, in their millions, rise up from thundering guns and mechanical horrors! Armies swallowed whole, the ruin of the world! Carnage spills from the cup of time! And it is here too! Fallen backwards through the psychic web. An inverted echo of disaster! Death is with us. Death is in this house. Death comes for us! Tonight!"

The curtains were flung open. "We'll keep an eye out for him then, shall we Alice?" said her sister Lady Jane. "I think that's enough, you know what you're like once you get hysterical."

Henrietta exchanged looks of arch disappointment with Danvers Carew. "Must you, Jane? Alice's hysterics are so entertaining."

"I agree," laughed Carew.

Mrs Stoppard leaned over the arm of a sofa, extending a hand in Alice's direction. "Are you alright, dear? How very disturbing. Jasper's sister has the gift too, hasn't she,

175

Jasper?" She turned to her weaselly husband, whose embarrassment was almost completely concealed. "Contact with the spirits can be unpredictable." Alice wordlessly agreed with her, fingers dabbing at blonde hair made wayward by the breath of the spirits.

Henrietta huffed. "Half the fun, in Alice's case, Mrs— I'm terribly sorry, I've forgotten your name."

"Enid Stoppard," she smiled humbly. "Jasper here," she said, indicating Jasper here, "is a senior bookkeeper at the War Office, working on His Lordship's behalf."

"As children," continued Henrietta, "our governess used to call her Alice Of The Apocalypse."

"Priceless," snorted Danvers Carew.

Lady Jane made a bee-line for him. "I'm sure the only spirits around here are those of the liquor cabinet," she said. "Danvers, come here please." He obeyed and she led him out.

Alice gave a brief sneer at everything in general before reaching across to Mrs Stoppard in return, her hand posed like a cherub's in the Sistine Chapel. "Thank you for your concern, Mrs Stoppard, I'm feeling better already. To those who won't believe, all portents are no more than grains of sand lost upon a beach."

"You really see a dreadful fate for us all here?" breathed Mrs Stoppard fearfully.

"It is inevitable." She turned and called loudly to the room and beyond. "Isn't Lionel back yet?"

At that moment, Lionel Chaney was pressed tight against the wall of the passageway leading to the basement, hiding behind the shelves of papers in case a passing maid should spot him. From his pocket he slipped a key, the one Moreau had given him.

He darted to the door and fumbled nervously with the lock. Casting an eye over his shoulder, he closed the door as quietly as he could and descended the stone steps.

His heart galloped and his mouth felt like a tract of desert. He arrived at the open area beside the entries into the cellar chambers and the boiler room. Yes, good, exactly as Moreau described. And here was the old bureau piled with books.

He rummaged through the bureau's drawers and compartments. Reports, reports, reports, where were these blasted— Ah! Was this it? Yes, dated last week and—

He jumped with fright as a sudden angry screech, like a large animal in pain, came from the depths of the cellar, beyond the second locked door. Another sound, too. Was that a man's voice? Calling out? Too muffled to be sure.

The noise died down. Chaney stood motionless for a few seconds, listening intently, feeling his heartbeat throb like the rhythm of a speeding train. He went back to examining a leather pouch he'd picked up. Skimming through the papers it contained, he found little he understood but enough to assure himself that this was the information he needed. Nerves turned to excitement. His worries would be over! Debts cleared, ruin averted! One in the eye for his bloody imperious father-in-law, too, now he came to think of it.

His fingers traced a lump at the bottom of the pouch. Inside he found a small vial, half filled with a dark liquid. His excitement bristled. This had to be the very stuff Jekyll was developing for the War Office! As he'd suspected, some kind of super pick-me-up, then.

He pulled out the rubber stopper and smelled the contents. Like ripe fruit. He put a finger over the open neck, tipped the vial forward and back, and licked the resulting droplet off his skin. Quite pleasant, reminded him of aniseed.

Quickly, he replaced the stopper, slid the pouch into a large concealed pocket sewn into the lining of his dinner jacket, smoothed himself down, and made his way back up the steps feeling a twinge of indigestion. Better hurry up, Alice would be asking—

"Isn't Lionel back yet?" She swung her gaze around the drawing room but nobody had an answer for her.

Lady Jane steered her husband to the threshold of the library, where the Earl was holding court on the subject of bicycles used in the recent Paris-Roubaix race, and Lady Violet was winning again with a Thirteen Orphans hand.

"Play," said Lady Jane, in a voice barely audible.

"I'll be thrashed again," whispered Carew testily. "It's bloody humiliating, losing to a woman."

She condensed several sentences into one short, effective scowl.

"Leave off," hissed Carew, "I can't do it."

"We have to do *something*," snarled Lady Jane, breaking off to thrust a beaming smile at Miss Augustine, the novelist, emerging from the drawing room. "You have a better idea?"

". . . Murder?" said Carew, pulling a comically shocked face.

"Can you not comprehend the monstrous injustice to be perpetrated if those twins inherit?"

"Wills can be contested, can't they?"

"Yes, for decades. The estate would be eaten up. I did

tell you about Thellusson and Woodford, and the Dineley-Gooderes, and the Acton Miser case, in quite some detail."

"Those were ages ago. I thought, these days, inheritances can be . . . what's the word? Partitioned? Pardoned?"

"My father is an *Earl*. An *Earl*. He is not about to dish out his estate in the manner of a common costermonger."

"Even so, I can't do it," muttered Carew. "Violet's a jolly handsome woman, but it's a bit . . . sordid. My reputation, you know."

"Whose side will everyone take?" whispered Lady Jane. "Yours or hers? You play the injured party, Father will explode as Father generally does, propriety will demand a new will, and the problem will be solved. I don't know what you're whimpering about, trash like her doesn't keep its knees together for a *Duke*. Now go and lose. And be nice."

Carew sighed and sauntered over to the square table where Lady Violet and three male guests were finishing a game. "Well now, Mother-in-law, gentlemen," declared Carew, taking a couple of steps in a comical gait, "might I be next into bat?"

Poole materialised beside Lady Violet, spoke discreetly to her, and she rose. "Dinner is served," she announced, before turning to Carew. "I'd be delighted, Danvers. Perhaps we can make a four after the fancy dress?"

Frederick Jekyll, 5th Earl of Westwych, and Lady Violet Jekyll took their places in the pairings of ladies and gentlemen who formed the line into dinner, a procession arranged automatically according to status. Eyebrows went quietly up or down when Lady Henrietta paired with her secretary companion Miss Augustine. Lady Alice poked her oh-*here*-he-is husband Lionel on the shoulder as he paired with Lady Delia Hapgood, to ask him where on earth he'd been. Chaney told her he'd already told her, and did he really have to tell her again, that he was taking a walk. He also told her he was feeling a little unwell. Mr and Mrs Stoppard found they only had each other to pair with and walked at the end of the line, Mrs Stoppard grandly, Mr Stoppard with almost completely concealed embarrassment. Everyone chattered as they moved into the dining room and were shown to their equally defined places at table.

". . . They've already had to sell off most of the paintings to pay the death duties, the walls are covered in blank rectangles, poor chap . . ."

". . . We saw her in *Macbeth* at the Lyceum, she was marvellous, better than Ellen Terry I thought. At home we started shouting 'out, damned spot' at the dog and laughing ourselves silly . . ."

". . . I tell you, the Treasury is well rid of Jumbo Harcourt and I thought Balfour was perfectly justified. High time the Irish learned their place . . ."

". . . With that many horses, you see, hundreds of tons pile up on London's roads every day. The recent committee to solve the whole problem declared it unsolvable. They gave up after three days. No, I assure you, motor carriages will present no such difficulties, we'll have cleaner and more fragrant streets, they'll be an enormous benefit to the city . . ."

". . . A lady novelist? Is she? . . ."

In the dining room, to emphasise the glitter of the electric chandelier, curtains had been drawn against the fading daylight. The ladies peeled their gloves, while everyone exchanged pleasantries, examined their menu cards and passed admiring comments about their hosts as the first course was set before them.

". . . Yes, the house was remodelled and extended by my father about thirty-five years ago, you'll notice a number of floral motifs which echo his love of the local landscape . . ."

". . . No idea what's happening to the world. These chaps, Chamberlain, that scoundrel Dilke, Lloyd George, not one proper gentleman among them, and some of the ideas of Cunninghame-someone and those people, the Independent Labour mob, well, I don't know what I think. At least Hardie's out of his seat now, I couldn't understand a word the fellow said . . ."

". . . Oh, brand new, quite a blood-curdler, and written by the man who's Sir Henry Irving's stage manager, would you believe? . . ."

". . . Brave to have it all over the house, I would imagine. If Mr Edison's own assistant can be killed in his own home by the electricity, what chance we, I wonder? . . ."

". . . Bankers? Odious breed. We went to a dinner the other week – one of the Marlborough House Set was doing something or other – and the table was lousy with them. Half a dozen Barings, some Currys, a brace of Lubbocks and a smattering of Huths, if you please. I hardly liked to shake their hands in case my cufflinks went missing! . . ."

". . . Hmm? The bookkeeper's wife? Good heavens, yes I see what you mean, she certainly plays a good knife and fork, doesn't she? . . ."

". . . Friends of ours were intending to be in last year's Emancipation Run, but in the end, they barely left the

Metropole, there were so many cyclists in the way, and the rain was lashing down . . ."

". . . Oh, cloven hooves are not required for admittance to the Fabian Society . . . Why, because I am a member, my dear Sir, and have no trouble finding shoes to fit . . ."

Cook had excelled herself and the croquette of chicken went down particularly well. Lady Violet's relief that everything was so convivial led her to drink more wine than she'd normally have allowed herself, and her voice drifted inexorably towards squeaky. Danvers Carew told her he found this wonderfully endearing.

Empty wine bottles found their way back to the kitchen, where the scullery maids checked to make sure labels were intact and then set them aside. Tomorrow, the bottles would quietly be sold on to one of the best hotels in Bristol, where they'd be refilled with a cheap Spanish import and re-corked.

Around the dining table, conversations ebbed and flowed. The state occasion which brought them together tonight, Her Majesty's imminent Diamond Jubilee, gradually pushed talk into a reflective mood. Some guests reminisced about better times, deploring falling standards and rising activism, some congratulated themselves on living in an era of steady progress and prosperity, some feigned shock at society gossip. Most quietly passed judgement on their fellow diners, either as rivals, or as useful friends, or as inferiors.

Thus, their time ticked away.

As the unseen sun dipped past the horizon, Frederick Jekyll – at a pre-arranged and just-remembered signal from Lady Violet – stood up to make a short speech. Guests turned replete faces to the head of the table as their wine glasses were surreptitiously topped up.

The Earl spoke of his pleasure at being among family and friends at a moment in history, a time when four hundred and fifty millions, across the entire world, had cause to rejoice in the secure sovereignty of Great Britain. There were noises of approval and a toast was made: to the Queen, and to the future!

The raising of glasses was followed by the withdrawal of the ladies to the drawing room and the serving of port and cigars to the gentlemen. Jekyll excused himself and his two War Office guests Major Ruck and Mr Stoppard – business matters to discuss – and expressed his regrets at missing the upcoming fancy dress.

Lionel Chaney barely noticed them go. He was concerned about the growing turmoil in his stomach and the agonising headache he'd developed in the last half hour.

Chapter 17

Out on the hills, the sunset threw spectacular streaks of red and orange across the sky. Grassy slopes and patchy woodlands alike were bathed in the muzzy, velvet gossamer of summer twilight, where insects zigzagged and the air was delicately warm.

Mr A. E. Jemmison, proprietor of Jemmison's Cabinet Of Curiosities, struggled for many minutes up a long, uneven ridge of land and stopped to catch his breath. He found himself at the end of a tall, crescent-shaped cleft which looked as if some giant knife had roughly hacked into the hillside. His lungs rasped, and his legs ached, and he took off his thickly-lensed spectacles to wipe the sweat from his round face with a threadbare handkerchief.

Cyril the Centaur was dead, curse him. Flat out in his stall last suppertime. The pride of the collection, gone without so much as a warning bout of colic. Dead as a doornail. And no tank big enough to pickle him in! Inconsiderate ruddy animal.

It would have been of no consequence to Jemmison, had

he known of Cyril's unusual longevity. Left without his prize exhibit, and with a landlord snapping at his heels, he was praying to an assortment of supreme beings that lightning would strike twice. To think that, for years, he'd dreamed of bagging one of the reclusive monsters said to haunt the high, deserted hilltops, and that *for five whole weeks he'd in actuality had one*! The day when fearful whispers, no more than ghosts of a rumour, had described a deformed horse glimpsed on a distant rise, he'd rushed out of the city in search. Luck had been on his side for once.

Jemmison felt the thin material of his shirt and trousers sticking to his skin. Wheezing, he heaved the net he'd borrowed into a more comfortable position on his shoulder. He thought about going home. What was the use? What were the chances of finding another one, ever, *ever*? Next to ruddy nothing. And now it was getting dark.

He shifted his bulk one way, then another, looking around and back the way he'd come. The emptiness inside his purse eventually spurred him on. You never knew, they might come out more at night? Maybe, after sunset, the hills were filled with prancing, ugly pony-monsters?

He had no inkling that he was being watched by bulbous, jet black eyes. The huge half-crab had lost its human name many days ago, along with its sanity, in the basement laboratory at Westwych House. Before being set free, to die on the wild, lonely uplands.

It had crawled, slept, lay in agony beneath the stars, snapped up unwary rabbits to eat, drunk rain from hollows in the ground. To survive, to cling onto life without knowing why, kept going by instinct alone, despite the self-horror that drifted around its mind, the phantoms of its past.

It had postponed death through cunning and willpower, but now it knew its time was finally ending. And here was a man. A fat and juicy man, a human man, a man like those who had stolen his life, who had stuck him with needles and put him in a cage. It shrank deeper into the bushes, out of sight, waiting for its chance.

Jemmison pretended to busy himself with one of the frayed ends of the net. Something had moved over there, behind all that leafy gubbins, he was sure of it. Too big for a fox or a dog, and a sheep was too stupid to hide. Perhaps, as may be, possibly, this something was just the right size to be a shy little pony?

The cords of the net scraped roughly around his arms as he tried to coil the ruddy thing. Why had he brought it with him? What did he think he was going to do, twirl it around his head like a circus lion tamer? Cyril had happily been led away with a gentle tug at his mane. He was—

It moved again. The something. No mistake.

He watched it from the corner of one eye, all casual like. A definite shadow, shifting slowly, slowly.

Bigger than he'd thought. Might be a full-grown one?

Jemmison began to whistle a tune, note by note. Nice and gentle. Friendly as can be, nothing to get startled over. He took a step or two closer to the bushes. In between his own wheezes, he could hear the something breathing. Sluggish and hesitant. Could be it was afraid?

The last rays of daylight were fading. As Jemmison's poor sight adjusted to the lengthening gloom, he saw a tall section of leaves slowly divide into two. For a moment, he thought they'd parted by themselves. It took him a second to perceive the large object which had moved the foliage aside. His blood turned cold, finally seeing the huge, curved upper section of an immense claw.

The half-crab suddenly lunged at him with a rattling screech, bursting out of the bushes, its claw wide open. Jemmison let out a yell and stumbled back, tripping over that ruddy net and landing on the grass with a hard thud.

The shivering creature was bony and emaciated, visibly on the point of death. What remained of its humanity – an arm, and part of its head and chest – were cadaverously thin, and of its six spindly legs only three could still move, the others left dragging.

Jemmison's continuous scream of terror was punctuated by short gasps for breath. The creature scooped him up in its giant claw and hoisted him above its head as if in triumph, staggering for a few seconds under the man's considerable weight. It shouted out, in a voice cracked like the dried bed of a river, something that sounded to Jemmison like no more than random words. "Obey! Obey-we! Die! Obey-we-die!"

With a loud, rattling rasp and a final burst of energy it turned and, tightening its hold on Jemmison, scuttled rapidly into the cleft in the hillside. The showman's spectacles flew off his nose and cracked against a rock, and his net trailed for a few yards before falling flat into a streaked shape on the grass. His screams quickly receded into the gathering night.

Chapter 18

Having donned their costumes for the grand fancy dress parade, on the theme of The Empire, the house party re-gathered and re-mingled, discreetly herded by various servants back into the drawing room. Lady Violet, suppressing a fit of wine-laden giggles, explained the procedure: in ones and twos, as and when prompted, each guest was to exhibit themselves by promenading through to the library, where-upon they would be judged, with the utmost gravity and sincerity, by the Jubilee Committee, who had all been given special licence to stay up late, namely the twins Claude and William, along with their little cousin the Honourable Albert Montgomery Carew. There would be prizes awarded to Best Lady, Best Gentleman and Most Likely To Please Her Majesty.

Everyone was enormously amused. The three boys were dressed like stern officials, including slicked hair and false moustaches. They sat at a card table positioned so they could see Mummy/Aunt Violet through the doorway and nod gravely to her whenever the next guest was wanted.

"Are we ready?" said Violet. She consulted some notes she'd hurriedly written.

Meanwhile, Jilks the footman very gently placed a black shellac disc on the new Berliner Gramophone. He'd practised keeping the handle turning at the correct speed, and was now quite skilled at it. He placed the tone-arm on the spinning disc. A lively, high-timbre tune sprang from the conical speaker and continued to play as a backdrop to the parade.

"Firstly," declared Violet, glancing at her notes, "we have Good Queen Bess and Sir Francis Drake!" Sir Godfrey and Lady Delia Hapgood stepped grandly past the young judges to appreciative applause. Their costumes were a dazzle of historical accuracy, and Sir Godfrey finished off the tableau by miming the bowling of balls and the scanning of a far horizon.

"Next, we have A Brave Defender Of The Colonies." Miss Augustine marched in an officer's uniform borrowed from a male friend, complete with regimental sword. She saluted the other guests and got several "Hurrah!"s in reply.

Lady Henrietta appeared festooned in a patchwork of colours, stripes and motifs. "The Flags Of Every Nation Of The Empire," announced Violet, and everyone agreed that this was an ingenious and original concept.

"Next, ladies and gentlemen, Britannia herself!" Lady Jane emerged swathed in white and a Union Jack, topped with a shiny helmet. Carew followed her, dressed entirely in blue, with paper cut-out fish bobbing in both hands. "Accompanied by The Waves Over Which She Rules." There were many cheerful whispers about what a good sport his Grace the Duke was.

Viscount Froome was next, clad in breeches and rouged cheeks as John Bull, a choice which the young judges thought appropriate because of the Viscount's round belly. He was followed·by his wife Lady Gertrude in green, adorned with floral garlands as Mother Nature, which the young judges thought pointless because she hadn't stuck to the theme.

"Ah! Now, The Lion And The Unicorn!" Edith Stoppard and Maude Ruck the Major General's wife, knowing in advance that both their husbands would be absent from the parade because of business discussions with the Earl, had devised a joint idea, Maude with furs around her neck, Edith with a *papier maché* horn pointing up from the top of her head, both with tails attached at the back. The judges concluded amongst themselves that although the costumes were poor, the acting was good thanks to all the roaring and galloping.

Lady Alice, in yellow, carried a very large fold-up fan which with a flourish she suddenly unfurled into a full circle painted gold. "The Sun Which Never Sets Upon The Empire." There was unanimous agreement that this was really very clever indeed.

Violet put on her horned helmet, and picked up her spear and shield, ready to end the parade with her Boadicea. One more to introduce first, Lionel Chaney. "And now, er . . ."

Her step-son-in-law's costume had been left upstairs apart from a sinister-looking mask which covered his face and looked ridiculous above a dinner jacket. The young judges muttered to each other that Uncle Lionel was showing a serious lack of effort and would not be in the running for any of the prizes.

Chaney swayed slightly in the library doorway. "I do

apologise," he mumbled. "Please excuse me, I'm feeling rather unwell." He turned, sped across the hallway and up the main staircase, followed crossly by The Sun Which Never Sets Upon The Empire.

He took the stairs two at a time, feeling as if he might faint at any moment. The earlier pains in his stomach had been replaced with a strange, crawling sensation across much of his skin. He was hot, and itchy, and wanted to sink into cold water.

He dashed into the nearest bathroom, slamming the door behind him and clicking the latch shut. Alice rattled the door handle and knocked loudly. "Lionel! What's the matter?"

"Go away please," he said unsteadily.

"I will not! Whatever is the matter? You made a complete show of me down there!"

"I am perfectly alright. Stop fussing, woman. I've eaten something that doesn't agree with me, that's all."

"I don't see how, I've eaten the same as you."

"Leave me to myself! I'll be down in a minute."

There was a long pause. "I'm going to wait here for you."

"Please don't, Alice."

No answer. He turned on the electric light and stood with his hands gripping the sides of the washbasin. Glancing up at an oval mirror he suddenly flinched at his reflection. He'd forgotten he was still wearing the mask. Impatiently, he pulled at the string holding it in place and lifted it away.

He let it bump to the floor. He frowned at himself in the mirror, leaning slightly closer, not quite understanding what he was seeing. His pulse started to quicken as his fingers slowly rose to prod cautiously at his face.

The flesh around his eyes and nose had become lumpy and discoloured. Raised, oddly-textured patches were developing all over his skin.

He edged closer to his reflection. The patches were patterned with tiny root-like tendrils underneath the outer surface. Growing, in his face, causing that infernal itchiness. It might be all over him! He ripped off his tie and tore at his shirt, exposing large areas of corrupted flesh, roughened and blooming.

He scratched wildly at his chest, his neck, his cheeks. The scratches seeped blood, which coated his fingers as he kept on scratching, digging with stark horror at whatever was efflorescing inside him.

Pain soon forced him to stop and think. He paused with his bloodied hands held up at his neck like claws, and he heard himself gasp for breath in stuttering bursts.

A truth was finally puncturing his earlier assumptions: that the vial he'd stolen, the one still tucked into the pouch concealed in his jacket, contained not a tonic but a poison. His first thoughts had been correct after all, that his father-in-law must be creating some kind of vile contaminant for the military, something to ruin enemy food supplies or drinking water. Well, so be it. If this filthy stuff had got into his system, then it could be got out again. There'd be an antidote. Of course, there'd be an antidote. There had to be one, in case of incorrect usage.

Chaney pulled himself up to his full height. He tried to stand firm but his whole body was shuddering. Now then, a plan of action. Should be return to the cellar? He still had the key, he could search for the antidote in secret and none would be any the wiser. But without guidance, or considerable luck, how would he know which antidote was the right one?

Should he come clean and throw himself on Jekyll's mercy? No, ridiculous, he'd face a ruin even worse than the one he was already facing thanks to his creditors!

Or, might he ride out the effects of this poison? He'd had less than a drop of it. If it was simply some hellish extract from Jekyll's vivarium, he'd already be dead, wouldn't he? How often had he heard the Earl mention the speed and potency of those nasty pets' venoms?

A muffled wave of laughter from below reminded him of the ongoing party. Outside the bathroom door, his wife was reminded too.

"Lionel? I'm going downstairs," said Lady Alice.

"Very well," called Chaney unsteadily. "I'll come along soon. I'm just going to wash."

She heard the basin taps squeak and start to pour, then hurried back to the library, where the young judges were finishing their deliberations. The Honourable Albert Montgomery Carew was informing his cousins William and Claude that his daddy was better than their daddy because a Duke beats an Earl. They had no means of winning that argument, and thus the matter of Best Gentleman was settled.

The twins ran over to Lady Violet and she bent to hear their whispers, the smile on her face radiant with love for them. Once a hush had fallen, William mustered his biggest voice and declared that Best Lady was Good Queen Bess, Best Gentleman was The Waves Over Which She Rules, and Most Likely To Please Her Majesty was The Sun Which Never Sets Upon The Empire. Claude distributed the prizes, thoroughly resenting his brother for always going first. The winners received the silver Royal Mint commemorative jubilee medal, with dated clasp on blue and white ribbon. The twins had their hands humorously shaken by one or two of the gentlemen, and were told how handsome and adorable they were by one or two of the ladies.

Lady Jane picked up the Honourable Albert Montgomery Carew, kissed him goodnight and handed him to the Jekyll's nanny, hovering in the background, who escorted all three boys up to the nursery. Danvers Carew caused much hilarity by swimming his medal through the air like one of his paper cut-out fishes.

Enid Stoppard, walking carefully so as not to dislodge the unicorn horn on her head, congratulated Lady Violet on a splendid entertainment. "Such a shame our husbands had to closet themselves away with business. Was there no persuading His Lordship?"

"Over the years, Mrs Stoppard," said Lady Violet with mock gravity, "I have learned that persuasion is something to which my Freddie has complete immunity. I gave up trying to tame him long ago, I simply let him get on with it. Dizzy duckling. It makes for a quiet life."

Mrs Stoppard twittered. She would never know how utterly unnerved her husband Jasper had become in the last half an hour, on business in the basement, or how her fate would soon be sealed by events taking place below her feet.

Chapter 19

Jack Utterson's journal

*Sat. 19th June. Westwych House,
from approx. 6:30pm.*

Jekyll and his rough servant left me locked in darkness. I stood frozen, dumbfounded, holding onto the bars of my cage, so shocked and so frightened that for some time not a single thought was able to enter my head at all.

My concern for Miss Prendick was what, at last, jolted me from this incapacitated state. I was greatly relieved she had not been with me in the passageway to the cellar, and so had avoided discovery, but I realised that she must, by now, be wondering where I had got to.

As I learned much later, she had swiftly returned to the Tethered Goat, believing that (since neither she nor her friend Ada had heard anything about an intruder being detained, as would be expected) I had been forced by circumstances to leave the house by another route.

Meantime, the pitch darkness threatened to plunge me back into horrified despair at any moment, a situation made worse by the unseen presence of the other captives. I could hear their harsh breaths, their low and piteous moans. Then from the inky blackness one of them spoke to me. "New man . . . new one . . . it slips not the veil, not I . . ." The voice must have been that of the woman covered in eyes. She said more, sometimes whispering about the future, but her mind was clearly no longer her own and I understood none of it.

Another spoke – which one this time I could not tell – but it too was unintelligible at first. "Obey," it said, over and over again in a guttural gasp. "Obey . . . We . . . Die . . ." Yet another took up the chant, and their voices became steadily louder until both were screaming with all their might, roaring their rage into the clammy, lightless confines of the cellar. I found myself crying out for help until my throat burned. As suddenly as it started, the shouting ceased and I was left trembling in terror, my thoughts squirming in remembrance of what the Earl had said would happen to me in due course.

Without reference to my pocket watch, I had no idea how much time passed before I heard the key in the basement door and squinted as the lights were switched back on. By crouching at the right hand side of the cage, with my right temple pressed to the stained bars, I could see with one eye what was going on throughout the greater part of the cellar's chambers while keeping myself largely hidden.

Of the two men who entered, one was the gaunt, bald servant who'd manhandled me on behalf of Mr Jekyll. The other was an unpleasant-looking type in a green workman's apron, who spoke with a French accent. They exchanged few words and it was immediately evident that there was no love lost between them.

The Frenchman set about tinkering with the stacks of scientific apparatus in the chamber closest to the entrance, adjusting taps and dials until various distillation columns were in motion and there was an audible trickle of liquid through a series of copper tanks. The tall man, who on closer inspection sported a glass eye as if needing further enhancement of his forbidding mein, distributed bowls of food topped with slabs of bread, and wooden cups filled with water. These he pushed through a narrow aperture at the base of each cage. Mine he delivered without a word or even a glance in my direction.

Beneath the bread were a few raw fruits and vegetables, along with a crudely chopped portion of raw meat, which I think was chicken, all of it presumably from the extensive kitchen garden I'd noticed behind the house. I dropped the bread back into place, having no stomach for even the finest cuisine, let alone this insulting animal fodder. I felt anger starting to heat my blood as the two servants left.

This time, although the door was firmly locked as before, the lights remained lit. The caged creatures ate noisily, save for the eyed-woman who appeared to be in an extremely sickly state and who stood with her arms outstretched as if in supplication to some unfathomable psychic power. The sickening horror resident in the cage beside hers, the fleshy mass which scuttled on many legs, pushed itself tightly to the adjoining cage-side and, unfurling what was in part an arm, reached out and offered up an apple to her. She seemed to notice the quivering limb poking between the bars, and indeed to personally recognise the horrible monster to which it was attached, but she made no attempt to take the apple. Eventually it was withdrawn, the monster mewling sorrowfully to itself. Having fed, the creatures either lay silent at the rear of their cages, or else adopted a rhythmic, circular pacing.

Here and there, one or another of them turned and looked me directly in the eye. I should have been repelled by such a thing, but suddenly was not, on account of the behaviour I had just witnessed – *a conscious act of kindness!*

I was greatly disturbed, for now I met their gaze I could perceive in them a quality I had been too horrified to admit seeing until this very moment, the same quality I had glimpsed in the grotesque Cyril at Jemmison's repulsive exhibition and had instantly dismissed as a fancy caused by shock, a quality which here forced itself upon my attention: it was *kinship*.

It was a commonality buried, very deeply, beneath insanity and physical distortion, beneath whatever process had twisted them, yet surviving. But a kinship quite separate from humanity, as such – for are not even the most beastly and incomprehensible of men still human beings? – it was the simple, benign fellowship of intelligent reasoning, of shared existence, of having deliberate, purposeful thought, which surely surpasses distinctions of destiny or species.

Perhaps I let optimism overwhelm my judgement at a moment of intense fear. Perhaps what I felt was no more than a mere empathy between living souls, but I was suddenly and most profoundly moved. My conscience filled with shame, for I had turned away from the so-called centaur in disgust, hardened my heart, despite my protestations to Jemmison at the time.

I could do such a thing no longer, no matter how unnerving or repulsive these creatures might be. They were individuals, as was I, our first origins in Nature.

Hesitantly, with my every fibre still knotted in terror of my predicament, I tried to communicate with them. "Your names . . ." I said, to none in particular, "can you remember? . . . How long have you been here? . . . What has been done to you? . . . Are there any means of escape from this place? . . ."

Upon my uttering the word 'escape,' the largest of the creatures, in the cage closest to my own, reacted with a grunt and reared up on its powerful hind legs. It understood me! In form it was somewhat leonine, but also somewhat simian and strangely crooked, almost a feline orang-utan of some kind, with elongated teeth and enormous, staring, saucer eyes. The very sight of it set me shaking with fright.

It struggled visibly to overcome the limitations of its palate in order to form words. "Ohbay- klee- woll-." To emphasise its meaning, it squeezed a forearm as far along the wall beside the cage as it was able. To show my under-standing, I also stretched as far as I could towards the small ring of keys the tall servant had hung up on a hook. For the creature, this hook was inaccessible by at least six or seven feet and a ninety degree turn in the brick wall. I, in contrast, had a clear line of sight to it but was even further away, some three yards or so.

Obtaining these keys seemed a hopeless endeavour but to show willing I scouted around for any object which might be adapted to extend my reach. Apart from a heap of straw, for resting upon, there was no material of any kind to hand, and to fashion the straw into an item of the required length was quite impossible. I contemplated throwing either my food bowl or water cup, so as to dislodge the keyring, but the curl of the hook made even a precise hit most unlikely to have the desired effect. In any case, I have never been proficient at that sort of activity. Furthermore, there was the subsequent question of how to retrieve the keys should a well-aimed cup knock them to the flagstones.

Pondering a problem of this sort was, at least, a distraction from the dreadful fear which continued to gnaw at my heart. After some minutes, a possible solution occurred to me but, before I could act, my stomach twisted at the sound of the cellar being unlocked once more. Instantly, with the Earl's threats to ensure my silence reverberating around my brain, I retreated to my obscured observation spot.

It was his Lordship the Earl who entered this time, accompanied by two men I'd never seen before. One was a spindly, weasel-faced person, the type to be found scowling behind a grille at a City bank. The other was a man of military bearing, rigorous and gruff, who walked as if led by the chin. He was smoking a cigar and all three of them were dressed for dinner. I surmised at once that these were War Office visitors, as I'd heard spoken of at the inn.

"Once the various proteins and neurotoxins are broken down," the Earl was saying, "what is then extractable is almost an entire biological pharmacology in itself, a broad spectrum of chemicals to be assembled or broken apart. For testing and experimentation purposes, this is both extremely useful and, as I'm sure you will appreciate, extremely time-consuming. You'll notice that this apparatus here, gentlemen, is distilling a basic formulation to which specific enzymes will later be added."

The weasel-faced man was trying to hide his reaction to the smell of the place, the combination of noxious substances and enclosed, much-used air which fortunately I had ceased to notice. By my pocket watch it was twenty-two minutes past eight o'clock.

"Be that as it may, Jekyll," said the military man, "the department is pressing for a date by which results may be fully deployed."

"I'm afraid foreknowledge of that kind requires clairvoyance, Major, not science, perhaps you should consult my youngest daughter?"

"Don't be absurd, man," grumbled the Major, "you know perfectly well what I mean. We expect more trouble from the Boers. Moreover, when the itchy trigger fingers of Europe take aim at each other, as they will, the conflict will be swift and decisive. Superior weaponry is what wins wars these days, the Prussians proved so in France twenty-odd years ago. You know what got us the African colonies? The Maxim gun. An advantage which has been lost, now every Tom Dick and Heinrich has one."

He stepped a little closer to the cages, his face swimming with undisguised revulsion as he looked over the six creatures. The weaselly man's face showed nothing but embarrassed unease via a tightly clenched jaw and continuous dry swallows. The Major's disdain was, quite transparently, intended to put the Earl on the defensive, but he remained as broodingly impassive as ever.

"These specimens," said the Earl, "show that even the tiniest variation in a formulation's construction or purity can produce widely differing results. Some test subjects revert to their former, fully human state after a few hours and can be re-used, but for the majority the change is permanent and, until further advances are made, irreversible. In all formulations, I include chemical inhibitors to restrict longevity and intellect. A shortened lifespan is for practical purposes, with lesions appearing on the skin shortly before dissolution, which can occur at any time between a few hours and a few weeks after injection, depending on what is now termed the mutational outcome. Cognitive ability is cropped because the shock of mutation caused problems in early experiments."

"Why not simply dispose of them?" said the Major. "This house's heating system must have a furnace? Save effort, surely?"

I could not gauge the strange look the Earl gave him. There was a pause before he spoke. "When the end comes, discards are allowed to die with dignity. I am not heartless, Major."

"Is your supply secure?"

"There is an arrangement with one of the local work-houses, my steward oversees it. No enquiries have ever been made, except for one occasion a number of years ago. A colleague of yours was impressively efficient in dealing with the situation."

The Major grunted approval. "We keep *our* end of a bargain."

I could see the Earl's lips purse amid his beard. "I've made significant progress in controlling metabolic absorption and the stability of blood proteins but, yes, consistency of reaction, relative to individual physical variables, is proving to be a difficult problem to solve. However, solved it will be."

"Why bother?" said the Major. "These hideous abominations would rout the enemy exactly as they are."

"For the same reasons that the armies of the world don't merely set massed packs of wild dogs on each other. Even the dullest military mind can appreciate the difference between a rock and a bullet."

"Either may bring victory," sneered the Major, "in the right circumstances."

"I must apologise, it's foolish of me to expect the War Office to understand my efforts from other than a simplified perspective," said the Earl. "The work of this laboratory will accrue benefits for the whole of Mankind, and not merely keep Her Majesty's government ahead of rivals. I am as willing to play my part in the defence of the Empire as any patriotic citizen, but my duty is to the world as well as to the nation. I have always made that explicit and you may not wish to step forward there, Major, you're placing yourself within its reach."

Like a scalded cat, the Major hopped back from the cage he'd been approaching. His face flushed crimson. "I fail to see what these benefits could possibly amount to, given the state of this place."

The Earl exuded a calm so icy I could have sworn to feeling a drop in temperature. "Science and industry," he said, with care, speaking as if to a bumpkin, "have given us advancements unparalleled in history. The telegraph, the steam engine, the artificial fertilizer, a thousand modern conveniences. These things are essentially mechanical, and have been since our ancestors wielded a stone axe and donned furs to keep warm. That is, they are tools, they in essence circumvent Nature, in order to overcome distances or accomplish tasks which Man the animal – and we are animals, as Mr Darwin has shown us, rooted in our landscape far more firmly now than when we were divine sparks – to accomplish tasks which Man the animal cannot complete using his delicate, hairless body alone. But consider, for a moment, if Man were not to circumvent Nature, but to *surpass* Nature. To leave behind the puny limitations of the human body. To dive like a fish, to climb like a monkey, run like a cheetah, lift like an elephant, even fly like a bird. It can be done. A human body can be remade, faults corrected, Nature defeated forever. *Then* Mankind will be truly free. An *absolute* liberty of identity and form."

"The department has been led down scientific blind alleys before," snorted the Major. "We got nothing useful from the Promethean Society, the Atun-Ra excavations, or the South Wales discs. You'll rewrite evolution, will you, when all you've got to show for almost nine years of government protection are *these* revolting monsters?"

"My formulation works!" roared the Earl, fists held tightly at his side, his bitterness enveloping the chamber like a cold fog. "I know it works! I have *proved* it! And at *enormous personal cost!*"

Whether it was the Earl's furious reaction to the Major's words, or their own anger at the words themselves, the creatures became restive and clamorous. I shrunk back, terrified.

Curtailing his emotions, the Earl seemed to deflate and regret his outburst. He slipped his hands into the pockets of his dinner jacket. "I assure you, my impatience for progress is acute," he said in a voice which teetered on the edge of agitation, "but impatience and progress are forever at odds. Never doubt that you will have your new Maxim gun, Major. You will have soldiers of infinite variety, of whatever size, shape or capability required. I imagine you'll expect them to retain a limited intellect, but they could be made as sharp as you wish. They will be the vanguard of a changed world. Are you familiar with the work of Francis Galton or Gustave de Molinari?"

"Galton, I've heard of," said the Major. "A relative of Darwin's, isn't he?"

"They both seek to improve the human race, Galton through what he terms eugenic methods, Molinari via political economy. Just as cattle or crops are hybridised to produce stronger characteristics, so Mankind, they argue in their separate ways, should be trained, or bred, even culled, in pursuit of a human population in which socially useful traits are spread while undesirable habits or people are eliminated. There can't be many in Westminster who wouldn't support the breeding out of unhelpful tendencies in the working classes. I doubt there's a government in the civilised world not interested in enacting Galton's ideas, I fully expect them to be the dominant topic of political debate come the new century. In fact, eugenic programmes have already begun in German East Africa and Togoland. What I wish to point out, Major, is that *my* work will make Galton's seem like the ham-fisted tinkering of a chicken breeder. Once the subtleties of moon—" He suddenly corrected himself, "the subtleties of more formulations are properly understood, over time, then there is no facet of either the human body or the human mind which could not be improved in minutes, let alone from one generation to the next. And improved for improvement's sake alone, guided purely by the aspirations and desires of every man, woman and child, for self-fulfilment, for the freedom to experience life in any way they choose. I do not seek to rewrite evolution, as you put it, but to sidestep it entirely. You call my experiments monsters? Eventually, they will be gods."

As if the flesh-creeping nightmare of their conversation was spilling outwards into physical action, the already aggravated creatures began to stamp their ground and strike at the cages surrounding them. The reptilian one suddenly thrust its long, crocodile-like snout through the bars and snapped its jaw an inch from the Major's face. He staggered, yelling, the cigar flying from his fingers and the reptile's saliva glistening across his cheeks and throat. The Earl quickly stubbed out the cigar underfoot while the Major and the weaselly man retreated to the workbench upon which rested one of the copper tanks.

The other creatures, apart from the eye-woman, began to cry out as they hurled themselves from side to side, their malformed voices rapidly unifying into a steady chant. "Die . . . we . . . human men . . . die . . . we . . . human . . . men . . ."

I was too frightened to do anything more than observe what was going on. The Major, wiping frantically at his face with a handkerchief, glared menacingly at the Earl. "They talk? You said they're made brainless!"

"I said they have a chemically impaired intellect. For ease of control, they have a basic set of rules drummed into them, to make them compliant." He moved, with complete confidence, closer to the cages. His mere presence seemed to subdue the creatures a little. "Silence!" he boomed. "Speak the First Command!"

They hesitated, but slowly became cowed and quiet.

"Speak the First Command!"

"Obey," they intoned as clearly as their bodies would let them, while a shudder ran down my spine, "obey our masters." It was the simian creature and the horrible wolf-like beast which led the response, and I surmised that they were the ones who'd been subjected to this conditioning the most.

"Speak the Second Command!"

"We are not masters."

"Speak the Third Command!"

"Die for our masters."

The Earl paused, letting their capitulation hang heavy and sombre in the breath-dampened air. He turned and rejoined his visitors. "The first rule encourages submission, the second emphasises their status, the third reinforces the first two. A firm frame of conduct helps their understanding and acceptance."

"I think we've seen quite enough," growled the Major. "Stoppard, your queries about logistics can damn well wait."

The weaselly man nodded rapidly. The Earl unlocked the door to the cellar and ushered them out, calmly entreating them to rejoin the evening festivities upstairs, and remarking that Lady Violet's fancy dress nonsense would be over by now.

The lights, fortunately, were left on. I spent some minutes in efforts to steady my shaking limbs and reeling mind, finding myself wary even to acknowledge that I was in a conscious, wakeful state and not mired in some hideous dream. Were it not for the sobering sight of those six unfortunate creatures sharing my captivity, I might have rejected the horrible revelations of the Earl's true activities as too vile for belief.

My pocket watch put the hour at twelve minutes to nine. My heart was racing and it was only with difficulty that I contained a growing feeling of panic. The Earl or one of his lackeys could return for me at any moment, to carry out his stated intention and forcibly administer his mutational potion.

The feverish urge to escape caused me to remember the idea I'd conceived before the arrival of the Earl and his War Office guests. With fumbling fingers I reached inside my jacket, around the waistband of my trousers, and undid the buttons on my braces. I separated them and tied the loops of one to the loops of the other, leaving me with one long length of material. Once I had stretched the button hole at one end, I had something with which I might, just possibly, be able to catch onto the ring of keys three yards away.

I leaned against the bars of my cage, my arms through them, and gathered the makeshift rope in both hands. I fussed nervously for a moment or two, not sure whether to cast it, in the manner of a fishing rod, or fling it like a ball at a coconut shy. Some of the creatures were, by now, watching my every move, which made me even more nervous. Settling myself, and keeping an eye on the wall hook, I swung one end back and forth then hurled it in a neatly curved trajectory— which fell far short of its target.

I quickly rewound the rope and tried again, with no better result. Assuring myself that the basic physics of the procedure were sound, I made more attempts, quietly cursing my incapacity for sporting prowess. Several tries saw the rope's end bounce off the key ring, the clinking of metal making my frustration feel all the more sour.

It was at the twenty-fifth attempt that the button hole caught over the hook itself. At first, I thought I had ruined my chances of success by snagging the rope in a position from which it could not be freed. However, a few sharp pulls showed that the hook would move and was not so firmly attached to the wall that it might not be dislodged. Holding my breath, I pulled a little harder, gritting my teeth in apprehension in case the braces should come loose in the middle.

Within a minute, the hook was shifting from side to side by at least half an inch with each successive pull. Seconds later, it slid out in a little burst of brick dust and fell to the ground with a loud clank. The creatures became agitated once more, but with a palpable excitement rather than anger.

My heart skittering, I carefully dragged both hook and keys towards me. Once they were in my hands I freed the key ring and – keeping my arms close to my sides to mini-mise their shaking – unlocked my cage.

Hurrying to the cellar's entrance, it became apparent that this set of keys operated the locks on the cages only. I turned to the simian beast who had communicated with me earlier, and my manner must have conveyed my question immediately, for the creature pointed down a long, gloomy corridor that lay at an angle just past the cage in which I'd been held. I ran along it and found a large, hatch-like door, as heavily reinforced as the one leading from the floors above but fastened only with a metal bar and a couple of stout latches. Clearly, a means of egress alone.

My actions, at this point, are ones which I now terribly regret. Looking back upon that ghastly night, from a distance of some weeks, I concede that I should have simply escaped the cellar and raised the alarm as soon as I was able. The hideous experiments being conducted at Westwych House would subsequently have been exposed, the perpetrators brought to justice, and the caged creatures in the cellar given whatever ministrations may have been possible.

In my defence, I can cite only my extremely troubled state of mind. I had just gained information which had shocked and upset me to the core. The caged monsters had at first turned my stomach but had, although my fear of them remained, by now elicited my sympathy as victims of an evil beyond my comprehension. And because of this change of heart, I had looked back upon my dismissive reaction to Jemmison's centaur and I had felt shame.

Thus, I had come to see the creatures as suffering and unhappy, capable of intelligence despite what had been done to them. I had neither the means nor the inclination to remove their suffering, as might be done for an elderly dog in pain or a racehorse with a broken leg.

Instead, I unlocked their cages and let them go free. I did not appreciate, at the time, that they were unlike the near-death horrors the Earl had been setting loose in the hills for years. They would not haunt the uplands for a day or two then die. A chance glimpse of them, by villagers from Hagstow or elsewhere, would not precede their deaths in some hidden nook among the rocks. All but one were still vigorous and strong.

If I could somehow reverse the hands of the clock and rethink the idiocy of my decision, I most surely would. They didn't harm me because I was their benefactor, and in that fleeting moment I took this as a sign of innate passivity.

I have since wondered, through sleepless nights, which side of themselves it was that lusted for revenge – the human or the animal. I tell myself I could not have known what they would do, but I have never been any more proficient as a liar than I have a sportsman.

I opened the exit at the end of the corridor, hearing them shuffle and growl behind me. I emerged between trees, with the house some hundred yards or more away. I skirted the grounds, making for the road at the front of the house and thence to Hagstow, the twilight dimming into ever-darker greys and blues above me. My immediate aim was to check that Lizzie Prendick had returned home safely.

Chapter 20

Leaning heavily on the fat, dark bannister rail, Lionel Chaney descended the grand, carpeted main staircase of Westwych House step by step. He'd tied his fancy dress mask back in place, to hide the disfigurement that was crawling over his head and neck.

Another wave of bonhomie rolled out from the library and drawing room downstairs. There was a clinking of glasses, and the soft bubble of conversation. Jilks the footman was turning the handle of the phonograph with precision, its tinny sound carrying a selection of popular comic songs into the hallway.

As Dan Quinn's recording of *Daisy Bell* gave way to Charles Godfrey's *Hi-Tiddley-Hi-Ti*, Chaney paused to steady himself. He bent slightly, the agony on his face hidden, a hand wavered at his chest. He turned, uncertain whether to carry on or return upstairs. Ada appeared below, heading for the library with a silver tray of crystal decanters, and jumped with fright when she spotted him.

"Very sorry, Sir, didn't see you there."

"Wait," said Chaney. "The, er, Frenchman, the engineer, Moreau, where is he?"

A frown flickered across her brow. "He's probably in the kitchen, Sir, in between minding the boiler."

"Fetch him. At once."

"Could Mr Poole be of help to you, Sir, he's in the drawing room?"

"No. Get Moreau. This instant."

"Yessir."

She hurriedly delivered the tray and scuttled off back down the hallway. Chaney held onto the bannister with both hands, feeling the strange ache of his skin and muscles slowly moving, slowly twisting. The phonograph went quiet for a second or two while Jilks swapped discs, then struck up a piano rendition of *Oh! For The Jubilee*. Chaney kept glancing at the opened doors below, hoping nobody would emerge and talk to him, least of all Alice. Dear God, what was he going to tell Alice?

Moreau was suddenly at the foot of the stairs, dressed in overalls and wiping oil from his fingers with a rag. Conscious that his appearance in this part of the house would draw comment, he silently beckoned to Chaney and vanished along the walkway leading to the atrium. Chaney caught up with him in the shadows beside Jekyll's collection of snakes, spiders and scorpions. The gradual onset of night was inking Westwych House's sumptuous entrance hall in dark greens and reds via the floral designs of the stained glass windows. Livid colour painted the reptiles and arachnids in their sealed enclosures. Chaney was close enough to the scorpions to feel the warmth in their habitat radiating out through the glazing.

"What is the problem?" whispered Moreau. "I gave you the correct key."

Chaney tugged hurriedly at the fastenings on his mask. "This is the damn problem," he hissed, tearing the mask away. "What the hell is that stuff? What the hell is it doing to me?"

For a moment Moreau was startled at the sight of Chaney's blotched, swollen features, before a smile spread across his saurian face like an underline. "You *took* some of it?" he sniggered.

Chaney grabbed Moreau by the collar and shook him. "It isn't funny," he spat through gritted teeth. "Get me the antidote. Now. Before this gets any worse. *Now*, I tell you!" He pushed him sharply and the Frenchman almost lost his balance.

Moreau looked him up and down for a moment, his smile unchanged, then tugged his overall straight and vanished into the lengthening shadows. Chaney was left staring at his hands, the skin bruised and beginning to erupt into sores, his fingers painfully fat with fluid. He leaned against the tall bulk of the vivarium, looking at the fading rays of iridescent daylight, his mind and his anxiety chasing each other in an unstoppable spiral. With luck, there'd be no need to tell Alice anything. He'd soon feel right as rain, he'd meet the chap from the embassy on Monday as arranged, he'd clear every debt. All would be well.

Out of the shadows, Moreau reappeared. Chaney was so wrapped in his own denial that at first he didn't see the significance of Poole and the Earl being at Moreau's side. "Well?" he said. "Have you got it? The antidote?"

"You're a fool, Lionel," said Jekyll in a low voice. "I've

214

often thought so, but to have such vivid proof of it is distressing, none the less."

Chaney felt a cold sensation in the pit of his stomach as he gaped helplessly at his father-in-law, an ice floe of realisation seeping through him. "Nothing has left this house," he stammered. He scrambled at his jacket and pulled out the leather pouch, which Poole took from him. "No harm has been done, Sir, my Lord, I'm sorry—"

"This will break my daughter's heart. Something I will not forgive."

"I will atone for my betrayal—"

"You misunderstand. Knowledge of your betrayal would sicken her and tarnish her name, of course, but it's your death that will break her heart."

"No, please, the antidote—"

"There is no antidote."

"Please, I don't want to die—"

"I've no wish for you to die either, but I'm afraid you will. The plant-based toxins in that vial are fatal and quite slow to act, but commonplace, just as the report you stole is nothing more than basic undergraduate chemistry. They're a mousetrap I baited a long time ago, on good advice, as a precaution against spies. The idea is to allow the spy to escape, then learn of his demise after his masters discover he's taken nothing of value. Tonight, however, breathtaking stupidity condemned you before you'd even left the cellar."

Chaney snivelled quietly. Tears dropped from his swollen eyes.

"I take it Utterson is your man? A decoy? A – what's the term? – a patsy?" said Jekyll.

"I've never heard of him, I swear—" He suddenly thrust

an accusing finger at Moreau. "*That* man took two hundred and fifty pounds from me!"

Moreau smiled and nodded. "I did. I showed it to His Lordship and gave him the sad news of your dishonesty. I didn't think you'd go through with it. I was wrong."

Chaney rounded on Jekyll, his face folded in fear and grief, spit gumming his teeth. "I was never good enough for you, was I? The high and mighty Jekylls, pissing on the likes of me, sneering at new money. Well, your time will come!" His head bowed and he slumped against the vivarium, mewling plaintively. "Oh God. When? When will I die?"

"Probably overnight," said Jekyll. "Certainly before lunchtime tomorrow. Lady Violet has put a great deal of effort into organising this weekend, and now you'll spoil it. You owe her an apology."

"You damned hypocrite," snarled Chaney. "The whole world knows she's nothing but a dirty street tart!"

Slowly, Jekyll bent to place his lips close to Chaney's ear. "Even if that were true, which it is not, she'd still have twice *your* moral fibre. You, Sir, are a whining scoundrel of the worst kind, and a coward to boot. Let's hope Alice's second husband has a little more backbone." He waited for Chaney to respond, but the fight had gone out of his son-in-law. "I suggest you go to your room now, Lionel, and stay out of everyone's sight. I'll send Alice up to be at your bedside. To spare her feelings and – although I don't see why I should – your reputation, you may tell her you drank too much and tried to handle the snakes."

Chaney slid to his knees, his head buried in his hands, shoulders convulsing in rhythm with his whimpering sobs.

He heard Jekyll and his servants walk away, Jekyll and Poole returning to the celebrations, Moreau to the boiler room to stoke the furnace ready to be left overnight, their footsteps loud on the atrium's polished floor.

His thoughts were a tangle of panic and loathing. Slowly, he stumbled to his feet, leaning heavily against the vivarium. Jekyll's parting offer of misdirection, which would have proved implausible under scrutiny, quickly twisted inside Chaney's addled mind into an alternative course of action. A necessary course of action.

He, Mr Lionel Chaney, respected London industrialist, had brought ruin upon himself through his own folly. A fatal bite from one of his father-in-law's hideous pets was the only honourable option within his power. His only possible penance. His necessary self-abasement. The shame of his many failures, past and present, would soon be laid bare to the world, but at least it would be said of him that he was man enough to do the right thing.

He'd once seen Jekyll open up the vivarium for cleaning purposes, after safely removing the animals to compartments in the structure's base. These large glass panels swung aside, he was sure of it. Jekyll had unhooked something, had he not, undone a bolt or two?

Chaney felt around the boundaries of the snakes' habitat, stretching to reach its upper edges. He could feel no catches or switches, no keyholes or sliding sections. Behind the glass, the snakes watched him briefly then retreated into their environment's densest foliage to hide.

He rattled at the panel in frustration. He tried to grip one side of its wooden frame, to wrench it open, but his fingers were too painfully swollen. A low growl rising from inside him, he battered at the frame with his forearms, then with his shoulders. He clasped his fists together and swung hard at the glass.

It shattered and he pulled back, taking the broken remains of the frame with him. It fell to the floor with a clatter and he looked down to see a rapidly spreading pool of blood. Several seconds passed before he realised that the blood was his.

He crumpled to a heap, tears welling in his eyes again. As he died, he became angry at the thought that not even *this*, this one final damn thing, had gone right for him.

Chapter 21

As Lionel Chaney's life ended, the creatures freed from the basement laboratory by Jack Utterson were considering their future. The eye-covered woman who had once been Bingham, the sacked maid, was close to the end of her life now. The thread-like rash, the mark of oncoming death for Jekyll's experiments, had covered most of the flesh not occupied by blinking, staring eyes. She walked up the steps at the cellar's exit and out among the trees, her skin seeing light and dark, the future and the past, distant landscapes and nearby hills, so many things. They clashed in her mind, suffused and melted.

A few minutes later, the other five creatures followed her out into the open, breathing the cool evening air and, if they were able, smelling the grass in the woods ahead and the sun-warmed gravel of the driveway behind them. The fleshy mass of legs and teeth, which had been Harris the footman, scuttled ahead of the bulky half-reptile and the sharply spined half-insect, once workhouse brothers James and Joseph Carter. The huge ape-lion and the elongated semi-wolf emerged last, but were the first to move cautiously towards the house.

In the new stable block, three hundred feet away across the rear yard, the guests' horses scented trouble and began to chomp and stamp. The eye-woman's hands swept in slow, symmetrical curves ahead of her, seeing into the known and the unknown. As the horses became more agitated, she sensed another presence close by, one she'd never seen before. She stopped. There was something trapped and terrible, down in the dark, very near. Leaving the other creatures, she turned and walked in the opposite direction, heading for the older, derelict stable block that, like the cellar, was forbidden to all.

She didn't veer from her path when the stuttering of the Earl's motor carriage could suddenly be heard on the breeze, coming closer. Monsieur Moreau's last duty of the day was to garage the precious Leon l'Hollier Anglo-French beside the Earl's brougham. He whistled tunelessly to himself as the automobile chugged crunchily around the side of the house and into the yard. Large, peculiar shapes shifted in the twilight, grey outlines which he thought for a moment were servants carrying piles of clothes or dragging rugs.

The eye-woman didn't hesitate at all when, behind her, Moreau's cry of horror was quickly stifled. She ignored the tearing of skin and bone. She felt the blood lust of her companions, the bestial swell of their thirst for revenge, their fury at humanity and all its foulness, but she kept walking steadily, drawn to the old stables. There was someone inside, a voice in the ether, plaintive and yearning.

She reached the stable door, its crumbling, cankered wood sealed with a shiny brass padlock. There was a way in, she could see, to one side and low down. Push the planking here, and it would break almost without resistance. Slip through.

Inside, the only light came through cracks and gaps in the wooden walls. There was the stink of offal, some of it coming from the eviscerated, near-skeletal corpse of a pig hung up on ropes attached to a system of pulleys. In the pulsations of her mind, the eye-woman could see Poole, last night, leading this pig away from the sty in the kitchen garden, his actions observed from the top of the house by Ada.

Ahead, there was a pit, dug into the ground, covering the area of what had originally been two horse stalls. Over the pit were bars, like those of the cages in the cellar, forming a secure lid. The eye-woman saw who was in the pit, and fluttered her fingers to see the heavy rods which held the bars in place.

When the rods were drawn aside, the thing in the pit reached up and pushed. The lid rose and the creature was free.

Chapter 22

Jack Utterson's journal

Sat. 19th June. The Tethered Goat,
Hagstow. 9:45pm – 10:07pm

I arrived at Hagstow in a state of complete exhaustion. The hurried journey back from Westwych House – mostly trotting, sometimes running (depending on the prevailing intensity of my fear), occasionally walking (to catch my breath after running) – was also a lonely one, since I saw no-one and passed no vehicles. I confidently assumed that I would find the villagers at the Tethered Goat in their usual fettle, that I would be admonished by Miss Prendick for my carelessness in being apprehended, and that I would have great difficulty in persuading anyone to accept the truth of what I had witnessed. In all three assumptions, I was immediately proven wrong.

As I entered the inn, gasping for breath and looking forward to resting my legs (another incorrect assumption!) the scene which greeted me was one of chaotic tragedy. A dozen villagers, fearful and thunderstruck, were standing around one of the tables talking across one another, arguing, jabbing emphatic fingers. On the table lay a stout man, moaning in agony and partly covered by a blanket soaked through with blood. At the other end of the room, another blanket covered a large, motionless hump on the floor, over which hovered old grandfather Bern. He caught sight of me and held a shaky hand over the hump, his face as white as his wispy hair and beard. "'Ere, London," he breathed in a trembling voice, "we got one."

At that moment, Miss Prendick seemed to appear from nowhere and flung her arms around me! I was so agreeably startled I returned her embrace without thinking. She tenderly held my face in her hands, and there was something in the kindness of her expression and the sincerity of her concern which, coming so soon after the nightmare I'd experienced, almost caused me to lose my composure.

I hastily enquired about the unfortunate man on the table and, on approaching him, discovered to my astonishment that I was able to furnish the villagers with a piece of information they'd hitherto been unable to glean. "His name is Jemmison," I said. "I met him in the city, he is the proprietor of a thoroughly unpleasant sideshow."

Even as I spoke, the poor man breathed his last and the room became silent for a moment. Tolly, one of those with whom I'd conversed the previous evening, peeled back the blanket to show me Jemmison's injuries.

He had horrible, open wounds around his middle, almost as if he'd been cut in two by a giant pair of scissors. "What on earth happened to him?" I gasped, while Tolly pulled the blanket over the poor man's face.

"This did," cried Bern, jabbing a finger at the covered hump.

"Not half an hour ago," said Lizzie, "we heard screams coming from the hillside out the back—"

"Like a soul in Hell's torment!" said Bern.

"—About a dozen of us ran out there and we watched this great crab-thing coming down the slope. Jemmison was held up in its claw, wriggling and bleeding."

"The monster was weaving about," said Tolly. "Unsteady. You could see it was dying. It almost got to the back field, then it just stopped and kind of flopped over. Just dropped dead. We couldn't believe what we was seeing. The man's shrieks gathered our wits, and Lizzie's da fetched a couple of blankets and we carried 'em in here."

"Jack? You know more than you're saying, I can see it in your face," said Lizzie hesitantly.

My revelations about the Earl's activities at the House were a shock but little surprise. Lizzie and the others had already deduced a little of what I had to tell them, from Jemmison's feverish mutterings in his last moments and from the horrifying actuality of the crab-like creature itself.

It was indeed a hideous thing, starved and diseased, all too clearly one of the Earl's failed experiments. How long it had clung to life out on the hilltops was something none of us could guess, but its emaciated form spoke of many days' struggle for survival.

The dreadful violence it had inflicted on the unfortunate Jemmison unified opinion among the villagers that these monsters of the Earl's should be dealt with by the authorities alone. And from this opinion, God help me, I found it hard to dissent. The room was gripped with an atmosphere of nervous resolution. My naivety in freeing the occupants of the cages was impressed upon me with the force of a hurtling train. Everything was slipping out of control, and I was suddenly terrified at the possible repercussions of my actions. My hands covered my head.

"Jack?" said Lizzie. "What is it?"

Her father, the landlord, was taking charge of the situation, the others deferring to the implied leadership of his steady manner and brawny physique. "We got to inform the proper authorities, and sharpish, 'cos it won't be long before young London's not being there is noticed, if it hasn't been already. I say we send two men out, on horseback, armed, to the constable up at Keynsham, they can telegraph there. The rest of us stay together in 'ere, or in our homes, in case there's more beasts about."

Amid the nodding of heads and grunting of agreement, I was compelled by conscience to speak up and admit that I had freed six others as well as myself. "I took pity on them," I said, wringing my hands in exasperation. "They were once as you or I, and have been so horribly mistreated . . ." My voice trailed away, my eyes drawn inexorably towards the mutilated body on the table.

A chorus of furious opprobrium sprang up all around me. Their braying words rained down like rocks.

"Listen!" cried Lizzie, hushing them while guilt soured my insides, "we got to warn them up at the House. There's some of our own people working there tonight, and we all got friends on the staff. Right?"

"I'll go there at once," I said. "Unarmed. Might I borrow a cart, I'm afraid I'm a rather poor horseman?"

"I'll drive with yer," said Tolly.

"We'll take your shotgun, Da," said Lizzie.

"You bloomin' well won't, missy," said Mr Prendick. "Tha's a dangerous weapon. Nobody fires that gun but me."

Plans were hastily made. I felt sick to my stomach. Lizzie, in secret contradiction of her outwardly censorious attitude towards me, briefly held my hand in so gentle a manner that the pain of my trepidation was temporarily eased.

Chapter 23

It was Lady Alice, searching in high dudgeon for her roving husband, who discovered his dead body beside the vivarium. Her piercing scream brought all the guests rushing from the library and the drawing room, and caused Jilks to badly mis-time the turning of the gramophone handle. The clatter of rapid steps and the rustle of skirts swelled up behind Alice as she fainted, her head caught an inch away from a heavy impact on the floor by Miss Augustine the novelist.

"Good God, it's Chaney!"

"Look at his face! Is he dead? What the devil happened—?"

"Those serpents of Jekyll's, that's what's happened!"

To rising, horrified cries about blood and broken glass, Jekyll marched around to where Chaney lay and raised his hands. "Please! Everyone! Remain calm!" A few swift glances into the shattered compartment were enough to tell him that the Inland Taipans weren't coiled at the other side of their habitat, as he'd hoped they'd be. His face lost all colour.

"There's bloody snakes all over the place!" piped Danvers Carew.

Lady Gertrude, Enid Stoppard and both the Hapgoods screeched in terror, lifting themselves as if trying to escape the floor. Viscount Froome's wine glass shattered at his feet.

"Stay calm!" boomed Jekyll. "They are *not* aggressive! They are *not* dangerous if you leave them alone!"

At that same moment, out in the old stables beyond the rear yard, the thing had now crawled from its pit. The eye-woman stepped back, seeing the creature's intent and fearing it, seeing the pain of its past and its future. She quietly left the stable the same way she'd entered. Outside, in the gathering night, her five companions were spreading out, surrounding the house. She turned and walked away, into the trees.

The Earl's motor carriage stood at the edge of the yard, Henri Moreau's body smeared over it. Nobody indoors had heard him die. As yet, the house guests were aware of only one danger.

"Do something, man!" demanded the Major. "We can't have snakes running loose!"

"I have told you," said Jekyll calmly, "all of you, there is nothing to fear if you stay out of their way—"

"Shouldn't the police be summoned?"

"Shouldn't we close this dead fellow's eyes?"

"—My steward Mr Poole and I will find and capture them. It won't take long, I assure you, I know their habits. They'll have found a quiet shelter somewhere. Everyone, please return to the library."

"And what if they're quietly sheltering in the library?" cried Carew.

"Then move to the drawing room," said Jekyll. He pulled open a drawer beneath the vivarium's broken compartment.

Inside were bags, flexible tongs and other equipment he used when dealing with his collection. "Poole!"

"How many of the damn things are there?" barked the Major.

"Seven," said Jekyll, and instantly wished he hadn't when a fresh wave of consternation crashed over the guests.

Lady Violet had already tiptoed away, holding up her skirts and switching on every light she passed, heading for the nursery upstairs. Lady Jane followed her stepmother to safeguard the Honourable Albert Montgomery Carew and, as she passed the family portraits on the staircase, coldly evaluated the possibilities of this unexpected situation in her head.

"Sir Godfrey?" said Miss Augustine to the nearest Hapgood. "Or Major Ruck? Would you help me carry Alice?"

"Of course," said the Major. "Stoppard, attend to the girl."

As Stoppard crouched and heaved the unconscious Alice into his arms, Danvers Carew stepped carefully into an open area of floor, eyes cast down and hands raised as if to ward off attack from below. "Well, father-in-law, much as I accept your assurances, I can't say I'm looking forward to a restful night's sleep any more. I've decided that the only place I'll be returning to is my landau, and thence a hotel."

"Sound idea, your Grace," said Sir Godfrey Hapgood, slightly too quickly. Like the other male guests still living, he'd wanted to avoid being the first to suggest retreat. "What do you think, Delia?"

"So dreadfully unfortunate, we should go, we mustn't

intrude on private grief," said Lady Delia Hapgood. Lady Henrietta and Miss Augustine exchanged glances containing an entire, protracted disagreement about the possibility of leaving and the wisdom of having turned up in the first place. Despite everything, Enid Stoppard felt miserably crest-fallen: she'd been so looking forward to her night in a stately home, and to being invited into all the neighbours' parlours back in Yardley Terrace. Jasper Stoppard, his knees buckling slightly, carried Alice away to the library with Lady Henrietta and Miss Augustine in his wake.

A distant thud, the sound of the old stables' padlocked door being forced open from inside, caught the attention of several guests but wasn't loud enough to distract them from the matter in hand.

"Where's Jane gone? Is she fetching the boy?" fussed Carew, drifting into the middle of the atrium to maintain the widest possible moat of safety. Other guests drifted alongside him. He raised his voice. "Will somebody call my valet?"

Poole arrived as Carew's words echoed off the high vaulted ceiling. He looked enquiringly at Jekyll, who sighed and gave a petulant nod. "Get the hall boy to open up the stables," he muttered, pulling on a thick pair of gloves from the vivarium's equipment drawer. "I'll begin searching. Find a sheet for Mr Chaney. And you'd better arrange for the doctor to come from Bath, first thing in the morning."

"Yes, m'lord," said Poole.

Sir Godfrey Hapgood's eagerness to get away spilled out of his mouth. "Perhaps, a stroll along the drive, buck up our spirits? Spare the ladies, um . . . this poor fellow. Clear our heads after all that excellent wine. While we wait. Take in the moonlight view down the valley and let his Lordship carry out his search unhindered, eh?"

The guests' casual consensus was tense with restraint. A footman appeared in the plant-filled vestibule and held open the arched front door. It crossed Carew's mind to add "thanks for a splendid evening, Freddie old chap" and pose his corded pince-nez in mid-air for comic effect, but he thought better of it.

Guests hurried unhurriedly out onto the wide front steps. Moonlight shone over the valley below, giving the landscape an ethereal quality, as if it was no more than a detailed model on a tabletop, painted in delicate greys and blues. Then clouds veiled the sky and the guests had to watch their feet as they negotiated the steps.

The half-insect creature was barely visible without the moonlight shining off its bloated, segmented body. It approached the guests slowly, on spindly limbs, the sharp spines clustered around its back and joints quivering in anticipation. They heard the crackle of its steps on the driveway before they saw the strange, twitching staccato of its movements and its fat, compound eyes. From the pinched warp of its once-human face curled a barbed proboscis, at the end of which glistened a needle-like sting.

"I say, is there someone there?" called Viscount Froome, narrowing his eyes as he took a few steps ahead of the others. They were suspended, like mites in amber, between their security as a group and their instinctive unease at the approaching shape. "You still in fancy dress, old chap?"

The half-insect made a rattling, sputtering sound. The guests' stillness cracked.

Viscount Froome retreated slightly. He had a momentary

impression of the creature's face filling his vision before it knocked him to the ground and buried its sting in his neck. He let out a strangled gasp, feeling paralysis coursing through his nervous system as he lost consciousness on the way to death.

Screaming, the guests fled back into the house. The half-insect caught the one at the rear, grasping her arm with the padded pincer at the end of its forelimb. It pulled her backwards with a sharp jerk and stung her twice, pulsing altered enzymes from its glands.

"Maude!" yelled the Major. "Maude!"

He was swept along with the others, through the vestibule. Jekyll, brandishing a thick hessian bag and a long grabbing stick with which to tackle the missing snakes, spun on his heels as guests scattered across the shadowy atrium, their screams reverberating off the painted plaster roses on the ceiling. He blanched, jaw slackening in disbelief, as the half-insect came into view under the vestibule's arch.

Instantly, he ran for the passageway leading to the cellar and almost collided with Poole coming the other way. "One of them's got out!" he snarled. For a split-second, Poole thought he was referring to the spiders or the scorpions, until the look on Jekyll's face put him right. "Get the guns from the plate room! I'll check the laboratory!"

"Yes, m'lord!"

It was a few moments more before the household understood that the tapping at the windows on the ground floor, and the scratching at the walls, indicated the presence of further horrors. Outside, the ape-lion, the half-reptile, the elongated semi-wolf and the creature made of legs and mouths were thinking of the blood that would soon be spilled.

The thing from the pit, having freed itself from the old stables, was making its way across the rear yard. It stretched itself to its full height and flexed the coils of its enormous, serpentine tail. It walked on six pointed, wasp-like append-ages, each as thick as a ship's cable, while four more served for arms. Much of its upper body was covered in snake scales, and the top of its head was smooth and domed. Its face and jaw had retained their human form, a visible testament to the hideous, cumulative transformations the rest of its body had undergone. Its chin was stained with dried blood.

Having never endured the chemical conditioning forced on the laboratory experiments, its thoughts plunged the depths of its own insanity. Its mind was clogged with painful, oblique memories, none of which it trusted, all of which it feared. It knew what it had been, and what it was. It believed its existence was no more than a nightmare, a dark whisper in someone else's fever. Its brain burned hatred and confu-sion, boiling itself alive.

The semi-wolf was in the yard, a low growl seeping from its throat as it reached up to scratch its long claws along the dining room's window sills. The thing slithered up behind it, hissing. The semi-wolf sprang aside, angrily baring its fangs at the newcomer looming over it.

The thing struck in the blink of an eye, piercing the semi-wolf's body from both sides and lifting it off the cobbles. The beast howled in pain and anger, kicking madly, scrambling to free itself, its throat quickly raw with wailing and blood.

As its dying scream pierced the night, every human being in Westwych House heard it and felt a cold stab of fear: Jekyll, racing to the cellar; staff gathered in the kitchen; guests fleeing to the library; Ada rolling with Carew's valet in her attic room. In the nursery, Lady Violet tightened her hold on her twin sons and knew the moment she'd dreaded for years had finally arrived.

Chapter 24

Jack Utterson's journal

Sat. 19th June. Westwych House, 10:39pm

The jolting, thunderous journey up to the House, with the road ahead of us barely visible and hideous portents of disaster sitting fixed and immovable in my mind, was one I hope never to repeat. While Tolly goaded his horse to a gallop, Miss Prendick, her father and I hung on in the cart as best we could. Nobody spoke.

Some of Westwych's ornate windows were aglow with electrical light as we approached, but the place seemed unnaturally motionless, as if held in some secret grip. My thoughts hung in anxious suspension, until we drew closer.

Suddenly, the air was rent with an inhuman shriek, a howl of agony so pained and bestial it might have turned the hardest man's blood to water in his veins. Tolly's horse shied in fright and he pulled the cart to a halt some thirty yards from the mansion's front door. The four of us alighted with trepidation. Our purpose had been to alert the household to potential danger, but such an aim no longer seemed necessary!

"We can get the servants away in the cart, if needs be," trembled Lizzie in the void which followed the scream's cessation.

"Or more, if the toffs can't get to their carriages," breathed Mr Prendick. "I reckon that sound came from round the back."

Lizzie nodded, quick and shallow. Her courage fortified my shaky resolve.

Keeping together, and with Mr Prendick loading his shotgun, we advanced towards the front steps of the house but slowed on realising that the door was wide open. Worse, voices raised in terror could be heard coming from inside.

At that moment, Tolly cried out and jostled us as he stumbled to move away from two figures suddenly appearing out of the dark a few yards to our left. One of them, I saw at once, was the saucer-eyed lion-ape with which I'd communicated in the cellar. The other was the grotesque, fleshy creature with many legs I'd seen offer up an apple to its mate.

"In God's name . . .!" spluttered Mr Prendick. Instinctively, he raised his shotgun.

"No!" I cried hurriedly, stepping forward to stand between gun and creature. "I know this poor beast, I have spoken with it!"

My knees felt as if they might give way at any second. The bulky creature seemed more terrifying than ever now that there were no bars between us. Raising my unsteady hands before me, in a gesture of caution, I moved closer to the beast.

"Jack!" hissed Lizzie. "Don't!"

I ignored her, my supposed bravado based entirely on

not giving the creature even a moment's inattention. "P-Please . . ." I said, my voice as unsteady as my hands. "You remember me? . . . I beg of you, don't harm the people here . . . You have been wronged, grievously wronged, but . . . Please, remember whatever may remain of your human self."

It lumbered towards me and I stepped back a little. I could feel the rapid thud of my heart in my chest. The creature glared at me, those huge eyes filled with murderous fury.

It forced the words from its tortured brain, and they chilled my soul. "Obey—Not masters!—Die masters—"

The other creature suddenly scuttled from the shadows and leaped at us. There was an almighty bang and it flew back, its mouths snapping and screeching. Mr Prendick took proper aim and a second shot killed it, leaving it sprawled in a pool of its own blood. The lion-ape bounded up the steps and was inside the house before I could stop it.

Our ears ringing, we hurriedly followed. Prendick cracked open his smoking shotgun and reloaded it from the supply of cartridges in his pocket.

Chapter 25

Some say that the thing from the pit, when it left the torn remains of the wolfish creature and broke into the boiler room from the rear yard, was fully cognisant of what it was doing. It can be argued that its actions showed conscious choices and technical knowledge, since it spent some minutes forcing the outer boiler room door (rather than making an easier entrance through the kitchens) and then proceeded to destroy the house's electrical supply without itself succumbing to electric shock.

But others say that fully conscious actions must have been impossible for the beast, that its mind was so tormented and broken by years of experimentation that it could not possibly have known precisely what it was doing. It retained memories of the house, that much is certain, but cutting off the electricity must surely have been the result of accident, not design.

The truth will never be known, but the thing from the pit did indeed break into the boiler room, and did indeed cut off the electrical supply, before breaking through the boiler room's inner door and gaining access to the rest of the building. At the moment when every light in Westwych House went out, Jack Utterson's party were racing up the front steps and Frederick Jekyll was leaving his basement laboratory for the last time.

He had found it wrecked. Papers had been ripped from the walls, files scattered, equipment broken, delicate apparatus flung against the cages, chemicals strewn about. The tap over a basin had been bent out of shape, leaving the floor's litter of data inches deep in water. A cool breeze flowed from the open exit beyond the cages.

Jekyll stood for a moment, fists tight to the sides of his head, unwilling to comprehend what was in front of him, fighting the urge to stamp and yell like a petulant child. All his experiments were roaming free, and before they'd left the cellar they had smashed it.

Ruined. His work, his *whole damn life ruined*!

He felt his gums strain as his teeth clamped hard to contain his rage. He turned on the spot and fled for the steps back up into the house, barely realising that the cellar's lights blinked out before he reached the switch, and oblivious to the thrashing sounds that came from behind the inner door to the boiler room.

Taking the steps two at a time, he emerged into the passageway and almost failed to recognise Poole, coming from the opposite direction with two loaded pistols taken from the plate room. Only now did Jekyll notice the near-darkness and look up at the unlit incandescent bulbs above him.

"Mr Poole," he gasped, taking one of the pistols, "all the cages are empty. Check the old stable at once. We can't lose her! Snap to it, man!"

For the first time in many years, Poole was afraid. "Sir, I-I can't."

Jekyll, despite Poole's height, seemed to occupy twice the space of his steward. "Then find Moreau! And get the bloody lights back on!"

Poole nodded, his lips shaking. He hurried past Jekyll and, brandishing his pistol, made for the cellar steps, to reach the boiler room and assess the generator. He thanked holy providence for sparing him from confrontation with the thing in the pit, for he was sure that, with all he'd seen and done, if she'd got loose too she'd have killed him on the spot without a second thought.

He was almost at the bottom of the steps, his footsteps tapping rapidly, when another heavy blow against the inner boiler room door suddenly splintered its lock and sent it violently slapping back on its hinges. Poole froze, one foot suspended over the next step. He felt his bladder let go as the thing quickly forced itself through the doorway, squirming, scaly, the pressure of its body cracking the door's wooden frame.

She saw him and hissed, mouth open to expose a ridge of pointed teeth. He couldn't move. The pistol dropped from his fingers and bumped down the last few steps.

The thing extended a pointed limb and ran him through. Then again, and again, until he buckled at the knees and fell forward, lifeless.

Chapter 26

Moonlight reappeared as clouds parted. It suddenly threw angular, blue-grey shafts across the atrium and for the first time Jack Utterson saw the bodies that lay on the polished floor. Sir Godfrey Hapgood and Viscount Froome's widow Gertrude, picked off and stung by the half-insect as guests ran screaming for the library, were spread-eagled beside the corpse of Lionel Chaney.

A loud bumping came from the far side of the room as Delia Hapgood tripped over her own feet and fell screaming into a moonbeam. Aware of her sudden visibility, she scrambled to stand but the ape-lion was upon her instantly and in a flash dragged her back into the shadows.

Over the sound of her bones breaking, the Major – strategically hanging back from the other guests – marched out of the gloom and grabbed at Prendick's shotgun. "Give me that!"

Prendick pulled away, tightening his grip. Jack, Lizzie and Tolly clustered behind him. "Leave off!" he hissed.

The major's hands clamped onto the gun. "That is an

order! In a situation like this, you people are to consider yourselves under my command!"

"Get to shite!" growled Prendick, flailing in panic. They grappled wildly, Jack and Lizzie trying to force them apart.

The ape-lion, its victim dead and the fire of vengeance burning all the hotter because of it, turned towards the noisy struggle and closed in.

"For pity's sake!" hissed Jack. He could hear the creature approaching, but fear gnawed too hard on his judgement to be certain, and shapes seemed to move in the dark on all sides. He extended a cautious hand. "Please, wait! Wait!"

The wrestle for the shotgun became more frantic. "I order you to hand it over! I am a senior officer of Her Majesty's armed forces, not some damn peasant yokel!"

"Nobody shoots this gun but me!"

Jack and Lizzie hauled helplessly at the two men while Tolly took hold of the end of the gun's barrel in an effort to wrest it from both of them. They scuffled close to the line of ancient monk's benches which ran along the wall beneath the windows. Under one of the benches, the seven escaped Inland Taipans huddled together, eyeing the panicked movement of feet in front of them, keeping themselves to themselves.

The ape-lion shifted from vague shape to solid substance as it emerged from the shadows.

The Major twisted and shoved, seeing the creature less than three yards past Prendick's shoulder. "Let go! Let go!" Prendick pulled hard and they spun to one side.

The shotgun fired. In the deafening blast of light, Tolly's face dissolved and the ape-lion roared in pain, blood flowering from its arm. It lashed out, knocking Prendick and

242

the Major off their feet and sending the gun spinning across the floor. It beat at the two men with balled claws, bellowing and pounding. Lizzie snatched up the shotgun, jabbed the barrel at the back of the creature's head and shot it into silence.

For seconds, there was no movement in the atrium. Jack dropped to his knees beside Prendick, his face frozen in horror. Lizzie, her eyes wide and her breath reduced to sharp snatches, sniffed and batted at her nose with the back of her hand. It didn't occur to either of them, as once it would, to run for their lives.

"Jack, bullets," she muttered through a throat clogged with stifled emotion. Utterson emptied her dead father's pockets and handed her the remaining cartridges.

Under the monk's bench, inches from their ankles, the serpents glowered.

From elsewhere on the ground floor echoed the hammering of the half-insect on the library door. All the fleeing guests had taken refuge there, bursting in as Jilks the footman was passing an opened bottle of smelling salts close to Lady Alice's face. She recovered from her swoon to find Jilks, Jasper Stoppard and Miss Augustine dragging furniture into a barricade against the door, leaving books and Mah Jong tiles strewn across the carpet.

"What is that horrible thing?" wailed Enid Stoppard, more to herself than the others. "It killed Maude, and Sir Godfrey, and . . ." Her husband, who knew perfectly well what that horrible thing was, having seen it in the cellar, heaved a chair onto the growing barricade and said nothing. Sweat beaded his forehead.

They could hear the half-insect tapping and scratching

outside the door. It knocked and hammered, pushing hard enough to rattle the haphazard pile of sofas and side tables but with nowhere near the force needed to topple it.

"That should be enough," said Lady Henrietta, the fingers of one hand working at the high collar of her dress. She glanced around the shadowed, abruptly disordered room, almost as upset by the damage done to the furniture as by the creature's efforts to gain entry. The tall display cabinet which held her grandfather's collection of Iron Age and Bronze Age artifacts stood untouched in the darkness.

"I saw it all!" sobbed Lady Alice, arms twisting around herself as if to ward off blows. "I saw disaster." Enid Stoppard, ashen-faced, rushed to her side.

"What the devil can we do now?" spat Danvers Carew. "We've got ourselves trapped in here."

"The animal will surely wander off," said Lady Henrietta unsteadily, "once it knows it can't reach us?"

"And then?" said Miss Augustine. "What about the others in the house?"

"How many of these horrors can there be?" said Lady Henrietta.

"I meant the other *people*, Henry!" cried Miss Augustine, taken aback.

"If they've any sense, they'll do the same as us."

"Where the bloody hell did it come from?" shouted Carew. "Do something!"

Lady Alice's sobs rose in pitch. "We will die, I saw it. And then dies half the world."

"Oh shut up, Alice!" spat Lady Henrietta.

Enid gripped Alice's arms in hers and whispered, her mouth dancing a tarantella. "Can you see a way out for

244

us? Can you?" In reply, Alice's face crumpled into misery and Enid looked frantically at Jasper with the same question. The almost completely concealed embarrassment at which his expression excelled had been replaced with one of overt terror. With their eyes locked, despite the lack of light, he shook his head, very slightly, and Enid's gaze lost its twinkle.

"We could break the window?" said Miss Augustine. "Get out that way?"

"Top idea! Do it!" cried Carew.

"No!" said Lady Henrietta. "If there are more horrors out there, the sound of all that stained glass breaking will bring them at once!"

Loud knocks and scratches came from beyond the barricaded door.

"Well, we can't stay in here!" wailed Carew, his fists pumping up and down.

"I seem to recall this window has vents, doesn't it, Jilks?" said Lady Henrietta.

"Yes, my Lady," said the footman, hurriedly unlatching the lowest of three slim, horizontal openings, which dropped level with the sill. "But they're made very narrow, to deter burglars."

"I'm not going to fit through *that*, am I?" said Carew.

"I might," said Miss Augustine. She marched to the window, pulling at the fastenings of her skirts. The others watched in dumb silence as she ripped at her clothes until she was down to her long underwear and corset.

"Well, help me, Henry!" she hissed. Lady Henrietta rushed forward and began to unlace the corset at the back. Jilks rummaged in his pockets and handed Henrietta a pen knife.

She unfolded the blade and quickly cut the corset's laces in a series of snicks and snaps.

"Take Freddie's motor carriage," said Carew. "No, you'll never get it started. Take one of the horses, go straight to the police."

Miss Augustine turned a disdainful glare on him. "Even my dainty brain *is* capable of the occasional thought, thank you, your Grace. I'm not some helpless damsel!"

"Oh really?" bellowed Carew at the top of his voice, his whole body twitching with indignation. "Thank Christ you packed your shining armour, Lancelot!"

Lady Henrietta took hold of Miss Augustine's legs and hoisted her up. Miss Augustine, hands first, aimed herself through the inches-high gap at the base of the window. Both women struggled and grunted, Miss Augustine using her freed arms to lever herself further out into the cool night, Lady Henrietta pushing from behind.

Sudden powerful blows at the door made everyone flinch. The half-insect was using something heavy to break in at the top, above the barricade.

"Wait, stop, I'm stuck!" hissed Miss Augustine.

"Shall I pull you back?" said Lady Henrietta.

"No. I need to . . . I can't move."

"Bloody well hurry up!" shouted Carew. "Hurry! Up!"

They instinctively crouched as a loud, hollow splintering suddenly filled the room. Shards of wood flew in all directions. Faintly discernable in the darkness, there was now a sizeable, jagged hole at the top of the library door.

At the other end of the house, in the kitchen, a dozen staff were gathered around the heavily marked wooden work table which dominated the centre of the room. They were so used to hearing strange things in the night, and so used to keeping quiet about them, that the unearthly scream from outside and all the noises from elsewhere on the ground floor had so far caused them only to gather in fear and morbidly suppress each other's suspicions.

A huge shadow slowly appeared beyond the glass panels overlooking the rear yard. The servants' voices rose into horrified mutterings. Several of them sprang to their feet, chairs scraping on the flagstones. The shadow, its shape amorphous in the shifting moonlight, moved in a swaying motion up to the back door.

The crash as the half-reptile shouldered it open suddenly jolted them out of their habitual ear-closing. For a moment, the creature stood framed against the night, a hump-backed clash of crocodile, lizard and human. It dipped its long, razor-toothed head slightly and let out a deep, rattling roar which thrummed through air and bone.

Emily, the new scullery maid, was among those who snatched up whatever pans or knives were nearest to hand and hurled them at the monster. It recoiled slightly as a skillet struck a glancing blow against its snout, but was otherwise untroubled.

It rushed at them, its body waving, hooked barbs at the ends of its crooked fingers splayed, jaw wide open and drooling, tail slashing. The servants retreated as one, knocking over chairs, yelling, grasping.

Cook grasped hold of a saucepan and swung it wildly, her bulldog frame directly in the creature's path. She battered at its head repeatedly, shouting about having had more than enough for one day, while the others shouted at her to stop.

The half-reptile twisted to clap its heavy jaws around her face and she dropped like a stone.

The creature flipped the kitchen table onto its side, placing itself between the servants and any hope of escape along the dog-legged conduit leading to the rest of the house. Their backs pressed against cupboards and warm ovens. All but cornered, they either froze in terror, curled into the smallest possible space, or broke into a useless, frenzied panic.

The half-reptile ploughed into them, its teeth and barbs tearing into whatever it touched. Its sinewy, ridged tail slapped from side to side, preventing those it hadn't yet reached from getting a chance to run. Gradually, the chaos of terror gave way to other sounds.

Miss Tippel, at the edge of the group, tightly wrapped her arms around young Emily, one hand over the girl's eyes. In that moment, neither of them made a conscious decision to duck down and crawl, but found themselves doing so. The creature's tail caught Emily on the side of her head, almost knocking her senseless, but the half-reptile was too intent on its task to notice. They crawled to the end of the connecting conduit and clambered shakily to their feet, each clinging to the other.

The creature, its mind bent on blood and retribution, never recognised the scullery maid. Emily, too horrified to look closely, never knew that the half-reptile had been Joseph Carter, with whom she'd talked pleasantly the day before, on the journey by brougham from the workhouse.

She fled with the housekeeper while the creature roared. When everyone in the kitchen was dead or dying, the half-reptile vented its fury on the room itself, breaking and smashing whatever it could, cracking open the sinks, shattering the glass roof.

Emily and Miss Tippel staggered into the main part of the house. They intended to find the rest of the household, and safety, but stopped when they passed the passageway to the cellar steps and saw Jekyll half way along it. He'd hurriedly emptied a tea chest in the plate room, dragged it here, and was clawing heaps of his father's books and papers into it from the archive shelves.

"Your Lordship?" whispered Miss Tippel.

He visibly started, and whipped around to glare at them. "I'd advise you to leave the house as quickly as possible, Miss Tippel."

Something large was coming up the steps from the cellar. It scraped along the sides of the narrow stairwell, apparently muttering to itself.

Jekyll spun with indecision, dithering between the cellar stairs, the tea chest and the open end of the passageway. Then, like some vast spider erupting from its hiding place, the thing from the pit squeezed out of the stairwell, into the passage. She reared up, almost to the ceiling, the coils of her serpentine body flowing behind her.

Jekyll was transfixed. He tried to stand his ground but slowly pulled away. The thing stared at him, shifting her weight from side to side, examining the Earl with evident glee, as if he was a prized exhibit.

Miss Tippel held her breath, her lips shaking. She knew that face.

When the thing spoke, her voice was high and rattling, human and animal. "Frederick," she breathed, grinning. "My dear."

"What the bloody hell is it?" shuddered Emily, peeping over Miss Tippel's shoulder.

"How can this be?" whispered Miss Tippel. "It's . . . it's Lady Evelyn. It's his first wife."

Chapter 27

Upstairs in the nursery, Lady Violet sat on the floor in the darkest corner of the room, an arm tight around each of her young twins, their nanny and the Honourable Albert Montgomery Carew beside them. Her eldest step-daughter took her ear from the door and groped her way back to them, colliding with a trunk of toys on the way and almost falling over.

"For heaven's sake, Violet, are there no candles?" she hissed.

"Frederick deemed them unnecessary, as we have electricity," said Violet.

Lady Jane felt her way to the floor. "I think that was gunshots. It came from the atrium," she whispered. "I don't know what can suddenly be happening, but it's far beyond anything Father's wretched pets have caused. I'll go and find out."

"No!" Violet clenched her fists and screwed up her eyes, but an involuntary sob shook her none the less.

"Mama?" whispered Claude.

"Don't be frightened Mama," whispered William. "We'll protect you."

"Oh, it's alright, boys, really. I'm just being a silly billy goat."

Lady Jane leaned closer to her, to make out her stepmother's face in the thin moonlight from the window. "You *know* what this is," she said quietly, "do you not?"

"I'm hungry," grumbled the Honourable Albert Montgomery Carew.

Lady Violet had long assumed she'd meet this occasion with more composure and decorum. After all, she'd had years to rehearse it. But now that the comfortable, genteel part of her life was soon to be over, she felt an aching nostalgia for it, an unexpected unwillingness to let go, for which she was completely unprepared. Her fingers touched at the dazzlingly jewelled choker around her throat.

"I was your mother's nurse, in London, during her final days. I was perfectly willing to tell you, and everyone else, the truth about my background, but your father said it would leave me open to awkward questions about your mother's death. I thought the snobbery which subsequently filled this lack of information would die down when the family became accustomed to me and could plainly see I wasn't some common bawd, but I was wrong. And it made me all the more determined to stand firm at Frederick's side.

"Our relationship was purely professional at first, then friendly, then one of confessor and confidante. I freely admit that I saw an opportunity in him, a chance to rise above the woes and worries of everyday life. However, our marriage was one of genuine love, not coercion or convenience. The extremity of his grief poured out the terrible story of his dark science, and my heart broke for him. I know he loves me too, both me and our boys, and we've had eight happy years. More than I had any right to expect, more than so many millions of souls in this world.

"He is a brilliant man. A true visionary, and this is why I have always been unswerving in my loyalty to him. But his achievements are not easily won. He has run horrible risks, and done horrible things, but all for the greater good. He is a good man.

"It must remain for him alone to tell you the exact nature of his research. He has never allowed me to witness its progress or its results, and I respect his choice. However, I'm aware that in the basement laboratory of this house he has bred . . . unspeakable things. For a long time, I have feared a breaking free of these experiments and . . . clearly, this has come to pass. What form of horror they are, I do not know."

William's little face, his eyes round and perplexed, squirmed upward to look at Violet. "There are no such things as monsters and ghosts and dragons."

"You said," whispered Claude.

Violet seemed to be about to answer them, but after a long pause returned her attention to Lady Jane instead. "Worse, I believe – I have no proof, I'm simply drawing conclusions based on unguarded utterances of Frederick's over the years – I am almost sure that your mother is still alive and among their number."

". . . I beg your pardon?" whispered Lady Jane.

"I haven't seen her since November of 1888. At the time, I had no reason to think her death was falsified, but I now believe Frederick and Mr Poole may have smuggled her in a heavily tranquillised state back to Westwych House. To find a way to return her to normality, to reverse her condition. But so far without success, I fear, since success has a way of announcing itself. I'm very sorry."

Lady Jane sat back a little. Her reeling mind almost overflowed, but then refilled itself with a whole new set of thoughts, coldly evaluating the possibilities of another unexpected situation.

A gentle creak of floorboards suddenly came from the direction of the corridor outside. Lady Jane quickly, quietly shushed for silence and everyone held their breath.

A soft clicking: the handle of the door, turning with infinite care. Lady Violet felt her sons' hands tighten on her sleeves.

"Is it a monster?" whispered Claude.

Moonlight reflected a gliding, vertical sliver off the door as it gradually opened. There was rustling, and a large gray outline which seemed to narrow and expand as it moved. "Anyone in here?"

Violet let her breath go. "Alcock?"

Ada bustled in, all but dragging Carew's valet, and soundlessly closed the door behind her. "Yes, m'lady," she whispered. "May we come in? There's summat funny downstairs."

"Whitton?" said Lady Jane. "What are you doing here, you're supposed to be with His Grace?" In the low light, she couldn't see the self-consciousness all over him. Without waiting for a response, she tugged the Honourable Albert Montgomery Carew away from the nanny. "I can't bear to be in here another second," she said. "I'm going to find Father, and Danvers."

"Jane!" hissed Violet. "It could be very dangerous—"

"I've heard all I want to hear from you. Whitton, you come with me."

The valet shook his head. "I ain't going down them stairs, after what I heard, y'Ladyship. I'll get out back, fetch the landau. You coming, Ada?"

Now her instinct to run was backed up by someone else, the nanny seized her opportunity and hurriedly rose to her feet. "I'm getting out too," she murmured.

"Well, I'm staying here," muttered Ada. "Hide, I reckon, let the rozzers sort it out. Or whoever."

Lady Jane hauled her son up onto her hip. "You must be quiet now, Bertie."

"I'm hungry," he grizzled, burying his words in his mother's shoulder.

Leaving Lady Violet, Ada and the twins to their fate, the others slipped out into the hallway. The valet and the nanny, aiming for the shortest route to the closest exit, turned left and headed for the servants' stairs. Lady Jane and the Honourable Albert Montgomery Carew turned right, for the main staircase.

Chapter 28

Downstairs in the library, the gap the half-insect had knocked through at the top of the door was now large enough for it to crawl through. It threw down the Aesthetic school pewter statuette it had used to crack open the wood.

Inside the darkened room, the surviving humans strained their eyes to see it emerge from the hole in sharp, sporadic movements. Outside the room, hiding in shadow, Jack Utterson and Lizzie Prendick watched it vanish from sight and heard a rising clamour of horrified voices. They tiptoed as fast as they dared into the dining room, fetched two chairs, and placed them by the library entrance to step up level with the jagged gap.

All Lizzie could see was the tall arch of moonlight at the window, and the outline of someone struggling at its base. "It's too dark," she whispered, "I can't get a clear shot at it."

The half-insect didn't bother to topple the heap of furniture blocking the door. It moved up the wall from the hole. In quick, scuttling hops it climbed past the room's elaborately sculptured cornicing and crawled across the ceiling.

"Watch out! Watch out!" said Lady Henrietta, gaze fixed upward while pulling frantically at Miss Augustine, wedged half-in half-out of the window.

"The bloody thing's going to drop on our heads!" cried Danvers Carew. "Move aside!"

Lady Alice let out a long, wailing howl. Lady Henrietta left Miss Augustine for a moment and slapped Alice hard across the face.

Jasper Stoppard held Enid close, one hand squashing her hairdo. "I do so love you, my dear," he whispered.

"I love you too, Jelly-bobble," she sobbed quietly.

Above them, the half-insect chittered and seethed, head twisting at acute angles to watch its prey below. It suddenly scrambled to the far edge of the room and began to descend, down the wall and over the window.

Henrietta pushed at Miss Augustine's legs. "Help me!" Miss Augustine shifted an inch or two, but no more. "Help me!"

The half-insect's silhouette scuttled down the glass in a zigzag, shuddering black against the ultramarine of night. Before Lizzie, outside in the hall, could take aim with the shotgun, it had stung Miss Augustine at the base of her spine and leapt at Lady Henrietta, who toppled over with a screech which cut out before she reached the floor.

"For God's sake," cried Carew, "are we going to let ourselves be slaughtered by a damn beetle? Gentlemen, there are three of us and one of it. If we rush it, we might bring it down, do you think?"

"I agree, Sir," piped up Jilks.

"There's four, including me," whispered Jack.

Lizzie grabbed his collar and held him back from clambering through into the library. "You stay put," she whispered through gritted teeth. She raised her shotgun and slid the barrels through the hole in the door.

The creature sprang to its rear legs, head cocked, curled sting flexing and shiny.

"I say we try!" cried Carew. "The fiend can't fight us all at once! We take it at the charge! Are we agreed? On three, then! . . . One! . . . Two! . . . Three!"

Jilks and Jaspar Stoppard flung themselves at the creature, yelling loudly. Carew yelled too but, in the deep gloom, it was difficult to see if he flung himself at the creature or not.

The half-insect's domed, compound eyes were less efficient than those it had once had. Smell and touch alone guided its sting into the necks of Jilks and Stoppard as they careered headlong into the creature and knocked it flying.

Lizzie took aim, guessing at the half-insect's position from the sound of it crashing into a bookcase and emitting a shocked, ululating shriek. The gun fired and the creature shrieked again.

"You got it!" breathed Jack.

She'd hadn't. Shotgun pellets had grazed its body, but the force of the blast had struck the books above it. While Enid Stoppard groped frantically along the floor to her dead husband, no longer caring about her own fate, the half-insect redirected its fury at the source of its injuries. It scurried up and around the barricade of furniture, racing for the hole in the door.

Jack and Lizzie jumped down from the chairs they were standing on, Jack letting out an involuntary yelp of fright. They ran for the dining room.

Half way down the sweeping staircase opposite, Lady

Jane saw them go and quickly crouched beside the bannister. The moonlight from the landing behind her was relatively bright, cutting geometric slabs of shadow and lucid blue across the hall. She watched, in abject disbelief, as the half-insect wriggled its way out of the splintered gap in the library door and skittered along the walls, following the two humans.

Urgently hushing the child in her arms and keeping the creature in view, she crept down the remaining steps, carefully levering off her shoes against the bottom one so her footsteps would be soundless. Treading in a slow sideways motion, she moved towards the wide walkway that led to the atrium.

The half-insect paused. From the library could be heard three voices rising in argument, and the drag and thump of furniture being removed from behind the door. The creature scuttled around on the wall, as if undecided, then resumed its pursuit of Jack and Lizzie.

As soon as she was in shadow, Lady Jane ran for her life. She stopped dead in her tracks the moment she emerged beside the broken vivarium, stifling a retch of disgust as she saw the blood and bodies littered across the floor. Her hold on the Honourable Albert Montgomery Carew tightened like a vice.

"Mumma, you're hurting my leg."

She didn't hear him. Her attention was on the far side of the cavernous room where her father, Miss Tippel and Emily were retreating out into the atrium ahead of a spiky-legged, serpentine mutation.

"Frederick!" hissed Lady Evelyn, baring her sharp teeth. "You were right, my love, I was so alive! Cursed with the life you gave me! Broken! Diseased! Defaced!"

Miss Tippel and Emily, entwined in peril, suddenly fell over each other and rolled to a squirming halt. Lady Evelyn, with a grin, raised a leg and stabbed them repeatedly, hammering until they were still.

"Evelyn!" cried Jekyll. "Listen to me! *Listen*! I did it for you! For *you*!"

"I am atrocity! I am the freak of nightmare! As I am made, so shall I be!"

She slithered steadily on, Jekyll stumbling backwards, arms pleading.

"I loved you! How could I end your life? By what right? I never meant for this to happen! I made a mistake, and it is my sworn duty to correct that mistake!"

"I am mistaken for my beauty," hissed Lady Evelyn. "The imps of Hell gather at my side and laugh. The witches of the hills dance my pain, feed all my sorrows. Death! Death!"

Jekyll's voice frayed, but somehow kept its commanding resonance. "Evelyn, think! *Think of how far we have come*! The moonwort which runs in your veins is a *miracle*! I *can* tame it! I *can* control it, if you give me more time!"

"Death! Death! Death!" she grinned. "A hundred needles! The crack of bone, the ache of twisting skin!"

"I know you've suffered, and endured a dozen forms. We've tried formula after formula, but every failure brings us closer to success. There *will* be a way back! I will *not* be beaten!"

"You will be dead."

"If you kill me, you'll have no hope! You'll be like this forever!"

Suddenly, a wailing shout halted them both. ". . . Mother!"

Lady Jane, aghast with horror and keeping her wriggling

son's face turned away, approached the Evelyn creature. "My father is an evil man," she said quietly. "What has he done to you?"

The sight of Jane sent memories cutting through Evelyn's ruined mind like shards of glass. She seemed to slump. Three of her pointed limbs rose in Jane's direction. Jekyll looked back and forth, from first wife to daughter.

"You can have justice, of a kind," said Jane. "If he ever loved you, clearly he doesn't now."

"Jane!" cried Jekyll. "That's not true."

"He told us you died! He told the world you died!"

"The funeral was a sham, but my grief was real!" cried Jekyll.

"We grieved your passing, Mother. While he remarried. An employee, a nurse. Did he not tell you that? They have offspring."

Evelyn's brain swam. Acidic waves of hate, bitterness, despair coursed through her aching heart.

"Come and meet them," said Jane, her voice cracking. "They're upstairs. His other woman and his— bastards, I suppose they must be? This child I hold is your true heir, your grandchild."

"Jane!" shouted Jekyll. "No!"

Evelyn slithered at Jane, who spun on her heels and raced back past the vivarium. The Honourable Albert Montgomery Carew, his little arms flung around her neck, peeked over her shoulder at the scaly terror spidering along behind them. A glimpse which might have haunted his dreams for years, had he lived that long.

Evelyn's body rolled over the corpses in her path, her coiling tail sliding in broad shapes. Beneath the monk's bench, the escaped snakes reared and spiralled, sensing hostility.

In the dining room, where Jack and Lizzie had hastily shut themselves, the curtains were still closed following dinner. The darkness was too deep for them to see that the half-insect was already in the room.

It clung to the upper part of the walls, moving slowly, getting steadily closer to them, drawn by scent and by air vibrations. Its progress around the room was silent, the fleshy pincers at the ends of its limbs biting into the patterned wallpaper until, as it neared the humans, anticipation sent an involuntary tick-tick-ticking from its deformed mouth-parts.

"It's in here," breathed Lizzie, voice wavering.

Instantly, the half-insect dropped to the floor right in front of them, its head level with theirs, mere inches away. In the darkness, they could smell the accumulations of blood and dirt on the creature, and the sickly, fruit-flower reek of its sting. It tick-tick-ticked.

It was, unmistakably, relishing the moment. It was enjoying its ability to kill both of them before the shotgun could be swung in its direction. Jack, the ice in his veins turbulent with the fear of death, realised with growing dismay that he couldn't tell if this was the mutated instinct of a monster or the calculation of the human remnants inside it. And in that moment of mourning he saw, finally and irrevocably, the true emptiness of the sympathy he'd felt and the true horror of what Frederick Jekyll had done.

There was a sudden commotion out in the hall. Jekyll's voice boomed, strident but faltering. Hearing it, the half-insect vanished into the dark.

On the staircase, Lady Jane ran ahead of the Evelyn-thing, who in turn was followed by Jekyll, demanding obedience from his eldest daughter, pleading for his first wife's attention. The library door was pulled open, forcing aside the last objects piled against it. Lady Alice, Enid Stoppard and Danvers Carew emerged, only to shrink at the sight of Evelyn. Alice launched into a fresh peal of screams.

Evelyn was passing the family portraits hanging beside the stairs. Her head arched to examine them. This one her perfidious husband's dead father, this one her perfidious husband's dead mother, this one her perfidious husband's . . . She looked at herself with disgust. Vile youth! Revolting grace! Painted for her birthday.

She ripped at all the portraits, hissing with despair. Frames and torn canvas were flung down into the hall. The picture of Violet survived long enough for Lady Jane's purposes. "That's her!" she cried. "His bitch! His whore!"

"Jane!" howled Jekyll impotently. "This is none of Violet's doing! Leave her alone! Leave my sons alone!"

Upstairs, in the nursery, all that could be heard was a muffled, approaching cacophony. Violet, Ada and the twins huddled closer together in the dark.

Down in the hall, Jekyll pulled out the pistol he'd been given by Poole and aimed it up the stairwell at Evelyn. "Stop! Come back!" He fired, but the shot rebounded off the bannisters, splitting the fat, polished handrail.

The three survivors from the library, about to rush across the hall for the imagined safety of Jekyll's firearm, suddenly noticed movement in the shadows behind the Earl.

"Daddy!" screamed Lady Alice.

He spun around to find the half-insect scuttling at speed

across the floor. "Obey the First Command!" he roared. "Obey! Be still!"

For a second, the creature was cowed, its conditioning unexpectedly reasserting itself. It twitched from side to side, as if startled into fighting some unseen enemy, then launched itself at a saucer-eyed Enid Stoppard, stinging her three times in the face before she could cry out. As she fell, the half-insect sprang onto Danvers Carew, wrapping itself around his upper body. He squealed in terror, arms flapping, twisting his head away. The smooth area of neck he exposed was all too tempting, and the half-insect plunged its sting deep, the pressure sending its paralysing bile flowing back up over the edges of the wound.

Carew's wife, fortunately, didn't see him die. She was busy leading the Evelyn-thing to the thickly carpeted landing on the first floor, where she stood pointing with her free hand, her whole body shivering with feral emotions. "In there!" she cried. A nauseous thrill ran through her. Evelyn smashed her way into the nursery.

Lady Jane had caught a momentary glimpse of the half-insect in the hall and had no wish to endanger either her own life or that of the Honourable Albert Montgomery Carew so, hoisting her son into a more comfortable carrying position, she hurried along the landing to the female servants' stairs, which would take her down into the atrium, not far from the entrance to Westwych House and safety.

She found the catch which made a tall panel in the wall click itself ajar. Treading with care, her shoe-less feet tapping for the edge of each wooden step, she advanced into the near-blackness, her elbows brushing at the walls.

"What's that horrid smell, Mumma?" muttered the Honourable Albert Montgomery Carew.

"Be quiet, Bertie darling, I'm trying to concentrate," murmured Lady Lane.

Descending step by step, her toes soon felt something wet and soft. Oh for God's sake, one of her father's slovenly maids must have dropped some food! Whatever it was, there was a lot of it. And it stunk!

She never knew that what she trod in were the remains of her husband's valet, Whitton, and the Jekylls' nanny. Her eyes were adjusting to the dark, and she could make out patchy shapes at her feet, but what exactly they could be, she couldn't tell. The half-reptile, having lurked quietly since hearing the click of the access panel, suddenly reared up over her, huge and bloodied.

Downstairs, Jack and Lizzie left the dining room as Jekyll put three bullets through the half-insect's head at point blank range. Lady Alice rushed to him, sobbing.

Lizzie was about to step forward, but Jack placed an arm across her. "I don't think the Earl should see me," he whispered nervously, "not while he has a gun in his hand."

At that moment, Alice's sobs rose into a fresh shriek of horror. Four human heads, torn from their bodies, came thudding, bouncing, rolling down the staircase. Lizzie, recognising Ada's, turned aside with a gasp, fingers tight over her mouth.

The heads were followed by Evelyn, racing to destroy the last living source of her torment. "Frederick! Frederick! Come to my arms, o my liberator! Join your army of the dead!" Violently, she tore at the walls and bannisters as she flew past, as if trying to injure the house itself, as if the death of its owner alone would never be sufficient revenge.

Jekyll shakily aimed the pistol and put two shots into his first wife's scaly body before his finger pulled uselessly at the trigger. He fled from the hall, Lady Alice at his heels. Evelyn, bullet wounds bleeding profusely, roared defiance and redoubled the speed of her clattering limbs.

They burst into the atrium as the half-reptile was emerging from the servants' stairs. Goaded into frenzy by the carnage it had wrought and the human blood covering its skin, it ignored Jekyll, charged directly at Evelyn with its mouth gaping, and sunk its long teeth into her side.

She howled and bucked, pulling the half-reptile off its feet. The end of her long tail whipped around to grasp the creature by its legs. She tore it free of her body and dashed it against the wall, snapping its neck and breaking apart the monk's bench under which the escaped snakes had been hiding. Their normally docile nature gave way to one of self-preservation. They slithered in a fast meandering fan.

Evelyn spun around to find Jekyll scrambling through the contents of the vivarium's equipment drawer, desperately trying to find the strong narcotic he kept for use on his animal specimens. From their undamaged habitats, the venomous spiders and deadly scorpions silently watched him flounder.

Evelyn snatched him up in her coils, curling him close to her. He struggled and kicked.

"Husband! Husband!" she hissed. "We'll squeeze the evil out of you!"

Snakes reared their heads up off the floor and made a dozen strikes at Evelyn's waspy limbs. With an angry shriek she flicked one away, high into the air. Jekyll's thrashing legs, perceived as an attack, were bitten innumerable times.

He gasped, his face filling with blood. He tried to speak, but his words – of destiny unfulfilled, of plans betrayed – were lost in a froth of spit at his quivering lips.

Lady Alice, weeping, ran out of the shadows and pounded at Evelyn's tightening coils, imploring mercy, but the sharp pain of snakebites at her ankles sent her staggering, then falling. Evelyn hadn't even noticed her youngest daughter, reptile venom and loss of blood steadily robbing her of sight and thought. With the remainder of her strength, she felt her husband's bones snap and, with an eerie suddenness, they drooped to the floor, entwined, and Westwych House became as silent as the grave.

Out on the hills, the eye-woman also breathed her last. She walked peacefully through the night, along ancient paths and over grassy slopes, her heart filled with joy. The freedom of the sky above and the earth beneath her feet! She felt the infinite variety surrounding her, and the beauty of it all. She felt the promise of life, and she felt a happiness she'd never known before.

On a hilltop, under the stars, she lay and died. The pulse of the earth softly lulled her into sleep, and she slipped away in acceptance and in love.

Chapter 29

The carriage which conveyed Jack Utterson and Lizzie Prendick into Bristol, five days later, was running twenty-two minutes late by Jack's pocket watch, but he was too preoccupied with other things to worry. Hagstow was behind them, sad but unbowed; London lay ahead.

Jack was preparing himself to report to his superior at the museum, Mr Bittlesham, that, sadly, his mission to catalogue Neolithic and Chalcolithic anthropological data along the Lulsgate Plateau, with reference to the transition away from a nomadic Mesolithic culture, had been a complete failure. However, the valuable maps given over into his care could, happily, be returned to the museum in pristine condition.

With her father gone, Lizzie felt little desire to remain at the Tethered Goat. A new proprietor would be readily found from among the villagers and she – like so many of her peers – couldn't help but seek the possibilities of a shrinking-and-expanding world. Jack assured her that his landlady in Battersea would be positively delighted to have A Self-reliant Woman Of The Modern Era among her paying guests, because she'd wanted one for ages. The gentle kiss Lizzie placed on his cheek went some way to relieving the nervous shock which still fluttered in his heart. He held her hand in his, and was rather pleased at his boldness.

The carriage passed close to Westwych House, and it was visible for several seconds between the trees. The police were gone, and the bodies were gone, and the estate had been locked up at the intervention of higher authorities.

The house was a dark and melancholy tombstone now, defiled and abandoned, rigorously sombre as if a silent death knell rang forever through its echoing halls and corridors. A palace of the dead, a hollow coffin to be picked at by flocks of fiscal and legal vultures circling a lineage ended, a family deceased. It was an infamous house of sorrow now, a house of haunted, empty rooms and the wailing of the past.

It slid from view and the carriage clattered on, its blinkered horses snorting. It moved steadily through a short, narrow valley, where Jack and Lizzie watched the steep and rocky hillsides passing by but had no inkling that they, in turn, were being watched from above.

Strange faces peeked at them from a crevice high up, a narrow gap in the rock. Inside, in the cold, black honeycomb of subterranean passageways and slimy caves, hid scrawny things who lived on wild plants and rodents. These were the sons and daughters of the sons and daughters of the tiny handful of freed experiments who, over the years, had survived long enough either to reproduce or to birth the litter already within them.

They were pale and stocky, and their lives were hard.

Their physical forms were unpredictable mutations of skin and bone. Those with too few appendages or sense organs to fend for themselves were cared for by the others. They'd lay twigs and leaves across fissures in the hills, to trap the occasional stray sheep or dog for extra meat. Sometimes, if food was short, they'd drag a young cow up from the lowland farms, but only at night because they were careful to avoid humans – humans, with their weird upside-down caves and their wheeled boxes for travelling in. The underground-dwellers made tools out of bones, and drew markings on dry stones. In time, they would come to tell each other stories about their ancestors, once fierce roamers on the outside lands, who one day vanished never to be seen again.

www.ingramcontent.com/pod-product-compliance
Lightning Source LLC
Chambersburg PA
CBHW050604190726
48283CB00007B/2278